THE CHATELAINE

This is the story of a little house in a little town to the north of
Paris. The house is a picturesque and pretentious little villa, but its
lady likes to call it her chateau because of its cone-capped tower and
the small garden of firs that surrounds it. Along the hills above runs
the deep Forest of Sainte-Marie, and in an opening chapter we see
from its fringes the town of Sainte-Marie-la-Forêt lying under the
sun in happiness and peace.

But it is 1939.

The English lady of the house, Sophie Burgermann, is one who
forever guards herself from the harshness of reality by a palisade of
comforting thoughts. She refuses to believe that any danger threatens
her strangely cosmopolitan household, wherein her husband is a
naturalized German, her step-daughter half-Scottish, her visiting
'nephew' (whose real relationship is clear to all) an English airman,
and her *bonne-a-tout-faire* an ardently patriotic Frenchwoman.

A year, and the War comes burning through Sainte-Marie on its
way to Paris. From that moment Sophie is never released from the
harshness of reality. German occupation; a German officer in her
house; menace and slaughter in street and forest; the sudden frightening courage of her step-daughter, her son, her mild German
husband, her maidservant, and the hitherto lazy and sensual Abbé
Belfort, Curé of Sainte-Marie; the coming of the secret British
agents, and the final rising of the town to swell the French Resistance
—all these things close in upon her.

At first, defeated by them all, she is driven to cowardice and a
betrayal. It is after this, and because of her secret shame and remorse,
that she begins to take on the colour of the courage around her.

BOOKS BY ERNEST RAYMOND

NOVELS

A London Gallery *comprising*

We the Accused	*Was There Love Once?*
The Marsh	*The Corporal of the Guard*
Gentle Greaves	*A Song of the Tide*
The Witness of Canon Welcome	*The Chalice and the Sword*
A Chorus Ending	*To the Wood No More*
The Kilburn Tale	*The Lord of Wensley*
Child of Norman's End	*The Old June Weather*
For Them That Trespass	*The City and the Dream*

Other Novels

Mr. Olim	*Don John's Mountain Home*
The Visit of Brother Ives	*The Five Sons of Le Faber*
The Quiet Shore	*The Last to Rest*
The Nameless Places	*Newtimber Lane*
Tell England	*The Miracle of Brean*
A Family That Was	*Rossenal*
The Jesting Army	*Damascus Gate*
Mary Leith	*Wanderlight*
Morris in the Dance	*Daphne Bruno I*
The Old Tree Blossomed	*Daphne Bruno II*

BIOGRAPHIES, ETC.

Paris, City of Enchantment	*In the Steps of St. Francis*
Two Gentlemen of Rome	*In The Steps of the Brontës*
(*The Story of Keats and Shelley*)	

ESSAYS, ETC.

Through Literature to Life	*Back to Humanity*
The Shout of the King	(with Patrick Raymond)

PLAYS

The Berg   *The Multabello Road*

ERNEST RAYMOND

The Chatelaine

CASSELL · LONDON

CASSELL & COMPANY LTD
35 Red Lion Square · London WC1
and at
MELBOURNE · SYDNEY · TORONTO
CAPE TOWN · JOHANNESBURG · AUCKLAND

Set in 11 on 12½ pt. Bembo type, and printed
in Great Britain by Cox and Wyman, Ltd.,
London, Fakenham and Reading
F.862

Contents

For
DIANA RAYMOND
in admiration

I

Sainte-Marie-la-Forêt

SAINTE-MARIE-LA-FORÊT lies across the Beauvais–Paris Road, its western houses climbing gently towards the Forêt on its undulating hills. Road and railway to Paris run side by side through the little straggling town. If you climb the hill to the forest and turn about before penetrating the dense trees, you can see in the distance the Tour Eiffel tapering into the haze and the domes of the Invalides and the Panthéon, and the cupolas of Sacré-Coeur, sketched against the noonday sky.

Come down from the forest and in the Rue de la Forêt turn into the first little avenue on its left, a brief narrow road, a 'voie sans issue', with a house or two along it. One of these, on the forest side of the avenue is a small villa in a small garden of firs. It makes a very French picture because, though small, it tries to look like a chateau, with sharp gables on its four sides and, if you'll only believe it, a round tower in one corner with a cone-capped roof. Has not the sixteenth-century Château de Chenonceaux just such towers at its corners? Why, some lively owner of long ago, contemplating that tower, has even painted a suitable name on the side wall, 'Castel de la . . .' but the rest has got washed away with time.

It is an April evening in the year 1939 and within those walls, bustling from room to room, or up and down the staircase in the tower, goes Madame Sophie Burgermann, the chatelaine. Madame always calls her villa her 'little chateau' and the quarter-acre garden with its fir trees her 'park'. She is a comely woman of fifty-eight with a once-pretty face and a plenitude of silvering chestnut hair. Her figure is dressed for company—except for the loose, pink, frilly bedroom-jacket which she will certainly discard as soon as the company is viewed behind the chestnuts of the avenue.

The 'company' which her dress is to please is one person only, Rennie Quentin, reputed her nephew. He is come from England, for Madame Sophie is English, though living in Sainte-Marie near her beloved Paris and married to a Dr. Klemens Burgermann, who is clearly German.

'Marie-Louise,' she calls from the first landing, and 'Marie-Louise' again, pitching her voice higher so that Marie-Louise, her 'bonne à tout faire', may hear it. 'Where is Monsieur? Where is Monsieur? Where has he got to now? Have you seen him? I need help. Where on earth has he got to?'

Marie-Louise Benoît, a petite dark Frenchwoman of thirty with a figure no taller, and not much fuller, than a twelve-year-old's, but skilfully, nay devotedly and admiringly, attired beneath her apron, is at her kitchen door with a glass cloth and a wine glass in her hands. 'Monsieur is in the garden, Madame.'

'Oh, dear! He always disappears just when I want him. Do tell him I want him. Monsieur Rennie will be here any minute. And where is Mademoiselle Jean?'

'Mademoiselle Jean went up into the forest with the dogs,' says Marie-Louise, polishing the glass.

'Oh, dear, surely the dogs could have waited, or done their business in the garden. There are several trees. Monsieur Rennie said he'd be here in time for supper. I should think he'll be tired out, travelling all night and arriving in Paris at some impossible hour this morning. He insisted on travelling third-class to save his money, and you know what your third-class coaches are like, Marie-Louise. Oh, dear, what it is to be young! And after all that he insisted on spending the whole day in Paris. He adores Paris, like me. *Your* Paris, and Frédé's——'

2

'Frédé is not a Parisian, Madame. Beauvais is his town. He was born and went to school there.'

'Oh, what does that matter. Paris is his capital. And mine too. My dear adopted capital. Do ask Monsieur to come and give me help. What on earth can he be doing in the garden?'

'Smoking, Madame.'

'Well, smoke him up here, for heaven's sake. He's never anywhere when I want him. Nor Jean either. Fancy taking off the dogs just when Rennie's coming. They were so looking forward to his coming.'

Let us explain, for this seems a household oddly cosmopolitan. Even the two dogs up in the forest are Scotch, two frisky, black, Aberdeen terriers, with bristling old-gentleman eyebrows and beards, and up-ended tails that signal in semaphore as their brief black-trousered legs go twinkling along. Scotsmen, they are called Wallace and Bruce.

Many years before this, at the beginning of the century, young Dr. Klemens Burgermann, a Ph.D. of Heidelberg, came to London to teach German literature and philosophy at the Royal Academy of German Studies. He was then twenty-six. Falling in love with one of his pupils, Helen McLeash, he married her the very next year, much against the wishes of her parents, but she was now twenty-one and all awash, yea drowning, with love for her little German professor whose pale blue eyes were so kindly and whose 'ducky little yellow moustache' turned up like his Emperor's. He was 'utterly sweet', she said. Adorable. Their eager love produced a daughter in eight months, but it was all in order because no one could be more 'correct' than this young German, and Helen was a child of the Scottish Kirk. Four years of love they enjoyed, and then Helen died giving birth to premature twins, who died with her, and lie with her in the cemetery on Highgate Hill. The baby Jean was then only four, but Dr. Klem (as most people called him, including Baby Jean) brought her up with the aid of house-keepers. Partly for Jean's sake, who was proud of her ancestry and chose to think that her mother was a McLeash of McLeash (whatever that meant), and partly in memory of a loved wife and two babies who lay in English earth, he got himself naturalized as a British subject. That was in 1909.

In 1916, when he was forty, and Jean a long, too tall, leggy girl of twelve, he met Sophie Kendal-Worth, a spinster of thirty-five with brilliant chestnut hair, a girl's pink skin, vivacious eyes, and a figure of generous shape. People might wonder why with such charms about her she was still unmarried. The answer to this question no one had ever heard from *her* lips, though many had bandied it about among themselves—but this didn't trouble Sophie so long as none of them spoke of it aloud to her. Only to Dr. Klem when he asked her to marry him and 'be a mother to his daughter' did she tell the truth, less from high principles than because she saw that he was bound to learn it some day.

This was the truth. In the year that Dr. Burgermann married Helen McLeash, Sophie ran away with Sir Hereward Ash to Paris. Lady Ash declined to divorce him for Sophie's convenience, so she and Sir Hereward had to remain in Paris, pretending to be a married couple but deceiving none, and, since this was Paris, offending few. They sought to avoid children but in 1913 a child arrived whom they called Ash at first, though legally his surname was his mother's.

Sophie, a great lover of pretty and valuable things (or, rather, of possessions which she chose to think valuable) laboured to find Christian names for him that were at once pretty and rare. The only poems she had read (and she was very proud of having read these) were Tennyson's *Idylls of the King*, so she sought a beautiful name among them for this exquisite child. Gareth she trifled with, and Gawain, and Galahad, and Percivale, but Sir Hereward, a big, un-poetical, lusty man, would have none of these. He forbade them under threat of instant departure. In the end he consented, not very willingly, to Rainald. Rainald 'Quentin' the child finally became— Sophie had read *Quentin Durward*, one of the easier of Scott's novels, and was proud to have done so. But the name Rainald never mat-tered much because from the first they called him Rennie, and he, when he came to years of discretion, spelt the name 'Reynold' and lived at peace with it. As Reynold Quentin or 'Rennie' the world knew him.

1913—and next year was the terrible doomed year. 1914. Not all Sophie's pleas to Sir Hereward, not all his affection for her and the baby, not the fact that he was now fifty-eight—nothing could stop him, a man of ancient family and a late major of yeomanry, from coming home with mistress and child to help save England. At fifty-eight not even he could hope for a combatant post but, being a man of influence, he got himself colonel's rank and the job of Commandant, Mudros West, when the Gallipoli campaign broke in storm. Mudros in the Isle of Lemnos was only the Intermediate Base for that bloody business, and in his ardour Sir Hereward insisted on being conveyed one day to the Gallipoli Peninsula 'to see some fighting'. There, during a sight-seeing tour of the Western Trenches, a sniper's bullet found his head in the Western Mule Trench. Sir Hereward was a tall man, and he had supposed he could walk erect in a mere communication trench.

Sophie and the child Rennie were left alone. So she gladly married the little German doctor when he asked her and when he listened sympathetically to her story, only smiling gently. Sir Hereward had provided for her a fair income, and after the war she had what she thought a wonderful idea. Loving her France, she bustled her doctor (because of that Ph.D. she always liked to refer to him as 'the doctor') across the Channel to the Touraine ('where the best French is spoken') that he might run a crammer's establishment there, teaching French and German to British students and making a pile of money. The infant Rennie she left with her mother, the only other person who knew for certain who he was. Her mother, still a year less than sixty, gave out that she had adopted the child, the orphan of her dear friends, Mr. and Mrs. Quentin, 'as a comfort for her declining years'. The cramming establishment made no money, so Sophie brought back all her 'beautiful furniture' and her Dr. Burgermann as far as Sainte-Marie where she could be near to her beloved Paris and yet live fairly cheaply in a sufficiently pleasing style.

Thus the doctor, on that evening in 1939 when Marie-Louise called him in from the garden, knew all about Rennie's relationship to 'Aunt Sophie', and Sophie for her peace and happiness chose to think that he was the only person in Sainte-Marie who knew. As if the merry eyes of Marie-Louise were blind, and the small smiling eyes of Frédé, her big fat husband, and Jean's when they were not concentrated on her dogs, and Rennie's, the most interested eyes of all.

§

'Madame is calling for you,' said Marie-Louise.

'Thank you, Marie-Louise. Is it that I am a little out of favour at the moment?'

'Oh no, Monsieur. She just wants help.'

'She just wants help,' repeated Dr. Klem as if to demonstrate to the house that he understood why he was entering it. 'And where is she now?'

'She is in her bedroom, dressing, I think.'

'Ah, yes, yes. She is catering for the public view. I quite understand. Even though the public tonight is only Monsieur Rennie.'

Dr. Klem, sixty-three now, was a much plumper figure than the slender professor who married Helen McLeash. When in the 'country', as he called Sainte-Marie, he always wore an old-fashioned knickerbocker suit which showed his calves swelling up from slim ankles till they were like two pillows, round and wide. His eyes behind rimless spectacles were a German blue and gentle and ready to smile. The yellow moustache had now greyed but its ends still turned up in the old German fashion. Usually beneath the moustache hung a decorated S-shaped Bavarian pipe, not necessarily alight. Rimless spectacles and serpentine pipe seemed to complete a perfect picture of one kind of German, studious and contemplative.

Hearing his step in the hall Sophie hurried out from her bedroom upstairs.

'Klem, where *did* you get to? Never do I want you but you're nowhere to be found, or else I see your coat-tails disappearing out of sight. I want you to lay the supper table. Nobody lays a table like you. And to chip the onion for the salad, please . . . please . . . nobody chips an onion like you. Or makes a salad dressing like yours. Rennie always says so himself. Isn't it wonderful to think that we shall have him for a whole month?'

'It is wonderful, dear,' said the doctor, coming up the stairs.

'I hope Jeanie'll be back soon. I want us all to be here when he arrives. Fancy going up into the forest just when he's coming.'

'She's been away all day, and the dogs needed a walk, I suppose.'

'Well, surely they could go alone and look after each other.'

'No, they'd chase the goats. And then the goatherd's dog. Each encourages the other.'

'Extraordinary having goats so near to Paris. We don't have them near London, do we? I don't wonder that Wallace and Bruce chase them. They smell. Now look, darling.' She hastened into the 'breakfast-room' ahead of him. This was a small front room on the first landing. It was simply furnished, holding little more than oddments: a small mahogany dining-table, a suite of old saddle-bag chairs, three portly easy chairs, and a cheap oak sideboard. From the sideboard she snatched some silver spoons and a polishing cloth and, tossing them on to the table, urged him gently down on to a chair before them. 'There. I know you'll give them an extra special polish.'

'Yes, dear. If you wish.'

'Nobody does it as well as you.'

'Nobody does it as well as me. Then the whole population of the world must be very incompetent.'

'Nonsense. You know how well you do it.'

'Yes. But it's not a difficult business.'

'No, but . . . I'm going to nip upstairs and see if he's coming.'

'And how, pray? You can only see a few yards of the avenue. You can't see the road from the station.'

'I can see a bit of it from the top tower-window.'

'"Sister Anne, Sister Anne, do you see anyone coming?"' quoted Klem, as she hurried towards the stairs. And he quoted

7

further, '"O lang will his Lady look owre the Castle Downe . . ."'
while briskly polishing in the breakfast-room.

Sophie made the family spend most of their days in the breakfast-room, and this may seem strange since she so loved all her beautiful chattels and furnishings. She would say frankly, 'I'm afraid I'm one of those who've always loved things more than people'; which was true enough if you allow that her husband was a pleasing thing which she could dress up and polish for visits to Paris, and that her shapely figure was an extraordinarily pleasant thing to ornament and decorate ('nobody has a figure like mine'), and that Rennie was a visiting property of which she could be proud—had not an old widow in Sainte-Marie described him to Sophie as 'le beau jeune homme?' Probably the lady was thinking her own thoughts at the time.

This house with its absurd little tower and its few firs around it was one of the pretty things, and in its salon on the ground floor were more loved possessions: Louis Seize chairs, a rococo Louis Quinze table, an upright Broadwood piano ('few pianos have a tone like mine') and a truly beautiful Louis Treize chaise-longue; but she couldn't bear these things to be sat on often or scratched in any way. In a satinwood glass-fronted Sheraton bureau there were many calf-bound volumes of English and French classics, all given to her by Klem in the hope that she would read them; but she never did so. 'Madame doesn't read the books I give her,' Klem would say to Rennie. 'But she does polish them up. With beeswax. So that they shine nicely behind the glass. Madame likes things nice.' In a word, the room was full of elegant ornaments whose chief purpose was to give her something to polish, to gaze at, and to shut the door on lest anyone hurt them.

For a woman of ample shape, and fifty-eight years, she 'nipped' very nimbly up the stairs to the tower's top window. From here she was just able to see a break between the houses of the Rue de la Forêt along which people came from the station. She looked long in the hope of seeing Rennie cross that break. But no; so she turned her eyes towards the forest stretched along its undulating hills. She was as proud of this view from her chateau as of the chaise-longue in the salon or the silver spoons in the sideboard. 'Few people have a view like ours.' And as she considered the view she saw Jean coming down from the forest—coming hastily and hotly because her two black terriers were dragging her enthusiastically homeward. Their little black-trousered legs were racing down the green slope, their prick-eared heads turning round to see why she wasn't coming faster, and their upright tails semaphoring towards the house as if signalling joyously to Sophie at the window.

Jean was now thirty-five, a long, lean, striding woman on flat shoes. A head taller than her father and stepmother, taller even than the big fat Frédé, her bobbed hair wispy and her narrow face untended, she was as little feminine as Sophie and Marie-Louise were conspicuously so; as little interested in self-decoration as they were devoted to it. Erik O'Healy of Sainte-Marie (whom we shall meet) an enormous expatriated homosexual, rounded as a white rhino and soft as a slug, used to say to his male friends, 'That Jeanie Burgermann. The Burgermann Girl. Diana Nemorensis I call her. Diana of the Grove. So apt, don't you think? For consider, dears, is she not always attended by dogs? Is she not usually in the forest? Is she not a head taller than all the other nymphs? And—forgive me, duckies—is there not something a shade masculine about her legs? What I mean is they are as long as those of her absurd little dogs are short. And she does *stride* so. Furthermore, consider this: Diana of the Grove was a patroness of chastity, and wouldn't you think our dear Jeanie is one too? Necessarily? But I'm very fond of Jeanie Burgermann.'

'Here's Jeanie!' cried Sophie. 'Oh, I'm so glad. Now we can all be there to welcome Rennie.'

The dogs came tearing through the garden gate, Jean still attached to them. Her face was sweating, her hair adrift, and her legs at full stride; it was as if she was on the leashes rather than the dogs. She only just managed to wave with one hand to Sophie at the window.

'Is he here?' she called.

'Not yet, dear. But I'm so glad you're back.'

'Wallace and Bruce insisted on being back in time to welcome him. I had little say in the matter. Like most Scotsmen they're disgustingly independent, only obeying when it suits them.'

'If only we knew what train he'll come by, we'd all go and meet him. Oh, let's go to the station—now—he can't be much longer. Oh yes, *come!* All of us.'

But just then the Broadwood piano in the salon spoke. The opening notes of a Chopin nocturne came out into the evening air. It was Klem at a favourite pastime of playing Chopin and Bach to himself, and the airs of old Germany, while he smoked a pipe above his rapidly travelling fingers. Sometimes the airs were those of old student songs which forty years before he would sing with others over beer mugs. He was the only person who went often of an evening into the salon, that closed state-room. Sophie suffered him to move there among the beautiful things because she knew he would do no harm to any one of them but just sit on the piano stool and send up a few dreams with his pipe-smoke and music and be careful with his ash. Besides she needed to believe that few people could play like Klem. 'His touch is so wonderful.'

But she didn't want him to play just now. 'Oh dear, now he's started to play the piano just when I wanted him to come out. Extraordinary thing, Jeanie: as soon as I want him to do something he disappears and does something else.' Proud of Klem as she liked to be, she seldom spoke of him to Jean or Rennie or Marie-Louise except as 'he' and 'him'. Or, in less approving moments, as '*he*' and '*him*'. 'Klem! Klem!' Now she had left the window and her voice was shrilling down the stairs while her feet came following it. 'We're all going to meet Rennie. Have you laid the table? Oh, yes!' She was at the breakfast-room door. 'Oh, beautifully! And the silver? Oh, lovely! Marie-Louise, Marie-Louise, we're all going to meet Monsieur Rennie. Come along, Klem. Leave that piano. Find your hat, twist up your moustache, and come.'

'But, Madame . . .' began Marie-Louise.

'Yes, Marie-Louise?'

At her kitchen door Marie-Louise was looking up with a mischief in her eyes.

'What is it, Marie-Louise?'

Marie-Louise did not answer. She seemed only ready to giggle. Then she turned her face and glanced back into the kitchen.

'It's all right, Aunt Sophie darling. I'm here.' And Rennie came from the kitchen to Marie-Louise's side, grinning and putting his arm around her waist, and making her look tinier than usual against his six feet. He'd had the lively idea of approaching the house by a roundabout route below the forest, entering through the open kitchen door, and surprising Marie-Louise from behind. He'd seized her, hugged her with a hand over her mouth that she might not scream, kissed her lavishly 'just before Frédé comes home', and then lifted her up like a child and sat her on the top of a kitchen cupboard, so that he could stand, arms akimbo, and admire her. It was often his habit, when in the chateau, to spend hours with her in her kitchen, helping her cook, helping her clean; when he was away he sent her comic—and dubious—postcards; never did he arrive for his holiday without a gay present for the beautification of Marie-Louise. Now at the kitchen door he held her against him, as a tall affectionate father holds a small daughter.

'Rennie! Oh!' The scream came from Sophie, and it stopped the doctor's tune. It brought him to the salon door. It brought the dogs too, scampering in and dragging Jean with them because she'd not had time to unleash them properly. Barking their joy, they pranced up at Rennie whose hand went down to find their ears.

'Rennie, my darling, where in the world have you sprung from? You were not in the road——'

'He came the back way, Madame, and wouldn't let me say anything.'

'Oh, Rennie!' Sophie was now hugging him. 'What a silly boy you are. *Down*, Wallace. You'll tear my skirt. And Bruce too: don't be a couple of idiots. You've seen me before today. Oh, but I've still got my dreadful old dressing-jacket on. Did you have a lovely day in Paris? We'll all go into Paris tomorrow, won't we?'

'Of course, darling. I've a whole list of new places that I want to go and stare at, places where scandalous things happened, such as you'll love.'

'Oh, how lovely. You're such a wonderful person to go about Paris with. *He* never seems to care much about anything—' she had jerked her head towards Klem—'he just trots along beside me smoking his pipe and thinking of something else. I used to say I was the best guide to Paris ever, but you're better than I am now.'

'I've my reasons for wanting to know all about every place in Paris, and especially the disgraceful ones.'

'*Monsieur!*' Marie-Louise looked up to chide him archly.

'It's all right, Marie-Louise, don't you worry; it's just that when I'm kicked out of my present job, I intend to be a professional guide to Paris, and I shall have all sorts of clients. English gentlemen on the loose. American gentlemen with needs——'

'And you'd do it wonderfully, darling,' interrupted Sophie. 'You speak French so beautifully. Nobody——'

He provided the rest for her. 'Nobody speaks French like me. My accent is so perfect.'

'Well, it *is*,' she insisted, pouting at his chaff. 'It is, because you got it from me and *him*. We're so lucky to have *him*. There's nothing he doesn't know about languages, and he never allows me a single grammatical mistake. And he has the most beautiful accent. So have I. Oh, here's Frédé.' She loosed Rennie from her hug. 'Frédé's here just in time. Monsieur Rennie's just arrived, Frédé.'

Frédé Benoît, a rotund and outsize Frenchman, in a workman's blue blouse and black Basque beret, was now standing in the kitchen doorway looking over the head of his small wife. There was no doubt that a smell of garlic and wine preceded him; and the smell of a heavy workman's sweat. Frédé was a warehouseman in the Entrepôt des Eaux Minerales de Sainte-Marie.

Rennie swung round to where he stood in the doorway, grinning. '*Mon Dieu,* I hope he's not been here long. I've been kissing his wife. Kissing her good and proper.'

'Frédé knows that you don't mean any harm, Monsieur,' said Marie-Louise.

'But I'm not sure that I don't. Not at all sure. I think Frédé should watch out.'

Frédé only laughed, breathing forth a somewhat stronger smell of garlic. 'You've done it often enough before, Monsieur.'

'Yes, Frédé, but you said I could only do it so long as I didn't enjoy it. And I enjoyed it a lot. In fact I enjoyed it like one-o-clock.'

'Monsieur will have his joke,' said Marie-Louise. 'Il plaisante sur tout.' And Frédé with a nod and a grin endorsed this explanation.

So, everyone satisfied, Rennie went forward and kissed Jean, to the approval of the dogs, who jumped up to join in; then went to Klem, who shook hands with him, bringing his other hand over so that Rennie's lay between both of his.

II

Paris, Spring, 1939

RENNIE, twenty-six now and a schoolmaster in a Sussex school, enjoyed long holidays at Christmas, Easter and Summer, all of which, as a rule, he spent near Paris with his 'Aunt Sophie' and Uncle Klem, partly because like everyone else in the world he loved the idea of Paris and partly to perfect his French and German so as to become one day a Senior Modern Languages master in some greater school.

Next morning he and Jean were walking together along a dappled glade of the forest, Jean with a dog-whip and the leashes in her hand. Two strangely tall figures they seemed for a glade in France. Wallace and Bruce ran ahead of them, visiting the shadows or the sunlight beneath the densely congregated chestnuts. The Forest of Sainte-Marie is almost a forest of crowding chestnuts, though you may see other trees standing solitary in the crowd— oaks and sycamores, beeches and ashes and pines. The dogs nosed and prospected among dead leaves and bracken and sycamore brush. If at any time they were still and Rennie and Jean had stopped talking, then the deep forest seemed to hold the silence of its immemorial years. Could this elemental silence really keep its place within a mile or so of Paris? It was only after a time that, in such a silence, Rennie and Jean apprehended the flutter of a bird or the stir of a bough; the hum of insects perhaps, or the slither and scuttle of some animal unseen.

'Shouldn't we turn back?' asked Jean, glancing at a wrist-watch on her long bare arm.

'Good lord, no. Has it ever taken my Auntie Sophie less than four hours to put herself in presentable order for Paris—one hour before breakfast and three afterwards? And when she's finished preening herself she has to put the finishing touches to the Deutscher. She has to arrange his waistcoat, and straighten his tie and touch up his moustache. And probably send him back to change his fawn waistcoat for a white one. She does so like him to look beautiful.'

'The Deutscher' was the nickname which, at nine years old, he had attached to Klem, on realizing suddenly that it was odd for an aunt to have married a German. It was now a term of affection but spoken only to Jean and Sophie.

'Are you going to call her your Auntie Sophie for the rest of your life?'

'Suppose so.' He said it with a lift of the shoulders.

'And do you really think she believes you don't know the truth?'

'Yes, because she won't let herself believe anything else. Mrs. Burgermann believes nothing that it isn't cosy to believe.'

'Well, I think it's all ridiculous. I suppose she even imagines that I can't see the truth. And that I've never had the gumption to ask Daddy for it. Why, I asked him at least twenty-one years ago, when I was fourteen.'

'Yes, and I tumbled to it all at about fifteen.'

'What mutts it must please her to think us. Have you never hinted that you suspect that she's your mother, and the great Sir Hereward your father?'

'No.'

'But why? Surely you have a right to?'

'No doubt, but I'm too like her. I dodge discomfort. I don't want any part in some embarrassing scene. Besides, she's always made such a devil of a fuss of me whenever I come that I've never once in twenty years had the heart to hurt her. If ever we've referred to the great Sir Hereward, she's always called him my guardian and I've always left it at that.'

'Well, I still say it's absurd. She ought to accept properly—and bravely—the consequences of her past. She's had her good time and she should be ready to pay for it.'

'Have *you* ever hinted that you're not quite blind?'

'No.'

'Exactly. Well, why not?'

'Because I promised Daddy I wouldn't. He's as soft as you are. Apparently she's obsessed with the idea that the great Sir Hereward Ash said she was never to be troubled. She argues that he made every provision for you so that she should never be troubled. And I say it's all damned selfish. Why *shouldn't* she be troubled? All this fussing over you is all merely verbal. She's prodigal enough with words, and there it stops. I've not much use for a love that's only verbal. She keeps all your letters tied up with pink ribbon and the prettiest of bows, but has she ever done anything for you that'd hurt her?'

'She lets me come here every damned holiday.'

'Oh yes, she gives you bed and breakfast and a cut from her joint. She salves her conscience with that. I've noticed that she always makes you pay your share of the meals in Paris.'

'Yes, but—hell!—I'm twenty-six.'

'Just so, and I wonder how soon she'll be charging you for your board here.'

'My dear, I see all that you mean. I see that she got quit of me as soon as she could, and that she now eases her conscience with a gush of pretty words, which are cheap enough. But there it is. She is what she is, and the words are charming. Let her be happy.'

'Well, I suppose it's all very noble of you.'

'Oh no, it isn't. It's mainly that I haven't the courage to tackle her, and that I much prefer a spot of liveliness, any day, to a horrible spot of discomfort.'

'What do you really feel about your father?'

'I suppose I'm sentimental about him, but I always like to feel I should have loved him. I keep his picture on my wall—one I got from Grandma, who always called him my guardian too, bless her.

I like to think I get my intelligence from him—which is rude to the good auntie, I suppose—and certainly my terrific longing for adventure and risk. After all, it was that which killed him.'

'But don't you ever feel angry with him?'

'No. No, I don't think so.'

'Well, I think it's generous and noble.'

'Not at all. I suspect I forgive him all his sins so as to keep a happy dream——'

But Jean was no longer listening. Her eyes were fixed on a bright powdered haze behind the trees, and after a pause she said, 'All I know is that if *I'd* had a child, I don't think I'd have deserted him, bastard or not.'

She had used the brutal word angrily, and in this moment Rennie perceived something that he'd never troubled to see before. He saw that Jean, tall and thin and thirty-five, was turning bitter at the thought that she was now likely to die virgin and barren—and never having known . . . He saw—why not before?—that it was this bitterness which now fathered her indifference to dress and her angry, careless inattention to the brown bobbed hair.

'We're getting too deep in the forest,' she said. 'Let's get back. Down, Bruce, down! Yes, I know you love me but that's not the point at the moment. There never was such a woman for keeping her head in the sand. I'm always asking her what she proposes to do if war comes——'

'As it will.'

'As it will, and the sooner the better. We can't go on like this. I'm all for having it out with this awful little man. Once and for all. But she won't listen. She won't believe there'll be any war because she doesn't want to.'

Jean put the dogs on the leashes lest they chased the goats down the green slope beneath the forest fringe. This done, they turned for home and instantly the dogs strained on the leashes as if they enjoyed the fun of pulling her along at an exasperating speed.

'Give me the beasts,' said Rennie.

'Gracious, no. I'm not so weak that I can't hold them when I want to, and I won't have them thinking so. I say the war became certain four weeks ago when the Germans marched into Czechoslovakia and stole a whole country. I'm not putting up with that,' she said, striding hard behind the drag of the dogs. 'Are you?'

'Not if I can help it.'

The forest glade opened out on to a rutted cart-track which skirted the forest. Above them now was the open sky, and below them the green slope falling towards the houses of Sainte-Marie. They halted, as always, to stare into the southerly haze where, not seen at first but then appearing like a picture on a film in its developing tray, stood all the domes of Paris and the tapering wraith of the Tour Eiffel.

'I wonder,' Rennie began, 'will they spare Paris or lay it flat.'

'Will it make much difference? It'll be the end of civilization.'

'Will it? I'm not sure. There's an awful lot of Paris—and London —to flatten out.' His eyes left the domes, and turned downwards to look at the little cone-capped tower of Sophie's chateau. 'Perhaps it's fairly safe,' he said, for Jean was looking at it too. 'All of fifteen kilometres from Paris.'

'Unless the swine get as far as Paris and come this way.'

'They may. Jean, I'll talk to the woman this afternoon. I feel more and more that I ought to dig my mother out of here. And your father too. If they get as far as here, his position as a German who's deserted the Fatherland might be far from a happy one.'

'Well, he'll never go unless *she* says the word. And she won't. Her home means too much to her. She'll hug it around her just as a limpet does on its rock. Leaving the sea to do what it likes. And there's something in me too that doesn't really want to go.'

'And what's that?'

'A rather mad craving to be here and see what happens. It'll at least be exciting, for a change.'

'And *I* feel exactly the same, Jean dear. I'm sure it's all very wrong, but there's a part of me that's hoping war will come—just for the fun and excitement of it. It's the bad old Sir H. in me, as I told you just now. Hurrah for some excitement and danger! But, on the whole, I hope for your sake—and the old Deutscher's—that they don't get as far as here. There might be rather too much excitement then.'

And Rennie continued looking down at little Sainte-Marie, lying there under the sun in happiness and peace for a while.

§

Sophie, dressed for Paris, and Rennie at her side, with the Deutscher in tow some paces behind, emerged from the Gare du Nord into the Place de Roubaix. The Place de Roubaix is not lovely. It is even grey and sombre, but Sophie spread her arms towards it and exclaimed, 'Paris! Paris in spring! How I love it,' and was nearly run over by a taxi tearing towards the station portals. Rennie pulled her back into life only just in time. The doctor, dressed for Paris as she liked to have him—in blue suit, fawn waistcoat and Homburg hat—saw nothing of this incident because his head was bent over his pipe-bowl and match flame, as he walked.

'Klem! Klem darling! I was nearly run over.'

'Were you, my dear?' he said without lifting his eyes from the pipe's mouth, because the tobacco was not sufficiently alight.

'Mercy, isn't he awful? If I were really run over he'd hardly realize it, even when the stretcher turned up. And yet he's fond of me.'

They were now walking along the Boulevard de Magenta towards the Métro so as to take the train to the Opera. Sophie went sailing a step ahead of Rennie in her enthusiasm, her broad breast well forward like a ship's prow. Nothing had pleased her more than when she heard that an épicier in Sainte-Marie had called her 'la grande dame anglaise', and she was now demonstrating a 'grande dame anglaise' to the citizens of Paris.

They came above ground, out of the Opera station, and there straight in front of them, decked out with its statues, and winged figures against the sky, and its roof like a combined tiara and coronet, was that ornate Second Empire palace. Sophie's delight in her trinkets spread outwards from her little chateau to Paris itself, which was one of them. And within the compass of Paris what more exquisite trinket than the Opera? She loosed a gasping 'Ah!' at the sight of it and worshipped, coming up the last few steps.

Then together, she and Rennie, with the doctor trailing behind, walked among the things she loved, from this big luxurious trinket of the Opera to the little luxurious trinkets in the shops of the Rue de la Paix. Klem had said to Rennie, 'I advise keeping her out of the Rue de la Paix or we shall never get beyond the shops,' but she had insisted on going along that jewelled way and past the Column in the Place Vendôme (Napoleon's trinket) to the Rue de Rivoli, where there were statuettes in the windows and engrossing blouses and hats. They attained at last the garden of the Tuileries where she sat herself in the broad central avenue between the plantations of chestnuts, so that she could see all the white statues and in one far distance the Louvre and in the other the Arc de Triomphe crowning the summit of the Champs Elysées. 'Everything in Paris is so clean and white,' she said delightedly.

The doctor, looking towards the Arc de Triomphe as he sat himself beside her, took occasion to say, 'Really the only difference between Sophie's trinkets and the Emperor's is a slight one of scale. Hers are on the mantelpiece and his in the Place Vendôme or on the top of the Champs Elysées. The top of the Champs Elysées provided him with an excellent mantelpiece.'

It was two o'clock. They had intended to have a cheap déjeuner in a bistro on the Quai de Montebello opposite Notre Dame, but Sophie's creation and completion of a grande dame anglaise had taken longer than her estimates, so they had decided to have 'a snack at home and save money', an achievement which could please her almost as much as a meal in Paris, even though—no, let us resist too much repetition and not speak of Notre Dame as perhaps the best-beloved of all her trinkets—even though that magnificent fane was permanently before her as she ate.

Spring was in possession of Paris. A week or two earlier, suddenly, overnight as it were, spring, like a silent army of occupation, had moved in and possessed Paris. The leaves on the chestnut trees about them were still a tender green but enlarging fast, and the buds breaking into blossom. In the tall buildings of the Rue de Rivoli before their eyes all the window shutters were open to the spring. In other streets the bright café awnings bowed before it, and their tables stood out on the terraces to enjoy it. Women passing Sophie in the garden had blossomed like the trees into new spring dresses and hats, not one of which failed to draw her eyes as it went past, no matter what she and Rennie were talking about.

Rennie was wondering how best to introduce the subject of war. She seemed so far from such a disrupting matter; and, to add to his difficulty, Klem was sitting on the other side of her. It would be necessary to speak of Klem.

'Where are we going this afternoon?' she asked after an interesting hat had passed beyond further study.

'To the Musée Cernuschi, and I'll tell you why. Because nobody else seems to have heard of it, and I've an ambition to know places in Paris that nobody else knows.'

Sophie, pressing up her lips, showed little enthusiasm for the Musée Cernuschi, till he told her that it was full of oriental bronzes, statuettes, tapestries, vases, and jade dress-ornaments. Then she thought she would like to come. The doctor offered no opposition, or indeed any comment; he just sat beside them and smoked.

At last, however, he knocked out his pipe, rose, and braced back his shoulders. He had complained in the morning of some slight lumbago, but no one had made any mention of this trouble since breakfast, so now he said, 'Rather than that you should pester me with inquiries about my back I am happy to inform you that it is a little better.'

'Oh my poor darling!' Sophie exclaimed. 'Has no one asked him about his lumbago? It's really better, is it, my precious?'

'It is. But it is still there and a subject for solicitude. I wouldn't wish you to think it had gone.'

'Oh, what can we do for it? My poor sweet!'

'Precisely nothing in the Garden of the Tuileries. I merely mentioned the improvement so that you could continue your discussion unworried by too much concern about me. I will walk up and down a little while you two settle your itineraries. Au revoir.'

He strolled away, and it was when his small figure beneath the Homburg hat was a good twenty yards distant that Rennie deliberately attempted a shock treatment. 'Better see all we can while we can. This may be my last visit for Heaven knows how long. For ever perhaps.'

'*No!* What are you talking about?'

'And all the museums may be flat in six months time.'

'*Flat?*'

'Yes, bombed flat.'

'Don't be absurd. Don't talk like that. You know you don't believe it.'

'I believe it enough to want to get you all away from this part of the world.'

'But what rubbish! How could I leave my home and furniture and everything?'

'There are firms that undertake to move furniture.'

'But do you mean go to England?'

'They negotiate seas and oceans.'

'Yes; and they'd smash half my precious things. *I* know them. Besides, where would we go? It'd take months to find a place where I could live. I can't live in any poky little hole.'

'There are such things as hotels where people can live a month or two, and warehouses where furniture can rest for a while.'

'Have my furniture ruined in some warehouse—no! No, no. There isn't going to be any war. They talked last year about war being almost certain, and I never believed it—or hardly ever. And I was perfectly right. They saw how terrible it'd be for everybody and patched up their silly quarrel—whatever it was. They'll do the same again.'

'Not again.'

'Why not?'

'Not since the fifteenth day of March last.'

'Why, what happened then?'

'My dear, do you never read a paper?' Rennie sometimes called her 'Aunt Sophie' but only rarely, because offended by the unreality and discomfort of it. 'My dear' came more easily. 'On the fifteenth of March last the Germans pinched a whole non-German country of fifteen thousand people and put it in their swag-bag. Not again. Not again without war.'

'Well, even if there is a war, they won't touch Paris. No one would.' She couldn't, wouldn't, believe that anyone would deal violently with Paris; was it not *hers?* 'They won't get near it. They didn't last time.'

'They did in 1870.'

'Yes; and they behaved very decently, *he* always says. And things were different then. Wars were wars of movement, he says. Now they're wars of attrition behind trenches, like 1914. Ask Klem.'

'They'll probably run over Poland in about fourteen days.'

'Yes, but . . . Poles. What are Poles?'

'Some of the grandest fighters in the world.'

'Well . . . even if by any chance they do come, wouldn't it be absolutely necessary for me to be in my house so as to look after my things? I don't want a lot of huge Prussian soldiers in it.'

'Among your valuable things there's the old Deutscher. What about him?'

'Klem?'

'Yes, what will the French feel about Herr Burgermann?'

'Nonsense. He's been a British subject for thirty years. And everybody in Sainte-Marie loves him. They'd never hurt him.'

'All right. All right. And if the Germans come?'

'They can think what they like. He's no longer a German.'

'I'll tell you what they'll think. And say.'

'What?'

'That he's a Traitor to the Blood.'

'Blood? What blood?'

'Oh my dear . . . doesn't the Deutscher ever talk about this?'

'He never talks about anything.'

'Well, they maintain that anyone with German blood in him is

23

a German wherever he lives or whatever he says. And if he tries to change his nationality he's a traitor. And they're not kind to traitors.'

'Oh, why do you tell me things like this? Why do you want to frighten me like this? You're spoiling my day with you, and I was so looking forward to it. I don't believe they'd do anything to poor Klem. He's much too mild and gentle.'

Rennie shrugged and said no more. He accepted that it would need mightier things than his words to make her believe something she didn't want to believe. And he now noticed, with some little hurt, that, in her unwillingness to listen, she hadn't even asked what *he* proposed to do if war came. He had wanted to tell her, to pour out, a private desire, but now he felt sullen and decided to keep it to himself. 'To hell with it, if she's not even interested. I'll stay alone with it.' This self-pity, pressing on the old grievance, made him increase his hurt by swearing that he wouldn't even tell Klem and Jean. 'They'd only tell her, and if she doesn't want to know, she needn't. I'm quite content to be alone with it.'

§

Now the three of them were returning through a sunset light towards the Gare du Nord. Sophie, enjoying an endless chatter with Rennie, sent the doctor ahead to find the platform from which a train would leave for Sainte-Marie; and when he was out of hearing, she clutched Rennie's arm, hugged it against her side, and said, as so often, 'Oh, you're the *loveliest* person to go around Paris with. *He's* very sweet, of course, and there's nobody like him when it comes to history or grammar or music——'

'Or chipping an onion,' suggested Rennie.

'Yes—chipping an onion—but when it comes to going about Paris from one lovely place to another he just tags along behind. You and I love it.'

In the station Klem led them to the platform he had found, and they got into a third-class compartment of a waiting train. Sophie, in her tenue of a 'grande dame', looked out of place in this dusty, wooden-seated compartment, but since there were only five stations to Sainte-Marie-la-Forêt she liked to save money by enduring a half-hour in the straitened comfort of the third class. For that brief time she was prepared to sit upright, her back hardly touching the vulgar wall behind her.

As the train drew out of Paris she looked from her window for what she always loved to see, the cupolas and campanile of Sacré Coeur, white as the towers of a celestial city, accosting the sky from the summit of Montmartre. Nor would she consent to be brought down to earth by Klem's assertion that, for him, it was all too like a wedding-cake. When the train had passed it, she picked up a *Paris Soir* which someone had left on the seat, and enjoyed a free read in it. Sophie seldom missed anything that was 'going free', because the sensation of getting something for nothing was so pleasant.

The trains to Sainte-Marie, ambling from station to station, were always slow, but this one today seemed to be taking such a long time to arrive that at last she looked from the window, hoping to see their forest lying dense on its undulating ridge. None of them had looked from the window for some time. The doctor had been reading the *Paris Soir* ever since Sophie transferred it to him, and she and Rennie had been chattering about things seen today. But now— why so long? Where were they? She leaned forward and looked through either window. They were travelling past houses extraordinarily tall and streets thickly populated. Surely the houses should now be small and scattered, and some fields be in sight? This couldn't be Saint-Denis; they'd passed it long ago. It looked more like Paris itself—and lo! Paris it was, for there was Sacré Coeur again, but now on the train's other side.

'Oh, my God! . . . Klem!'

Much as she liked to see her beloved Sacré Coeur at the end of a day in Paris, she didn't want to see it twice the same evening, first from one side and then from the other.

'Klem! What have you done?'

Clearly what he had done was to put them into one of those trains which leave the Gare du Nord, amble slowly among the stations of the Banlieue and turn round in an interesting curve so as to arrive back in Paris at the Gare Saint-Lazare.

'Klem! You put us in the wrong train. Oh, Rennie, he's impossible.'

'I looked at the indicator,' said Klem, now in his turn looking anxiously from the window, his brow creased, his eyes distressed. There was no doubt that that *was* Sacré Coeur. No amount of staring at it would abolish it from the top of Montmartre. 'I looked at the indicator and it certainly said Saint-Denis.'

'Of course it said Saint-Denis. Why shouldn't it say Saint-Denis? Not every train that goes to Saint-Denis goes on to Sainte-Marie. Some of them do this ridiculous business of turning round and coming back to Paris.'

Too true. Here were all the familiar features of Saint-Lazare station.

Klem slumped back into his seat just as Sophie rose furiously from hers. 'Well, here we are. Back in Paris. Get out, Rennie. Go on. And *he* too. Perhaps *you'll* get the tickets this time and we'll begin all over again. Perhaps *you* can get us to Sainte-Marie; it's only ten miles. And perhaps you can explain to the ticket collector why we've all got tickets from the Gare du Nord.'

All the way from the door of their compartment to the ticket barrier she discharged a hot running jet of reprobation at the head and the face of Klem, as he came walking in disgrace at her side. Rennie, walking on her other side, suffered for him. He was always uncomfortable when she started bullying Klem. 'She does go on and on so. On and on and on. Why the hell doesn't he tell her to shut up? *Shut up*, woman! Poor little man. All he's done has been to give us a nice round trip, so that we can have a new view of Paris. . . .' And then, walking by the side of this continuing rebuke, he began to wonder why he was always a little pleased to be censuring her and, after a time, to be shrugging the censure helplessly away.

III

The Abbé and Erik

For once the door of the salon stood open, and all the furniture within it, the Louis Seize chairs, the beautiful chaise-longue, the Sèvres vases, the marquetry commode, and the inlaid ormolu cabinet, stood newly dusted and polished. Even the books in the bureau had been given a touching-up by Sophie's feather duster. On a silver tray stood her silver teapot, milk jug and sugar basin, all of which the doctor had been given the task of polishing, because nobody did it like him. He had polished them in the kitchen, sitting with Marie-Louise and explaining, 'I'm taking my time about this, Marie-Louise, or she'll be sending me out to polish some of the stones in the drive.'

And now, above the salon, in her bedroom, she was putting the finishing touches to her own appearance. And, at intervals, to Klem's.

Rennie came down the tower stairway and joined them. She loved to have him in the room when she was seated at her Louis Quinze marquetry poudreuse which served as her dressing-table (and which she had convinced herself was worth many hundreds of pounds).

'I hope you're looking your nicest, Rennie darling.' She rose, came towards him and touched his hair into beauty here and there 'You've got such lovely hair. And you've got to be very nice to both of them. I know you think my poor Erik revolting but he can't help being what he is. And he's always charming to me. And

27

he's so pathetically huge.' One more touch at his hair, and she hurried back to her happy craftsmanship at the poudreuse. 'Besides, he admires you. Of course we know he can't help admiring any young man who isn't hideous, but he did stop me in the market-place yesterday and say "I see you've got the delightful Quentin boy back. What a sweetie he is".'

'How perfectly foul.'

'Yes, but surely you can't help liking someone who admires you. Who thinks you a sweetie. *I* never can. And I just had to ask him to come and meet you after that. The Abbé'll be here, and you like him. So be nice to both of them. You can be so charming if you want to.'

Rennie was now standing by the window. 'It's raining.'

'Oh, *no!* Not enough to stop the Abbé coming. He's such fun, and he delights in our Erik. Extraordinary how these Catholic priests never seem to mind what anybody is or does. In fact they seem to like you best if you're a shocking sinner. Erik's a Catholic, of course, like all Irishmen—so's *he*, come to that—' she jerked her head towards Klem who was disappearing through the door—'but Erik never goes to church any more than *he* does. Of course *he's* an unbeliever but Erik isn't; Erik says quite frankly that it's just his sloth and he's deep in mortal sin.'

'"Erik" with a "k"! It's damned affectation.'

'Oh, I know it is. And so does Erik. But he wanted to write, you see, and he thought people'd take his work more seriously if he spelt his name with a "k". He says nobody could possibly take an "Eric" seriously. And I think he's right in that. I don't think I could.'

'He'll never write anything.'

'Oh, I know he won't. And he knows it too, now. But he's grown so fond of his "k".'

'Here's someone coming.'

'Oh, no. I'm not ready. He's early. Who is it?'

Beyond the garden hedge an umbrella was sailing up the avenue towards the gate.

'It's—it's the Abbé.'

The great bulge of the Abbé Belfort's paunch was now advancing between the piers of the gate. It was so ample a paunch that it lifted the frayed hem of his black soutane far off the ground, uncurtaining his coarse grey socks and thick black shoes; it was so weighty that its carriage through the world required that the Abbé's upper parts leaned back as he walked; and thus it came through the gate with the Abbé's head lagging behind it, and the umbrella coming last of all. Buttoned all the way from collar to hem, the soutane had no cincture, cord, or belt about its middle; it was as if no girdle was long enough to encircle that huge periphery.

Shutting his umbrella, the Abbé disappeared beneath the porch. On the front door he dropped a single knock as a peasant might. Marie-Louise's steps clicked towards the door.

'Bonjour, Marie-Louise.' His voice came up the stairs. 'Bonjour, my dear child, and give me your blessing, Sainte Marie-Louise of Sainte-Marie-la-Forêt. Put me somewhere where I can sit down. I am exhausted.'

Sophie said, 'Oh, go and look after him. Oh dear, where's *he* got to? He was here a moment ago. Dash down and do the honours, darling.'

When Rennie got to the salon, the Abbé was already spread over an easy chair and puffing out enormous breaths through lips parted in a narrow slit. Marie-Louise, looking very small before that bulk on the chair, stood in front of him listening to the remarks that intervened between the puffs.

'Time was, Marie-Louise, when this road from the Presbytery to the forest seemed but a gentle slope, but things, alas, are not what they were. . . . Phew. . . . The road has tilted steadily upwards in the years and is now a most damnable incline. . . . Dear me! Tell me, Marie-Louise: to you it is nothing; you can dance up slopes like a child; you are but a baby; but Frédé? Your Frédé? He is getting fat; you feed him much too well; tell me, tell me for my comfort, that it's beginning to tilt for him too.'

'He hasn't said so, Father.'

'Oh, well . . . a pity . . . but he's not yet a sexagenarian like me. Ah, here is the young man. Oh, qu'il est grand! Bonjour, Monsieur Rennie. Don't ask me to get up. No, *please*: as you love me. Just imagine that I've stood up to greet you.'

There was no doubt that each exhausted breath expelled the odour of a red wine recently absorbed, but whether a burgundy or a claret Rennie was not connoisseur enough to learn from this bouquet. 'No, don't you move, sir,' he said, forgetfully speaking in English.

'And don't you call me "sir". I know what it means in English: it means you think I'm a hundred. Alas, I'm forty years older than you, but just call me "Abbé" or "Father". Or, better still, "Georges" because then I could feel like a contemporary, which would be absurd, but pleasant.'

'My aunt will be down in a minute, Father.'

'Yes, yes. It's a touch of this, isn't it?' And the Abbé gave an excellent demonstration of a woman wielding her lipstick before her glass. He pushed out his lips and pencilled them delicately with an imaginary stick of Guerlain's best; he drew the stick away to consider the reflection of his artistry; he turned his head this way and that to see the triumph from all angles, and then dabbed with imaginary powder his nose and the deep, sagging pouches of his chin. 'Tout pour la beauté. Comme ça.'

'That's precisely what's going on, Father.'

'Splendid. Let her take her time about it, and may the good God guide her hand. The result should be worth waiting for.'

As he prattled on breathlessly, Rennie suddenly realized that he was alone in the room with him, and that here was a good chance to ask his help; to ask him to do something which he himself had failed to do. Time pressed, and he said abruptly, 'Father, can I ask your help in something?'

'Indeed yes, dear boy.'

'First then, is it war this year?'

The Abbé shrugged. He did not speak at once. He was still breathless and the short breaths were like a smothered snoring in his throat. 'War? . . . Yes, I should think so. . . . But who can say?'

30

'I think so too. So does everyone in England.'

'Then God help us all. God help my poor France.' Abstractedly he made the sign of the cross over the whole wide front of his breast. 'And your dear England too.'

'And don't you expect, Father, that in the first months the Germans will carry all before them, as they did last time?'

'Alas, yes. I await exactly that.'

'They will try to get to Paris, as before?'

'Naturally. I fear for Paris. Unless Sainte Geneviève sees fit to save it again. She saved it from Attila and his Huns, God bless her, and again, at the last moment, from the Kaiser and his Huns. I pray she has not wearied of helping us. But sometimes I think there are all too many reasons why she should be entirely weary of us.'

'Will they come this way?'

The Father lifted one of two fat hands which had both been laid against the sides of his stomach; and after a few seconds he dropped it despairingly. 'Some will come this way if Sainte Geneviève doesn't hold them back. We bestride one of the great roads into the capital. My church opens its doors on to the Rue de Paris.' He sighed. 'In August, 1914, I was the curé of a village, Autheuil-les-Eaux, near Beauvais and we expected them among us any minute. We always said that it was only your noble British army that saved us. God bless me, that was twenty-five years ago, and you were in your voiture d'enfant.'

'If they come, will they just pass through Sainte-Marie or will some stay?'

'What do I know? I am a man of peace. But we are only a few kilometres from Paris, and'— he gently pushed down Wallace whose forefeet were on his knees—'no, no, dear beast, I have no lap—down, dear, down—and I can only imagine that they'll occupy Sainte-Marie.'

'But in that event, my God!—pardon me, Father——'

'No need of pardon, my dear. If that's to be the event, you may well call upon God.'

'Just so, and what I wanted to ask you was, will you speak to my aunt and tell her all this? She won't listen to me. She will to you.'

'To what end do I speak?'

'I think she should get the family out of here. Uncle Klem was a German once.'

The Abbé fetched a black snuffbox from somewhere under the wrinkles of his cassock. He offered a pinch to each nostril and, snapping the lid shut, said, 'But, my dear boy, if the Boche gets as far as here, I suggest he'll get to England too. Would the good doctor be any safer there than here?'

'At least he could get farther away.'

'You mean that Madame should leave this house and Sainte-Marie for ever?'

'Or at least till the war is over.'

'I have sometimes thought so, sad as I should be to lose her and the doctor and Mademoiselle Jean. But she will never do it.'

'Then what about Uncle Klem?'

A smile made the Abbé's broad face a little broader yet. 'Madame Burgermann loves her good doctor, but there's so much more of her furniture than of Monsieur—if you see what I mean.'

'I see only too well; but you *will* speak to her?'

'Certainly—hush! Is this her coming?—certainly I will, but with little hope. Maybe I shall have a chance to introduce the subject this afternoon. Ah, chère Madame, for *you* I do get up.' He began to heave his mass out of the chair. 'Not for your young man, but——'

'No, no, chèr Abbé, don't move, don't move.' Willingly he collapsed back again. 'How could I be so late with *you* coming?'

'Dear lady, I was early. I began early because of the terrible slope.'

'And where is Klem? Why hasn't he come down, Rennie? Oh, he's awful.' She went to the door. 'Klem. *Klem!* The Abbé's here. Been here for hours. You must think us awful, Father. Jeanie, if you'll only believe it, has gone off to swim at Enghien, now that the bathing place is open. Swimming in April. Extraordinary. And where is Erik? He's late. He *is* naughty. I'll not wait tea for him.'

'Don't you, Madame. Monsieur Erik O'Healy has been indulged too much all his life. Ah, bonjour, Docteur. Comment allez-vous——'

'Now sit down, Klem; you allezvous very well. And we were just going to talk some interesting scandal about Erik O'Healy. I'm glad he's late because we can now get on with it. Yes, it's clear to me, Father, from what he tells me, and he tells me everything that's ever happened to him, that he was idiotically indulged in England by a doting mother and sister. Does he go to you for confession?'

'He doesn't need to confess to me, dear lady, because he confesses to everybody. Of course there's the little trifle of absolution which he doesn't get from the others, but——'

'He doesn't confess to me the one thing I long to know. Don't you think, Father, that he only got to Sainte-Marie just in time?'

'You mean? You would say . . .?'

'I would say that he had to leave England as quickly as he could.'

'Now then, Sophie darling,' Klem rebuked.

'Nonsense, Klem, why shouldn't I say aloud what everybody believes?'

'But why, dear lady, should he need to leave England quickly?'

'Oh, now, come, Father! Need you ask? I know he's kept here by the mother and sister. He's told me so. He says he loves being a kept man; it's what he's always wanted. He says the only pity of it was, they wouldn't give him enough money to live in Paris proper.'

'I wonder,' said Rennie, perceiving a chance to give the Abbé his opening, 'if he'll be able to go back to England if there's a war.'

And instantly a loud knock on the door—*ratta-tat-tatta-tat-TAT*, unlike the Abbé's single bang—closed that opening.

'That's him,' cried Sophie. 'Oh, what a pity. It was just getting interesting. That's him. No one else knocks like that. Never mind, Marie-Louise, I'll go; it's only Monsieur O'Healy. Bring in the tea.... Ah, Erik my dear, come in. You're late and you're naughty. No, there's no time to kiss. Here's the Abbé been sitting there for hours and wanting his tea. Get you in and sit down.'

From behind she was pushing him into the drawing-room while he was lifting a big plump hand in protest and saying 'Gently, beloved. I cannot be pushed'.

'Rubbish. Go in.'

'I must never be hurried.'

'Well, you shouldn't be late. Hurry in.'

'Dear lady, you're bullying me. Let it be understood: bullied I'll never be.'

'Rubbish. Go on,' said Sophie, still pushing.

'I protest I'm not one to be shoved around by women.'

'Oh, yes, you are, Mr. O'Healy. Get inside.'

'To be shoved is an indignity.'

'Well, go and sit down. You're so enormous.'

Erik O'Healy was a huge man encompassed in soft flesh but with no such vast promontory as the Abbé Belfort's stomach. His big head and features above the big, broad-hipped body, suggested a touch of giantism, contradicted however by the terminals of his body, the hands and feet which were small and delicate. He did not lessen this appearance of size by keeping his hair long and curling down to the nape of his neck, nor by his customary wear of pale fawn knickerbockers, wide and long and drooping.

'My salutations, Doctor,' he said to Klem while still being pushed. 'And to you, Rennie my sweet. Here I come, propelled from behind by Auntie. And there—' this was on sighting the black mass of the Abbé in his chair—'there is the good Monsieur Belfort. Sophie, I adore the Father.'

'So do we all, Erik dear.'

'And yet,' objected the Abbé, 'not one of you ever comes into my church.'

'That's quite untrue, Father,' said Erik. 'I was there last Christmas

Eve for Midnight Mass, and, what's more, I made Sophie come with me. I told her how absolutely divine it looked with the candles all over the place and she immediately insisted on coming and tried to make the doctor come too.'

'Erik, *do* sit down. You're so enormous,' Sophie begged with a little more pushing.

'Not yet. Not yet. I adore your Midnight Mass, Father, and above all, I adore going to it with our Sophie. But, Sophie, where's Jeanie? Where's my Diana of the Grove? My Diane Chasseresse?'

'Swimming with Françoise de Brienne.'

'Swimming? Did you say *swimming*? Oh no, it's impossible. Why, we're not half-way through April; or are we?' He went to the doorway from which he had been pushed. 'Marie-Louise, dear, bring the tea. I've arrived. And the Abbé's hungry. How's Frédé?' But, not waiting to hear how Frédé was, he came back and put himself into the chair nearest Rennie. To whom, when the clatter of tea things, and Sophie's and Marie-Louise's talk covered his words, he said softly, 'Can't get over that Jeanie swimming. Swimming in April. Is she a mermaid? She's not as petite as most chic little mermaids but, besides the swimming, there *is* one thing in which, in my view, she has affinities with the mermaids.'

'What's that?'

'Well—no, perhaps I shouldn't say it to you, ducks, though you're not her brother. Not even a blood relation, are you?'

'No. Say what you like.'

'I always think of you as her half-brother, but you're not really, are you? Just Grannie's adopted son? If we may call our Sophe's mama Grannie.'

'Just Grannie's adopted son. Say what you like.'

'I may be a little naughty, may I?'

'You may.'

'Well, if you study the structure of a mermaid you'll see that she can't really be of much use to a man, and—but hush!—tut, tut!—not in front of the clerisy.'

The clatter had stopped. Tea was being passed round by the

doctor. Rennie leapt up to help him. Talk around the cups was about local people at first and scandalous, both Erik and the Abbé being of those who will slaughter any reputation if thereby they can achieve a tea-time witticism. Indeed Erik admitted as much after they'd dealt with Madame Dubois in the Rue de la Forêt. 'It may be we all tell lies,' he said, 'but we do have fun. Both the dear Abbé and I are good Romans and ready to butcher anyone to make a Roman holiday. Actually I have a passion for Lucille Dubois.'

'You're a shocking man,' said Sophie who'd been delighting in the scandal.

'I know.' Erik shook his head as if deploring the truth of this. 'It's sad. And the trouble is you don't half know the worst. I turned fifty last year, and there's no doubt I began to deteriorate after that. Rapidly. I think I'm horrible now. I wander about the forest distressed by it all and wishing I were nicer. I'm getting so frightfully touchy. In fact I'm getting exactly like my Auntie Glad, who's just on eighty. I keep feeling I'm not wanted at parties any more, and that nobody wants to speak to me, and so I go away in a huff. If I go away suddenly this afternoon, you'll know that it's the old amour propre.'

'Never mind about your amour propre, Erik dear.' Sophie waved it away with a discouraging hand. 'We can't worry about that this afternoon. And it's probably no worse than anyone else's. It couldn't be worse than mine.'

'But then again, Sophie dear, I'm a most awful liar. And the trouble is one can't admire oneself if one hears onself lying and lying, and one does so need someone to admire. The person I want more than anyone else to admire is the party I have to live with all day and all night—Erik O'Healy, to wit—and, Sophie, I really can't. No, I'm quite clear about that. There's something awfully sly and nasty about him that I don't care for at all. One could wish——'

'Never mind about what one could wish. There's a lot that's quite nice about you, and we're all very fond of you. So now let's talk about something other than you, you silly man.'

'Certainly. But what else is interesting? There must be something. Abbé, what?'

'What,' said the Abbé, 'are you going to do if there's war?'

'Oh, but there mustn't be a war. It'd be *too* boring. Why's there got to be a war?'

'I think you never read any papers, do you?' asked the Abbé.

'Of course not. Why should I? It's so unnecessary. I know that if there's a war someone's sure to tell me.'

'Oh, I hate this talk of war,' interrupted Sophie. 'Rennie's been getting at me about it. There's not going to be a war.'

'And even if there was,' said Erik, 'they'd never get as far as here, I sincerely hope. Could they, Abbé?'

'They could.'

'Oh *no*, please! That'd be so upsetting. You don't really mean it, lovey, do you?'

'I do most emphatically, Monsieur Erik O'Healy.'

'Oh, gracious me! How extremely repellent.'

Rennie quoted the Abbé. 'It was only Sainte Geneviève who stopped them last time.'

'Sainte Geneviève! Oh, but she's my patron saint as well as Paris's. I adopted her very soon after I arrived here—in fact, it was immediately after I saw her picture in the Panthéon: "Sainte Geneviève watching over Paris while it sleeps". *What* a pet! I gave my heart to her at once. And *what* a picture! All in the cold colours of moonlight. She'll do her stuff again, the dear girl, I feel sure. I have the utmost faith in Sainte Geneviève. And, somehow, I always have the feeling that she knows it. She knows that I adore her. And she watches over me while I sleep. I truly believe it.'

Somewhere amid all this persiflage the Abbé's effort to instruct Sophie lay still-born.

IV

Paris, Autumn, 1939

'No, no, darling. I must go at once. Tomorrow. I must get back while I can.' Rennie spoke with a young man's excitement at the certainty of war and with pride that he was needed to help save his country. At the same time he was suffering an ache of irritation with Sophie that she should be belittling this great hour and his place in it.

'And he's right,' said Jean. 'Absolutely right. I only wish I could go back with him. Why on earth didn't I get to England and join the Army or the Air Force when there was some chance of it? It was Wallace and Bruce that stopped me. Now I suppose it's too late. Perhaps I shall find something to do here.'

'He's right, my dear,' said Klem.

They were sitting, the four of them, under the red awning of Fouquet's on the sunlit side of the Champs Elysées, sipping their evening aperitifs, Sophie her Guignolet, and the others their Pernods. Rennie was in the uniform of an aircraftman in the R.A.F. To join the Air Force and volunteer for aircrew, if war seemed certain, had been that secret resolve which he had hidden from them all because he was angry with Sophie for not being sufficiently interested even to ask what he'd do in a war. When a few days ago he'd arrived at the chateau in his smoke-blue battle-dress with an eagle for a shoulder-flash, she had screamed with admiration, turned him round and round to look at him in uniform, and said he looked beautiful. 'Though they ought to have made you an officer,' she began. 'Your——' Then she stopped. She had been about to say, 'Your father was made a colonel in the last war, and he looked beautiful. Magnificent.'

It was August 25th, one day after the world had learned, with a stunned bewilderment, that Germany had signed a pact with Russia, which would leave her free to crush Poland and then turn her might against the West. Against France, first of all, perhaps. And yet the Champs Elysées, in the softened evening light of Paris's heure bleue, with the sun falling behind the Arc de Triomphe, looked no different from a thousand yesterdays. August it might be when Paris is said to be empty and half asleep, but the cars were speeding in several lanes abreast up the broad carriage-way and down it—speeding, racing happily, as if their one ambition was to be anywhere but in the Champs Elysées; while pedestrians streamed up and down the broad sidewalks under the autumn-tinted trees, all apparently confident and happy. These crowds seemed different only in the absence of young men with their girls on their arms and leaning against them. And in the diminished number of middle-aged men. This because men of military age had received their mobilization orders yesterday or the day before.

Yesterday while all were abed in Sophie's chateau except Marie-Louise who was preparing petit déjeuner amid a smell of coffee, and Frédé who was already in his blue blouse and beret before departing to his usine, there had come a sharp knock at the door. Frédé went to open it, and there on the threshold stood a policeman.

'You are Monsieur Frédéric Benoît?' he demanded.

'Benoît? Yes.' Frédé's eyebrows had risen towards the rim of his beret.

'For you, monsieur.' And the smiling policeman presented him with a document that was waiting in his hand. He seemed to think this an occasion for friendly and reciprocal smiles.

Frédé took the document and read it. It summoned him to report to his unit 'immédiatement et sans delai.'

'I see,' said Frédé and nodded; then pulled off his beret and scratched his head. 'This is It,' he said.

'Yes,' said the policeman. 'Cette fois nous y sommes. Bonne chance, mon vieux. If faut en finir.'

'Oui,' agreed Frédé, though somewhat sadly. 'Il faut en finir.'

'C'est ca.' And the policeman went down the steps and out of the garden to find the next on his list.

And yet the Champs Elysées, on this pleasant evening, was full of happy voices. The cars speeding in opposite directions seemed like two excited but mutually indifferent chariot-races. Slowly, by the side of the downward race a fiacre behind a piebald horse went clopping along, its wheels white, its coachwork red, and its cocher in a low black Pickwick hat. It might have been the nineteenth century clopping along at its own reasonable pace beside the feverish and desperate speeds of the twentieth. Within it were a pack of merry young men, coming in this traditional fashion to the Bois; American students on holiday perhaps and untroubled by all this war business. Mobilization was not for them.

Not yet.

'They'd never have given Rennie two weeks leave,' said Sophie, 'if they thought there was any danger of war.'

'It was compassionate leave *because* of the danger,' Rennie explained impatiently. 'I told them a tale about my interests over here, and somewhat to my surprise, they believed it. I came quickly before they changed their minds. Of course their minds weren't reckoning with this German–Russian pact. Nor was anybody's.'

'If they gave you leave to the end of the month, I don't see why you've got to go,' said Sophie, having, as usual, hardly listened to his explanation because she didn't like it.

'The end of the month will see the beginning of things.'

'But surely, then, they'll summon you when they want you.'

'No doubt that'll be their idea when they recover from this slight attack of shock. At present I imagine they're in about as big a flap as an ant-heap that's just been kicked over. I'm not waiting

for any summons. I'm acting on my own,' he announced proudly.
'They might even forget me. And I'd miss all the fun.'

'Well, I still don't believe that anything will happen.'

'It will happen in a few days.'

'Nonsense. You just want to think so because it's exciting.'

'And *you* won't think so because it's worrying.'

'It's no good, Rennie.' Klem had drawn his dead pipe from his
mouth and was knocking its bowl against the heel of his shoe.
'No man's ever persuaded your Aunt Sophie of anything she
didn't want to believe. Dynamite might achieve something.
Nothing less.'

'He doesn't have to persuade *me*,' said Jean.

'No, but your good stepmother likes to live like a tortoise in its
carapace.'

'What in Heaven's name is a carapace?' laughed Sophie, who
always enjoyed a discussion of her weaknesses, so long as people
were treating them as attractive weaknesses.

'The hard but very attractive shell of a tortoise, my dear. It
protects him from almost any impact from outside, and he must
be very cosy in it.'

'Oh, look at that poor gendarme!'

The day, though fine, was windy with the promise of autumn,
and a gust, coming up the avenue, had swept the gendarme's cape
all round his head and his peaked hat. Rennie was angry again that
her interest should have drifted so easily from the war and her
weaknesses. He went silent. All were silent till she started to make
fun of their war talk. 'I tell you what, Rennie darling: if the
French really are going to war with the Germans, *he'll* have to
turn his moustache down. Turn it down a little now, Klem, my
pet. And we'll have to knock that second "n" off our name.
It looks so horribly German. Erik's already become "Eric"
again. He said it was a bore, but he'd do anything rather than
be worried by Germans and their silly war—oh, what's happening
now?'

Most of the pedestrians had stopped and were gazing down the slope. Police were shepherding cars towards the sides of the road. Half the gay voluble voices had sunk into silence.

'Oh, look!'

A squadron of cuirassiers on their brown matching horses, and splendid in their plumed helmets, were coming at a slow, processional pace up the avenue towards the Arc de Triomphe—why they should pass at this evening hour no one knew. Returning perhaps from some ceremonial occasion.

An admiring silence climbed the hill-slope with them, as they went by.

'Such beautiful men!' said Sophie. 'In their lovely plumed helmets. They just complete the picture. The Grande Armée marching up the Champs Elysées to the Arc de Triomphe through crowds of delighted Parisians. That is Paris.'

'Once,' said Rennie, 'the Germans marched *down* the Champs Elysées from the Arc de Triomphe past empty pavements and drawn blinds. That was Paris too.'

'Oh Rennie, why are you always so depressing? If the Germans come Klem must just turn his moustache up again. And Eric must become Erich—if that's the way the Germans spell it.'

Jean spoke. 'I agree entirely with Rennie and Daddy. If we'd been sensible we'd have gone from here months ago. But I was just as bad as Sophie, I didn't fancy having to put Wallace and Bruce in quarantine. They'd have been miserable, poor loves. Besides, I had a fancy to stay and see it all.'

'See what-all?' asked Rennie.

'Why, the war, of course. I've told you so before. It'll at least be exciting. Something happening at last. If I were a man like Rennie, I'd certainly have joined the Air Force, *and* aircrew, just for the hell of it.'

'My feeling is,' said Sophie, 'that, if the Germans come, they'll behave correctly. They may be brutes, but they tend to be correct brutes. They worship order and correctness. *He* always says so. And for the same reason I don't believe they'll damage Paris. Not seriously. No one ever does. Actually, I've met and liked a lot of

Germans. Didn't I go and marry one, and find him a treasure?'
She patted Klem's hand at her side.

'They may damage *me*.' Rennie had pretended to laugh as he
said this, but really he had thrown it at her because so fretted by
her complacency.

'Oh no, darling, they mustn't. You mustn't let them.'

'I happen to be aircrew.'

'And what exactly does that imply? Will you have to do anything very dangerous?'

Rennie seized upon this purblind question to justify himself
in some boasting, though he tried to make it sound modest. He
let them understand that it was an honour to be selected for aircrew;
that one had to show a high educational standard and pass aptitude
tests. He reminded them that, as he was not a pilot officer, able to
fly solo, he'd do his service in bombers, and the bombers would
start the war and be in the front of it before anyone else. And then,
because she only remained silent and thoughtful, and said no word
in praise of his distinction and his bravery, he added without
mercy, 'Danger? Nothing to speak of. Merely the danger of being
shot down in flames and burnt alive.'

'*No!*' She turned to him and her face had blanched.

Instantly, ashamed of this self-centred bragging and of this ruthless harrowing of her, he said, 'But don't worry. I exaggerate. If the
old crate catches fire you can always bale out.'

'What's baling out?'

'Jumping out of your bassinette with your parachute and drifting
pleasantly down through the clouds and the summer air. Smashing
views of the countryside. A mild bump as you touch down, and
all's well that ends well.'

'But, darling, you'd never jump out of an aeroplane thousands of
feet in the air?'

'Better to bale out than to burn—as St. Paul said about remaining
a bachelor or a spinster.' He'd hardly said this before he wondered
if it could have hurt Jean. Did she burn at times, and without hope
or chance of baling out?

'Oh, bale out if you have to,' begged Sophie. 'Bale out at once. I'm glad you can do that.'

Silence fell between them again, and in it Rennie was fighting a battle with himself. The more generous side of him had the notion of inviting them all to an expensive farewell dinner, the more selfish side, and that part of him, inherited from Sophie, which disliked spending too much money, had been arguing against the pleasant idea for a hour. But at last, thinking, 'God! We may never see each other again. Don't be a stingy cad,' he said aloud, 'I don't know whether you people know, but I'm giving a little farewell dinner to you all—and in some style. Not at the Meurice or the Continental—I can't afford that—but very definitely at the Delmonico.'

'Oh, but you can't possibly afford that, my darling. There are four of us.'

'I can, and I'm going to. We aircrew lads get better pay than the lesser breeds. After all, when shall we four meet again?'

'Of course he mustn't afford it,' said Jean. 'We mustn't let him.'

'But if he really wants to . . .' began Sophie, who loved sitting in expensive places and feeling well-dressed and expensive.

And yet again Rennie was displeased by her too quick readiness, not only to enjoy his beneficence, but to let fall, without further comment, the matter of his bravery. But, shrugging, he thought, 'Oh well, let it ride. My respected father, Sir Hereward, said stoutly that she was never to be troubled. Come, all my guests to the great farewell banquet.'

§

Sophie, Klem and Jean sat in that plainly furnished breakfast-room, with the dogs lying near them before the empty grate.

Nine o'clock, and the room was a cube of light hidden behind thick black-out curtains, and surrounded by the almost total darkness of Sainte-Marie and of the slopes to the forest. In Sainte-Marie there was not even a glimmer from the windows of the railway station though its booking office was active, and no more than pricks of light along the platforms though the trains, blacked-out too, were running through. Because of this black-out there was a silence in Sainte-Marie—a silence like a sister of the darkness. The great forest above the little town was hardly more silent. No voices could be heard gossiping in doorways or laughing at street corners. Occasionally one heard the sough of a car or lorry making what headway it could along the Beauvais–Paris road. One knew that its lamps were blacked down to narrow slits like hooded eyes half shut. Of course there was the drip-drip of the rain from the fir trees in the garden, but this was so continuous that they heard it no more than the ticking of the marble clock on the mantel. Now and again there was a shuffling of fallen leaves on the gravel when a flurry of wind came down from the forest.

'Ninette Duquesne says that Paris is quite incredibly lovely in the black-out,' said Sophie, as she darned a sock taken from a basket beside her.

'Forgive my somewhat clouded perceptions, dear,' said Klem, pressing down the tobacco in his curled Bavarian pipe, 'but how does one see its loveliness in the black-out?'

'Oh, don't be silly, darling. Of course I mean when the moon's up. She says it's entrancing. We simply must go and see it. When is the moon up again?'

Klem, after finishing with the pipe and hanging it from his mouth, drew his diary from a vest pocket. 'The moon's at the full eleven days from now.'

'Oh well—only arrange for it to be fine—you're so clever, you can manage that—and we'll go and see. Ninette says it's quite easy to get about in the moonlight. Who's coming? What a pity Rennie can't be here to see it. Nobody has such a feeling for things like that, as he has. But it's something he'll never see because, as soon as this horrid war is over, there won't be any black-out. Klem, how long before it's over? You know everything. Do you think it'll be over soon?'

'I do not.'

'Nor do I,' said Jean, without looking up from the book she

was reading. It was the poetry of Charles Péguy who fell in the first months of the previous war, defending the approaches to Paris.

'But nothing's happening. It's been going on weeks now, and not a single thing's happened.'

'Only Poland has been annihilated,' said Klem. 'That seems to be something.'

'Yes . . . but . . .'

'Britain and France'll never settle for that.'

'I pray God—*not*,' said Jean, though apparently still reading. 'Either this German madman gets out of Poland or the war goes on till he's driven out.'

'Certainly.' Jean's terms too.

'Well, I don't know . . .' sighed Sophie, and indeed she didn't for this brightly lighted room with a black-out around it, and strips of gummed paper on the windows to protect them from splintering if a bomb fell, was no bad picture of her mind—a lively, personal, domestic mind, comfortably shut in from the night by curtains of embroidered velvet. 'If it's going on, why doesn't something happen?'

'It's getting late in the year,' said Klem. 'Caesar goes into winter quarters.'

'Well, I hope he stops there,' laughed Sophie.

'*Tres legiones ex hibernis educit,*' said Klem. 'Or, in other words, he'll emerge in the spring with all his legions.'

'But surely it'll be over long before that?' said Sophie. 'Oh, I feel sure it will.'

It was with Erik—now temporarily Eric—that Sophie went to see Paris under the moon.

She had met him on the next morning when she was buying flowers for her chateau in the market place; this she liked to do on market-days because they were cheaper at the stalls and she could save money. The market place of Sainte-Marie was a broad and elevated area next to the Mairie Square and facing the schools. It was shadowed by files of marching lime trees between which stood rows of permanent iron roofs for the collapsible stalls. She saw Eric at the fruit stall next to her flower stall, a large loose figure in baggy jacket and knickerbockers; and he came with his apples towards her, explaining, 'I'm getting these things, my dear, because of my madly costive condition. It's this war. I can't imagine anything more constipating. Honestly, can you?'

Very soon Sophie, paying no attention to the state of his bowels, was suggesting that he should accompany her to Paris. '*He* won't come, you see. At least, he obviously doesn't want to. He never wants to come and see anything jolly. Oh, why isn't Rennie here?'

'And is our Rennie really going to fly? How incontestably brave of him. I wish I were brave like that. I do so admire bravery in boys. But if there's one thing I should dislike more than another, Sophie, it'd be flying about in a disgustingly thin-skinned compartment and being shot at. And then being steadily shot at again when you jump out and come down, swinging around at the end of a parachute. I should offer much too large a target to these deplorable Huns. My beloved Saint Sebastian wouldn't be in it with me. And I should look so ridiculous swinging like a pendulum. But Sophie, my pet, I ache to come to Paris with you. How angelic of you to ask me. We go quietly in the evening, do we? Just you and me? That'd be divine. I'm afraid I can't treat you to a nice meal in Paris because I'm wildly unhappy about my money just now. I'm so afraid my mother and sister won't be able to get my little remittance over to me. I'm a remittance man, pure and simple, as you know. It's a delightful occupation, but only provided the remittance arrives. Do you think it will? I mean, it's important.'

'Of course it will, Eric dear.'

'I think so. I mean, France and England are still allies in the tedious business, aren't they?'

'Of course they are, silly.'

'It's just as well. I can't see these Frogs keeping the Germans out, unless we stiffen them up a bit. I mean, we can't have a lot of unpleasant Fritzes roaming about Saint-Marie. I feel that, in the words of that charming boy, John Keats, their identity would *press* upon me so.'

Sophie, not listening any more, cried, 'Ah, there's my dear Abbé.'

'Now don't rush it, ducks,' said Eric, putting forth a hand to stop her from running towards the Abbé. 'He's bucketing along towards us all right—like a good ship homeward bound. Keep calm. And please don't get me excited. I'm in no condition to be excited.'

The Abbé Belfort, in a black beret and with the globe of stomach lifting up his black-buttoned cassock high above his coarse black shoes, was waddling past the stalls and occasionally speaking to parishioners as they chaffered with stall-holders or gossiped in couples and groups. He was carrying home to his presbytery, where at present he lived alone, two portly jars of Bordeaux Rouge, bought cheaply at a stall, and now nursed like two fat twins against the width of his breast. It was whispered in salons and doorways that the Curé was wining himself far too well while living alone in the Presbytery.

Eric watched him and said, 'Have you ever thought, my dear Sophie, that if only the good Abbé's cassock were white he'd be extraordinarily like the central dome of the Taj Mahal walking around our market place? Or perhaps one of the oniony domes from the Brighton Pavilion. I mean, he swells out so gracefully from the neck downwards and curves in again so pleasantly lower down. I take it you've noticed that. Father, come and talk to us.'

The Abbé, rolling towards them, raised his eyebrows in recognition, and said, 'My children, good day.'

Eric greeted him with, 'Monsieur Belfort, believe it or not, Sophie and I are going on a pilgrimage to Paris so as to see it under no light but the moon's. I'm escorting her because God alone knows what goes on in the black-out. The possibilities seem to me illimitable. I'm told the ladies simply don't know who it is that's embracing them. It must be interesting at times, but there's always danger that things might go a shade too far. Haven't we had enough of this war, Father? We've had several weeks of it now, and I pray it'll finish soon. I hope you spend a lot of time in your church praying really hard for it to end.'

'I try to do that, dear boy.'

'Well, it's angelic of you; but keep at it, lovey, for the Lord's sake. Personally, and between ourselves and the flower market, I have more faith in prayer than in your great and glorious armée. The Huns obviously have the Devil on their side, so if you could get us the Bon Dieu . . .'

'And it wouldn't do *you* any harm, Mr. O'Healy, if you came to church and put yourself in a state of grace. It would be good for you, yes? There's some excuse for Madame Sophie. As an English Protestant she may be assumed to be in a state of invincible ignorance, but you are a Catholic born, so it looks to me as if she'll be beaten with few stripes, but you with many. That, I suggest, is the position.'

'Oh, heavens, Father, do you really think so? Oh, dear! Perhaps I'd better come to my duties again. I'd love to be in a state of grace. But I can't be hurried. Definitely I mustn't be hurried. A confession after all these years, Father—after about twenty years of open and notorious sin—would be a pretty distinguished affair.'

'It would be a most happy occasion, Monsieur. If necessary, I'd give up a whole day to it.'

'Oh, yes, it'd be an occasion. A triumphant occasion both for me and for Holy Church. And therefore I think, my dear Abbé, that it should be fully choral.'

To this remarkable suggestion the Abbé could only reply with a smile, 'I imagine the choir will be provided by the angels in Heaven, dear Mr. O'Healy'; and, nodding to both of them, he waddled away, the two jars of wine nursed against his breast.

So Eric and Sophie went off to Paris together on an evening when the moon would be full and high. At first they were but two of the invisible figures moving in totally dark streets and now and then switching on a shaded torch to see where their feet were going.

Often a torch showed a figure in uniform, and once a woman soliciting the uniform. Cars went by creeping strangely through Paris instead of racing, their slits of light from blackened head-lamps piercing the darkness like thin knives. On the river the whistles of the tugs were cutting a way through the pitch of the night as they brought their coal barges from Rouen or Le Havre. But gradually the moon lifted above the high roofs and lightened as it rose. Sophie and Eric were now in the Place de la Concorde, standing in the tempered darkness by the Chevaux de Marly. These Horses of Marly, usually rearing on their high pedestals at the entrance to the Champs Elysées—two of Sophie's best-loved objets d'art—were now cased in high sandbags. The Avenue, under the moon, was all that people had said it was. Moonlight sprinkled the leaves of the climbing plane trees and of the chestnuts in the thick plantations at their sides. The shutters of the tall mansions, all tight-closed, gleamed in the blanching light. Not a street lamp glittered up the whole great slope; only the wide carriage-way mounted like a road of white stone to the firm grey shape of the Arc de Triomphe, and a few blue lights showed under the trees.

'And *that* is my Paris!' said Sophie, almost in a whisper to match the darkness. 'Who ever expected to see it like that? Fancy *him* not coming to see it. Oh, I *am* glad I came.'

'Well, I find it all rather ridiculous. I mean'— Eric looked up the Avenue—'what a strange way for a city to behave.'

Sophie too looked up the avenue. 'Is there really any need for this, do you think, Eric?'

'Don't ask me. The minds of the makers of wars bewilder and bore me. But there they are: nine-tenths of the human race.'

'But surely you want your country to win?'

'Only in the sense that I want this dreadful German man stopped in his tracks and put away in the asile d'aliénés.'

'But haven't you any feeling for your country?'

'I'm not sure that my country is at war at all. I'm Irish; and we Irish aren't at war, are we?'

'*You* are. You're from Northern Ireland.'

'Bah to that, lovey. These Huns don't know the difference. For the purposes of this war, I'm from Cork, and that's south enough.' Then he suddenly added a curious thing. 'And, anyhow, I've no particular reason to love my country.'

There was a mystery around this remark like the barely penetrable darkness around them. Sophie, not liking to seek illumination, turned at once to another question. 'But what about France? France has given you a home.'

'Dear lady, that's only so much pretty talk. I've learned to like a few French people and to dislike heaps more. The gayer Parisians are good fun, but France as a whole—well, speaking generally, I find her a conglomeration of oddly unlovable people, all too many of them sour and grasping and ready to rob me whenever they can. I like the Italians much better, though without fervour, you understand—but they're fighting against us, aren't they?'

'Not yet. But *he* says they'll come in against us later.'

'How tiresome of them. What on earth for? No, my precious, I can love a few persons—you and the doctor, for example—but any loyalty to abstractions like "France" and "England" which don't really exist at all apart from concrete individuals—this, though apparently built into everyone else, somehow got left out of my system.'

Sophie had not heard such words before. Or if she had heard anything similar from Klem, she had not listened to it properly or not found it easy to understand; and anything she found difficult to understand she would always thrust aside and discard. So she turned now to easier things. 'I think we've seen enough now, don't you, Eric. Are you ready to come home?'

'I am,' he said. 'I think it would be divine.'

And soon they were travelling from a pitch-black Gare du Nord through the unaided moonlight to Sainte-Marie.

V

Reality Comes By

SOPHIE, entering her little chateau, shut its door on the quiet darkness around; and that darkness was a symbol of the impenetrable and sinister peace that surrounded it for another seven months.

Seven months of autumn. Of winter—the coldest winter for half a century, the winter that broke into 1940, and what would 1940 bring? Of spring breaking suddenly in leaf and blossom over Paris. And still Klem, gazing between strips of gummed paper on his window at garden or avenue, or up at the forest, would quote, 'No war or battle's sound. Is heard the world around; The idle spear and shield are high up hung.' He and Jean might wonder what would yet happen; Sophie chose to believe that nothing would happen, or, at any rate, nothing near to them. She liked to say romantically that she was standing on guard over her house and furniture, but this really meant nothing, for the only guard she could put around the chateau was her palisade of comforting thoughts. Already the phrase 'phoney war' was being used to describe this general silence, but Klem preferred to call it a 'phoney peace' or a 'loaded peace'. To this she didn't listen, preferring to think that this daily normality beyond her hedges was proof that she was right. Other things sustained her in this pleasing optimism. No restrictions except the black-out regulations had been imposed. There was no rationing. Food was abundant in market and shops. France and Britain being allies, there were no difficulties of movement for British citizens; Sophie, Klem and Jean could travel as they liked. There was no breaking of communications with Britain: Sophie had many anxious letters from her mother and affectionate if slightly boasting ones from Rennie. Marie-Louise received plenty of comic and slightly bawdy cards from Rennie. And the censorship in Paris suffered nothing but reassuring news to be purveyed to the people; all journalists knew that they were now dishonest tradesmen. By order of the Republic.

Certainly April saw fighting begin, but only in Norway—the Germans invading Norway and driving northward—and northward was away from France. Certainly in May it swung southward, but only to Holland . . . Belgium . . . Luxemburg . . . and these were not France. 'La France n'a pas été envahie.'

But then—mid-May and the Germans were over the frontier. They had forced the Meuse at Sedan. Sedan: name of terrible memory. Sedan where seventy years before a French emperor had surrendered with eighty thousand men and left open the ways to Paris. Still . . . still. . . . Sedan was still two hundred kilometres from Sainte-Marie. . . .

Boulogne has fallen; all Belgium has capitulated; the British have been driven, literally and exactly, into the sea at Dunkirk; the Germans are at Abbeville. Abbeville—Beauvais—Paris—the road is straight. And straight through Sainte-Marie. What now? Why don't they bomb us? Why don't they bomb Paris? Is it that they want it as a lovely place for themselves? Is it that they hope the Parisians will take their side and turn against the British? Marie-Louise has heard from a sister that leaflets have been dropped on Paris, telling the girls that the Germans hope to dance with them in the streets on their next festival day, the Quatorze Juillet, 1940.

What now?

Only this, that at dawn on a day in June the Germans attack along the whole line of the Somme: Abbeville—Amiens—Péronne. And that means Paris.

But the Somme held them before. The Somme held them last time. Twice last time they failed to get to Paris.

One afternoon there is a tremor in the air, and a tremor of the little chateau which is a simultaneous tremor in their hearts. Only in Jean's heart is it almost a pleasing tremor. 'Guns?' she asks excitedly. 'Is it guns?' But no: they listen and learn that it is but the rolling of a small dry summer storm away to the north.

All were nervously quiet in the chateau these days. Jean and Klem walked about it, saying little or nothing; Marie-Louise stayed silent in her kitchen, wondering where Frédé was; Sophie, pale-faced, looked often from the window of any room she chanced to be in. Always at any sound she had been one whom curiosity drove to a window to peer out, or to the corner of a door to peep round; but what was she looking for now? She did not know. None knew what they were waiting for.

And all these days a splendid sun watched and waited too. The skies were empty except for this hot, staring sun and a few white stationary clouds which seemed too high up to care. If Jean walked up to the forest with two happy dogs, she saw the green of June springing high in peaceful fields and the cattle munching impassively across their pastures. Their slow munching was as indifferent to the war as the springing of the crops. Sometimes she climbed high enough to see a portion of the road to Beauvais, and it seemed to her that the lime trees along it were on the watch and waiting.

'Come and see, Madame! Madame, come and see!' Marie-Louise was crying up the stairs. 'Marcel Dreux says they're pouring down the road. Thousands of them. Thousands.'

'Who?' Sophie dared not say more; dared not ask, 'Is it *them?*'

'Les réfugiés. Mon Dieu. Mon Dieu. Oh, what is happening? And where is Frédé?'

Jean appeared on the landing above. 'What is it? What is it?' With the defiance that Sophie lacked she asked, 'Is it *them?*'

'No, no,' Sophie answered hurriedly, for her own peace. 'Marie-Louise says it's refugees. But—oh, Klem, where *is* he? Klem, come with us. It's refugees. Coming in crowds.'

Sophie was not one to stay away even from an excitement that was terrible. All four of them ran out into the brilliant morning and hurried down the Rue de la Forêt to the carrefour of the Rue de Paris, which was the Beauvais–Paris Road. They saw the refugees before they reached the road. They were pouring through the town as if in their panic they hardly saw it; as if they cared nothing for these villagers at their doors and windows or lining the trottoirs to stare at them as they went by. Cars, some new and expensive, others old and valueless (save today) tried with angry horn-blasts to force their way through the farm wagons, the hay wains, the dung carts, all loaded high with mattresses, trunks and kitchen ware, and sometimes with small children, old shawled women, and birds in cages. Dogs padded along by their familiar carts. Some of the refugees hurried by on foot, pushing bicycles, hand-carts or prams overhung with suitcases, sacks, bags and bedding. Sometimes they were priests leading their flocks to safety or shepherding them from behind.

The west front of the church of Sainte-Marie faced the Rue de Paris, and on the steps of its central doorway, watching this wild cavalcade, stood the Abbé Belfort, his hands in the pockets of his cassock and his shoulders pulled back as if only thus could they uphold the protrusion of his stomach. His lower lip also protruded over the drooping sacks of his chin as he watched.

Sophie and Klem hastened towards him, followed by Marie-Louise.

Klem said, 'Bonjour, Father'; and the Abbé, loosing a bitter laugh, answered, 'A good day indeed, Monsieur. Yes.'

'What's it all about? What's happened? Quoi de neuf?'

'New? Didn't you see them coming yesterday?'

'No. Why are they coming?'

'They tell me a hundred different things.'

'Who tells you?'

'Those who stop to pour out a tale to me and then go on.'

'What do you gather from them?'

'I gather that this is the end. There *was* a line covering us from Rouen to Compiègne, but the Boche has smashed it in a dozen places.'

'*No?*'

'Even so. There was an Armée de Paris yesterday or the day before. Where it is now, or what it is, God knows.'

'Frédé!' It was a cry from Marie-Louise, who'd had no news from Frédé for a month though she'd written to him day after day. His last letters had suggested that he was in the Maginot Line. 'Monsieur Belfort, cette Ligne Maginot? Cette Ligne Maginot? Où donc est la Ligne Maginot?'

'Yes, where, my dear? Left behind and forgotten, I should say. "Où sont les neiges d'antan?"'

'Oh, Frédé! Frédé!'

'How long have they been going by?' asked Klem, while Sophie stood there to listen. Marie-Louise had slid down into a bog of private sadness.

'Hours.'

'And where are they going to?'

'South. Just south.'

'But where to? Where?'

'Anywhere away from the Boche, I suppose. There are centres d'accueil in Paris, but they can't cope with these thousands and thousands. Millions, Monsieur. Millions from Belgium and all the north. Maybe they think they'll be safe in Paris. Our good General has declared it an open city. In other words he won't fight for it. Perhaps they'll try to stop there, or perhaps they'll just go on and on.'

'But where can they shelter? What can they eat?'

'There's always grass.'

Klem turned again to look at this desperate procession driven ever forward by fear, but with no known goal or haven ahead. The Abbé pointed to a couple of weary soldiers straggling by. 'Look, Monsieur. Two more poilus without their weapons. Lost or, more likely, thrown away. It's the end. Others have gone by without their arms. One told me he was going back to his farm in the Beauce, and they could look for him. He said "A bas la guerre" and went on.'

'The end?'

'Mais bien sûr. La fin de tout.'

'No, no, Monsieur! Your beautiful France. No, no! Elle ne peut pas mourir.'

At these words the Abbé broke into tears. The tears streamed down his broad fat cheeks. 'I thank you for that, Monsieur. I thank you. But it's only your England that can save us now.' He had drawn a huge soiled handkerchief from his cassock pocket and was wiping his eyes with it. Behind the drooping handkerchief he sobbed and gulped. 'I am ashamed. Of France. Of France. So ashamed. I cannot look you in the face.'

'I am German, Monsieur.'

'It is good of you to say that. I had forgotten it. I always think of you now as an Englishman.'

'Nevertheless I am German-born, and I ask you to forgive me and my country.'

'Not you, not you.' He was now wiping eyes, mouth, cheeks and chins, and getting the tears under control. 'Nothing to forgive *you*.'

Sophie, to ease his embarrassment, turned her eyes northward along the road and asked him, 'Where are *they*?'

He blew his nose resoundingly and put the handkerchief back into his pocket, from which a long corner of it dangled down. '*They*, dear Madame, are at L'Isle-Adam, Auvers, and Méry-sur-Oise. Or so I'm told.'

'So near?'

'So near. I imagine they'll come along at any moment.'

Her mouth dried even as her hands grew moist. 'And what'll happen about us? Shall we be interned? We shall be interned. Oh, what'll I do?'

They came even as she spoke, but not along the road. Overhead. A dozen Stuka dive-bombers screeched out of the northern sky. They dived towards the stampeding refugees with their sirens at full blast so as to enlarge the panic. Sophie's hands had rushed against her ears, for the sirens were stunning thought out of her.

The Stukas dropped no bombs but played jets of machine-gun fire on the carts and the cars and the screaming, running people. Merrily, for the joy of it.

'Oh, Mary Mother of God! . . .' It was Marie-Louise's voice. 'Jesus . . . Jesus. . . .!'

Wounded men, old women, children, fell across the bundled furniture on the carts and down on to the road. A horse screamed, slid on the cobbles, and lay bleeding. One old touring car, its driver hit, swerved on to the trottoir and crashed into the wall of a boucherie.

'Oh *no!* Oh, God!' Sophie, covering her eyes, rushed into the church. Marie-Louise followed her. Others on the trottoirs nearby also rushed in. The Abbé, stepping on to the pavement, lifted a fat beckoning hand and called to all who could hear beneath the sirens' din, 'Come in, my dears. Come.' They obeyed, crowding past him as he stood shepherding them into the church as into a fold.

Neither he nor they noticed, or remembered, that the picture in the tympanum of this arched central doorway represented Christ with his hands outstretched in appeal towards all passing people in the road and saying, 'Aimez-vous les uns les autres.'

One who came quickly to the church door, a big fleshy figure in loose knickerbockers, was Eric O'Healy. But when he saw the Abbé still on the pavement, he stopped by him—or, rather, he put for the present only three quarters of his big body under the shelter of the church door.

'What was the sense of that?' he asked. 'Father, what sort of game was that?'

'It's the Boches, Monsieur,' said the Abbé, not recognizing who he was in these dire moments. 'I have seen them before.' And he walked out to an old woman lying wounded in the middle of the road. The cart from which she had tumbled had gone on, either unknowing or seeking safety in a side-street. He knelt beside her and, laying one hand on her brow in comfort or blessing, lifted the other to divert the traffic around them both. None of it stopped for them; it swirled round them and raced on.

The Stukas, their fun over, swept northward again.

Now that the firing had ceased, the road became loud with voices, and Sophie and Marie-Louise returned with other excited women to the steps of the church. Bewildered out of thought, blinking, speechless, Sophie looked at the street with a thumb-nail against her teeth: blood on the cobbles and trickling to the gutters; blood splashed on the trottoirs and house walls; men carrying the wounded or dead into houses or shops; the Abbé still in the midst of the carriage-way, and the stream of refugees still hurrying by. A dead man lay beneath the window of a pois-sonerie, looking like a tramp asleep in the sun. For the sun, never, as it seemed, so brilliant, looked down upon it all. And already the blood smelt in the sun.

Sophie made a movement to go and help those who were help-ing the wounded but suddenly cried, 'No, I don't want to see. I don't want to'; and turned back into the twilight of the church.

But just then the ground beneath her shook. Her curiosity stopped her and brought her back to the threshold. From higher up the road came a clatter and a drumming—caterpillar tracks rattling and bumping over cobbles. And motor-engines at the roar. Tanks.

'Is it *them?*'

Yes, they. They came round the bend of the road, slowly roaring behind the refugees, scattering them as they came. Tanks. Tanks with steel-helmeted men in green-grey uniforms sitting on the hatch covers or standing in the hatches of these monstrous, iron-skinned, belly-flat reptiles grovelling by. One of the terrible Panzer divisions? Yes. One of them, for sure. Flanking their mighty armour came motor-cyclists with side-cars; in each side-car sat two helmeted men, one holding an automatic rifle erect, the other pointing his gun at the people in the road. From windows and pavements fists clenched to be shaken at the steel helmets, but eyes saw those levelled guns; and the fists dropped. Safer not to hiss out, 'Swine! Murderers! Pigs of Boches!' or to spit at their rear as they passed, for others were coming behind. Armoured cars were coming behind. Thus the long procession, endless, it seemed, went thundering through the heart of Sainte-Marie. To Paris.

Suddenly all eyes shot from this passing armament to the sky. A single German reconnaissance plane, flying high above the houses, had an engine on fire.

'Bon! Bon!' cried the people. 'May they burn. May they fry.'

It was going to attempt a landing. It was curving down towards the fields beyond the railway line. The railway line ran like a fringe along the skirt of Sainte-Marie, there being nothing south of it but a ribbon of orchard, a few lonely houses, a road, and then fields as flat as adjoining table tops for a mile around. Thus the people had but to run down the Avenue de la Gare and over the line to see the plane land, or crash, on the wide invitation of these fields. The butcher from the boucherie, having started to run with the others, stopped, went quickly back into his shop, and came out with his butcher's knife. Some shop-women, inspired by this action, slipped back into their shops, came out with knives and ran with the rest. Sophie's curiosity was equal to any of theirs, no matter how hysterical her state; so was Marie-Louise's; and they were two in this wildly running hate-intoxicated crowd.

When the foremost and the fastest had leapt the village outskirts, they saw a man in a field racing to meet the still unlanded plane with his fowling-piece held in both hands. Clearly the pilot of the plane was bringing his machine down as near as possible to the village in hope of help. The plane would land in a field where the shoots of corn were high and the new scarlet poppies bright among them. The poplars lining the railside road seemed, as always, to have turned their backs on the town and to be watching the earth yield its young green wheat—and to be waiting, just now, for the sky to yield what it would. The plane, with its wing ablaze, tore its long cauterizing way through wheat and poppies. And stopped. The pilot, a lieutenant in handsome grey uniform, with his padded boots zipped up this morning for anything that might happen today, staggered and stumbled out. Two others, sergeants, followed him. And the man with the sporting gun knelt in the wheat and shot them down one by one as they appeared—while the people cheered to the sky each attempted execution.

But a fowling-piece does not necessarily or instantly kill, and the butcher who had arrived with his long knife, ran forward, stabbed the fallen lieutenant through his body to the earth which he had invaded.

'That,' he said, 'is for a few friends of mine just murdered in front of my shop. And for others who happen to be my country-men.'

Forcing the knife out, he went to the two other shot men and, whether they were dead or alive, impaled them in the same way to his French earth, and gave them the same words through his set teeth.

Then he drove the knife three times into the clean dry earth to wipe the reeking blood off it and, rising erect, said, 'Mission terminée.'

Sophie had arrived in time to see this. Pale as the men now dead or dying, a hand pressed on her breast, she cried to Marie-Louise, 'Come away. Oh, where is Monsieur? Come away. Come home.' And Marie-Louise came following her and murmuring, 'Oh, Madame. . . . I've never seen anyone killed before.'

'Come. Come away from it all.'

'But I'm glad they killed them, Madame. I'm glad. I wish *I* could have done it.'

VI

'Ils Sont Corrects'

A STRANGE quiet possessed Sainte-Marie after the passing of the German armour. No more armour, no motorized infantry, passed through the village on the Paris Road. Only the tank marks on cobbled and macadam were there to remind Sainte-Marie of yesterday when the enemy went through.

One could imagine an even stranger silence up in the forest—almost as if the forest were guarding a secret for its friends below. Jean in the forest with her dogs knew that somewhere in its deeps, where there were many sunless hollows massed with tall attenuated trees, four German airmen lay buried (a fourth had been found dead in the wrecked plane). All Sainte-Marie knew it, but only a few men knew the hollow where they lay. Jean in her secrecy, hiding from all a so-called 'morbid' interest, hoped with some shame that the dogs might lead her to the place, but since they nosed everywhere, among leaves and bracken and brush, she never knew.

Meanwhile the plane's burnt skeleton still lay in the wheat. Should Germans come to it and ask, 'What became of the crew?' the citizens would say with shrugs, 'How should we know? Presumably they escaped,' and think, 'Let them look for them.'

Then, one morning later, Klem returned from the shops with his string-bag full (Sophie often sent him shopping). He placed the string-bag in Marie-Louise's kitchen and climbed the stairs to Sophie in the breakfast-room.

'Paris is gone,' he said.

'Gone?'

'Yes. Taken.'

Sophie could only sigh a helpless, inadequate, 'Oh, dear.'

'Yes. Our Paris received them with her shutters closed and her streets empty. Almost all day there were only Germans in the streets. It was rather like '70. And there it is: there you are, my dear: the most civilized city in the world under the feet of louts.'

'And what is going to happen to us? Klem, what will happen?' Sophie was still striving to comfort herself with the notion that the Germans would take no steps against anyone of Klem's distinction. Was he not a Ph.D. of Heidelberg?

'We should know soon. They're coming here.'

'*They?*'

'Yes.'

'Coming *here*? To Sainte-Marie?'

'Yes, their billeting officer has been at the Mairie and is now going from house to house requisitioning rooms. There's to be a battalion quartered here.'

'You don't mean they'll want to be billeted in *this* house? I won't have them. I can't. We've no room.'

'Maybe they'll have all our rooms. When we're in our prison camp.'

'Oh no, Klem, *no!*'

'We'd best please them all we can. There's Rennie's room. And there's the salon downstairs which we hardly ever use. There's my workroom.'

'I *won't* have them in the drawing-room. They'd ruin everything. Lovely things I've been collecting all my life.'

'That's rather what war does. You can move your precious things. I suppose, or hide them.'

'How many will they try to inflict on us?'

'Four to a room, I dare say. They're billeting whole divisions in these small towns round Paris.'

'Can't one refuse to have them?'

'Certainly not.'

'Four to a room! Oh, but my carpets!'

'It may be there won't be so many. This is a small house on the edge of the town. And I'm told they've been ordered to behave with the greatest correctness and courtesy. Just as in '70. They've arrived, you see, and they want to be loved.'

'Was that correctness and courtesy when they massacred helpless refugees before our eyes?'

'They apparently think it correct. Correct when they're invading. That was invasion. This is occupation, my dear.'

Nothing to do but shrug and wait. Wait for these visitors to knock at the door. The little brass knocker on Sophie's door was a model of a Flemish caravel in full sail, a trinket which she had once brought with joy from Bruges. Now it would provide this knock for her.

Nothing to do that night but go to bed, sleep for a little, and awake again to the last agony of France and to their own jeopardy. And to lie there in the dark thinking of these.

§

It was not till late the next afternoon that the billeting officer appeared in the garden. From the garden's lattice gate a tongued bell hung on an iron bracket and rang as the gate moved. Always it started an indignant barking by Wallace and Bruce. So now. Soft bell and fierce barking drew Sophie and Klem to the break-fast-room window, and they saw a lieutenant, old for his rank and small for a German, with peak-cap upthrust in front, holster on hip, and his little legs in high field-boots. Behind him came a young corporal in *feldgrau* uniform and steel helmet who limped incongruously in *his* high boots. Hardly less congruous with boots and steel helmet was the file of documents under his arm.

'The bookie and his clerk,' said Klem. 'Honest Joe. The old firm.'

'Those boots on my carpets,' said Sophie.

'I'll go to them. They may frighten Marie-Louise.'

'It'd take more than these two to frighten Marie-Louise.'

And indeed, as the knocker fell on the door and he went down the stairs, he saw Marie-Louise approaching and warned, 'No, Marie-Louise. It's they. Go back. You're a comely girl, and we don't want you to suffer a "fate worse than death".'

Marie-Louise's lips were grim, but she only answered with a show of cheerfulness, 'That won't happen easily, Monsieur I, assure you; but if it has to happen I can't see that it's worse than death; and if some dirty Boche thinks I'm going to kill myself to avoid it, he'll be just the silly romantic fool they mostly are. I shall just shut my eyes and think it's Frédé.'

'Yes, but sometimes they are more than one, my dear.'

'Oh well, Frédé is often not content with once.'

'Marie-Louise, it's *you* that should have been the Doctor of Philosophy. Still, get you back, and leave these gentlemen to me.'

She went, and he opened the door to them.

Instantly the officer clicked his heels and bowed slightly. 'Guten Morgen, Monsieur,' he said, with a small, uncomfortable smile at this deliberate mixing of two languages; and Klem saw that he was one of those basically solemn men who think their efforts at humour funnier than they are. This middle-aged man had been ordered to be correct and courteous, but he would have been correct and courteous in any case. He was no tough bully and had doubtless been rendered uncomfortable and unhappy by the steel-cold reception he'd met at every door. Sainte-Marie's only weapons now were eyes that communicated hate and voices that answered only 'Yes', 'No'. One by one the inhabitants of Sainte-Marie had struck with these weapons.

By his next words the visitor explained his small, ingratiating jest. 'You are Doctor Burgermann and you speak German, I think, Monsieur?'

'I do.' Who had told him this? What more did he know?

'You are German?' This was asked in German.

'Nein.' Why expound further? What sense in saying, 'I am a British subject resident in France'? Let them find that out for themselves. Why prompt Fate to act one moment too soon? 'What can I do for you?'

'You speak German very perfectly.'

Klem replied in French. 'That may be so, mon lieutenant.'

'We are sorry to disturb you, but we must billet our soldiers wherever we can. You will permit me to see over your house?'

Klem spread a hand inward to the house. He said nothing, but the gesture said, 'I can do no other.'

They walked in, the two of them; into the salon, whose sacred door Klem flung widely, sarcastically, open; out again and towards the open kitchen door round which Marie-Louise had been peeping. Tramp, tramp. For the first time Sophie, listening upstairs, heard that characteristic sound of the Occupation, the peculiar tramp, tramp of strong iron-heeled German boots. In the kitchen Marie instantly turned her back on the intruders and gazed out of the window, motionless, hands at her sides, erect. If there is an exact opposite of 'standing to attention in honour of a passing officer', this was it. They went upstairs to where Sophie stood waiting. And on the officer asking, 'This is Madame?' and Klem admitting it with the briefest of nods, he clicked his heels and bowed. Sophie did not bow; she, like Marie-Louise, remained erect—and then turned away.

They went upstairs to Klem's workroom and Rennie's guest-chamber. Here the officer, in his turn, looked from the window. He looked down at the garden of firs and over the lifting fields to the dense forest. He looked for a long minute and more; then said, 'You have a most pleasant position, Herr Doktor, and this is an enchanting view. I think you will be fortunate in that I need hardly incommode you at all. I would like to assign this room to a Major Clauss—Major Wilhelm Clauss. He is an officer of much distinction and he has just been made Town Major of Sainte-Marie. He will be responsible for the reasonable comfort of the troops billeted here and their local administration. I would wish him to have this room, and his orderly the workroom you showed me. There, I think, they will not greatly trouble you. They will just sleep here and take their meals in their respective messes in the village, but it may be helpful to him occasionally to have someone at hand who speaks such excellent German as yours. I confess I had this in mind from the first when I heard that your German was so perfect. Thank you, Monsieur. That will be all.'

A little later, and they heard in silence that quick smart tramping in the garden and down the avenue.

§

It was dark when the Major came. The black-out curtains were drawn in the breakfast-room, so that Sophie, Jean, and Klem did not hear him come. Only they heard the slap of the brass knocker and the ringing of the bell, both of which sounded imperious to their heightened imaginations but were probably not so; they may even have been diffident.

'This'll be he,' said Klem, almost in a whisper. 'Who goes?'

'You go,' the two women enjoined.

Klem rose, saying 'Heil Hitler'. But before he had gone down two stairs he saw Marie-Louise walking towards the door. 'This'll be our new guest, Marie-Louise,' he said. 'A person of high distinction. Put out your most welcoming smile.'

But no answer came from Marie-Louise. It was as if her mood tonight had become one of anger with her country for its defeat, an anger which she felt forced to project on all in the house. This house, her home, stood for France. France defeated. She did not switch on its light to admit its conquerors. She merely opened the door as far as it would go, as if to say, 'Come then. Take all. You are the victors.'

But in the half-light admitted by the widely opened door she saw that two tall men had stepped in. The foremost, the taller, in officer's green uniform, peered and saw her and instantly saluted, hand touching his peaked cap, though she was obviously only the bonne. But strange—it was his left hand that had touched his cap. Against all usage he had saluted with his left hand. 'I think you are expecting me, Madame. My name is Clauss. Major Clauss.'

Not a word from Marie-Louise. She just kept the door wide open, and when she saw Klem at the foot of the stairs, immediately left them all and, walking quickly to her kitchen, shut its door with a perceptible slam.

It was Klem who switched on the light. It showed him that the tall Major was a young man, hardly thirty, with the round cheeks and smooth skin of youth. When this young man politely removed his cap with his left hand, Klem saw that his hair, straw-pale in colour, had been convict-cropped for war; and in the same moment he perceived that his right arm was hardly more than a stump; its sleeve slept in the side pocket of his tunic.

'I am sorry to disturb you, Monsieur Burgermann, but I am informed you have a room for me.'

'That is so.'

'You will allow my orderly to bring in my field trunk and a few other things?'

'Yes.'

'You will not treat me as an enemy, I very much hope. We all trust that that unhappy relationship is for ever over. As you have doubtless heard, our General Keitel has declared that it is in no way our intention to humiliate a gallant foe but rather to try to win him as a friend.' Evidently the Major was thinking of Klem as a Frenchman. He was smiling awkwardly and seemed most anxious to speak words of comfort to this household, before taking his place within it.

Klem acknowledged the strained comfort with an inch-deep bow and a spreading, as in doubt or question, of the hands hanging helplessly at his sides.

And the young man went on, 'The Führer firmly believes, and I assure you we all believe with him, for the Führer is the voice and will of us all, that, if Germany and France cease fighting one another and act in concert instead, they will be able to establish in Europe a civilization that could last for a thousand years. France is not our enemy. Our real enemy is Great Britain. It is her power that we must destroy now, but that will not take us long. So there's little likelihood that I shall have to incommode you for more than a few weeks. We fully expect to be in England in a very little time.'

'You think so?'

'Yes, Monsieur. In two months at the latest. She should be on her knees by then. I hear that the Führer has said he'll be in London on August 4th or the 12th, and the Führer does not err. All that he has foretold so far has happened so far. England will then have to choose between surrender and annihilation.'

'Come upstairs. I will show you your room.'

'It is kind of you, Monsieur.'

'You may need it for quite a long time.'

On the stairs Klem was guessing from the young man's age and rank and empty sleeve that he was a regular officer, able and gallant. Possibly he had lost his forearm after one of those daring patrols last year before the Maginot Line. Possibly he had been promoted to his field rank for bravery and given, at his own request, this administrative job instead of being invalided home. Later Klem was to learn that these guesses on the stairs were almost the exact truth.

On the first landing they passed the half-open door of the breakfast-room; and the Major, observing Sophie's and Jean's eyes peering out, bowed as he went by.

In Rennie's room he looked around him—at Rennie's comfortable bed, at his table and easy chair, and out of his window. 'This is certainly all I could wish, Monsieur. A most charming room. And my orderly next door? Excellent. I am very grateful to you. We will do our best to derange you as little as possible.'

Once again Klem spread open his palms, as one who would shrug and say, 'Derange us or not, we have no choice.'

'You speak German, Monsieur, do you not? I think Lieutenant Gaertner said you spoke German?'

'I do.'

So the Major now spoke German. 'I am glad. My French is all too inadequate. My purpose it to make our unavoidable occupation of your town as little troublesome as possible, and if I may ask you questions now and then it will be of real help to me in this.'

Now Klem's bow was an inch or two deeper. It said, 'If that is all you ask of me, Herr Major, I will certainly do my best.'

§

The Abbé Belfort, puffing, blowing, waddling, brought his great stomach up the stairs to the breakfast-room because the salon below was stripped of its fine furniture. Sophie guided him to one of the large easy chairs, and when he had collapsed heavily into it and could speak, he breathed out to them all, Sophie, Klem, and Jean, 'My dear friends, I have come to apologize.'

It was the morning after the French Government had asked the Germans for their terms of surrender.

'It can't be helped, cher Abbé,' said Sophie.

'It could have been helped, and it should have been helped. We vowed to you English that we would never sue for a separate peace, and France, my France, has broken its word. He paused, and his breathing snored in his throat. 'How do I face you, please? Tell me how I face you? You who have been betrayed.'

'It is not *you* who have done this, Father,' said Klem.

'No, by my God, it is not,' declared the Abbé, leaning forward, almost as if the passion in the words required that he should rise to assert them; and then collapsing back. 'Nor, I swear, has it been done by the greater part of my countrymen. We have been betrayed too. Are those his footsteps overhead?'

Booted steps were sounding across the ceiling, this way and that, softly. There was a creaking under the tread.

'It's either him or his orderly,' said Sophie. 'Probably the orderly tidying up his room.'

'Our house is greatly honoured,' explained Klem. 'We have the Town Major.'

'Well, it is *they*, at any rate. In *this* house, my God! My presbytery is almost the only house they haven't occupied. Is it possible that they feel a presbytery of Christ's Church is no comfortable lodging for them? Dear Madame, I have come to assure you that at least nine-tenths of my people feel that they have been betrayed like you and therefore are with you, heart and soul.'

Jean said, 'We know it. We can feel it everywhere. They have been stopping me in the market place this morning, knowing I was British, and saying they were sorry and ashamed.'

'Bless them. They are my people. My children. But, Jeanne, to think that it was our Marshal Pétain who sued for mercy, the man who fought them to a standstill last time at Verdun, the man who gave us for our battle-cry, "They shall not pass".' Sadly he spoke the great words to himself. '"Ils ne passeront pas." And now he has flung open the gates, and he bows to them as they pass. They pass at ease, while he bows to them in courtesy. Jeanne . . . Jeanne. . . .' His mouth was twisting as he forced back tears. He sought in a cassock pocket for a handkerchief, but it proved to be unnecessary. He was in command.

'Never mind, dear Abbé,' Sophie comforted. 'We understand, don't we, Klem? Personally I can't see what else France could have done. And now Marie-Louise is going to bring you a cup of tea.'

He smiled lovingly. 'God bless you, my dear friends. I know that when an English lady suggests a cup of tea it means both her absolution and her benediction.'

'Benediction, yes,' said Sophie, 'but not absolution. My good Abbé doesn't need that.'

'Well, I will accept it as benediction for those of our people who are loyal, but not as forgiveness for this present government of France or for any who support it. Do you know, Doctor, some of the people—I see it clearly—want your England to be defeated, and quickly, because it will make their own surrender seem less guilty.'

'That is natural,' said Klem, 'and perhaps one can feel some compassion for it.'

'For the people in their shame and guilt, perhaps, but never for the thing itself. The France we love should have fought in every street and slum of Paris instead of proclaiming it an undefended city; and when Paris fell she should have fought the whole way down to the Mediterranean coast and the sea. And, after that, from Africa.'

'But, Father . . .' Klem began an objection—and was interrupted by Marie-Louise bringing in the tea. The Abbé turned to her. 'Bless you, my child. I know one who would never ask any favours from the Boche, and her name is Marie-Louise Benoît. Isn't that so, Marie-Louise?'

'Yes, Father . . . but does this mean that Frédé will come back soon?' she asked, as if considering wearily the one small gleam in the darkness. She had heard that Frédé was a prisoner-of-war in Germany.

'I don't know, my dear. I imagine the release of prisoners will have to await a Treaty of Peace. An armistice is not the final peace. But perhaps if our acceptance of their terms is abject enough, it will come soon. Meanwhile, if he's a prisoner-of-war, he's at least safe.'

'Is it wrong then to hope that he will come back?'

'No. Hope. But hope too that your country doesn't cringe and fawn and lick its conqueror's boots too shamefully. I don't believe even Frédé in his prison camp would wish that.'

'No he wouldn't. Nor I, nom de Dieu. Oh, well, Father, I'll stick it out. I'll wait.'

When she was gone, Klem took up his objection again. 'But, Father, do you really think that France could have fought all the way back to the Mediterranean when all her industry would be in the enemy's hands, or from Africa when all her people would be left behind in his power? He could have threatened to massacre them all, if she didn't yield.'

'Maybe, but her position was much stronger than she chose to think, and his much weaker. She had her fleet at Toulon and an army in Africa and your England behind her, while he stood between two threats, Russia and England. Oh, their behaviour to us is being very correct, but it is not out of generosity or love, it's because they need us to keep quiet, and because, in their own good time they're going to ask our help against England. And when that happens, dear people, I go cheerfully to the wall and the firing squad. I thought I'd like to tell you that.'

'*Dear* Abbé,' Sophie acknowledged in a low voice, so moved was she.

'Even as it is, this foul government seems ready to help him all she can against you, her ally of yesterday; ready to give him our Channel coast so that he will then face you all the way from the North Cape to Brest. How you will survive I can't imagine. I can only pray. And pray. At every Mass for England. Every day.'

Sophie said one thing that had been troubling her. 'But do you mean, Father, that you would have accepted the total destruction of your beautiful Paris rather than give in?'

'Yes, I do. I do. Even that. It would have been terrible but—
'A quoi sert de lui sauver la vie si l'on perd son âme.' Paris stands; we have saved Paris, and lost our soul. How can we look any more at those words on the great monument in our Panthéon, "Vivre libre ou mourir"? I suggest we wipe them away for ever now.'

This syphoned up the tears into full view, and they averted their eyes while he regained control.

VII

Monsieur Belfort and his Church

A BIG German swastika flag drooped above the Abbé Belfort's church in the Rue de Paris. The doors of the church were tight shut behind heavy, threatening padlocks. The bells were silent, forbidden to sound except for a Mass on Sunday. The Angelus sounded no more over the roofs of Sainte-Marie—at morning, noon, or evening.

This was the Abbé's punishment for what the German O.C. Troops in Sainte-Marie called his 'persistent oppugnancy'. Some of the higher clergy had been advocating not only an acceptance of all Germany's terms as a kind of National Penance for the nation's corruption, irreligion and other deadly sins, but also a collaboration with Germany as an ally in the battle against Communism, 'pour lutter contre l'esprit révolutionnaire, communiste et bolcheviste'. But not Monsieur Belfort in his little church at Sainte-Marie. After France had accepted the Armistice with its heart-searing terms he had preached a sermon in the church advocating, not active disobedience but certainly a passive, hostile resistance whenever and wherever possible.

In his white cotta, filling his small round pulpit like an egg too big for its cup, like a plump duck's egg in a normal cup, he had said to a crowded congregation, trusting that there were as yet no German observers among them, 'Mes enfants, the Enemy—or perhaps I must call him, since we have signed this dreadful capitula-

74

tion, the Conqueror—is in our midst. How are you to treat him? Some collaboration there must be, for you must live, you and your children. You must obey his regulations, because disobedience of them, as the posters outside this church tell you, can be a capital offence. Can mean death. You must obey also because you will need your ration cards for such food as he will allow you, and your permits to go where he will suffer you to go. But I enjoin the minimum of collaboration. They are wooing us to win our support and goodwill, but I suggest that our hearts are not in the market for the winning. My own goodwill lies elsewhere.' Here he halted, looked at the sunlight pouring down from easterly windows, and lowered his voice for his next words; it was as if fear and courage were at war within him, and the courage had some difficulty in conquering. 'It lies to the northward, across twenty-two miles of sea.'

As he said this, the fear forced him to make, unconsciously, a tiny sign of the cross amid the big spaces of his breast. Perhaps this strengthened him, for he went on, 'Here in this your church I feel compelled to remind you that these people are not only the conquerors of our country; they seek also to be the conquerors of our faith. Have no doubt of that. Their prophet, Friedrich Nietzsche, has said it plainly enough. "Happy are those who wage war", he has said. "They shall not be called Jehovah's children but the children of Odin who is greater than Jehovah."' The courage rose, passion exalting it. 'What they worship now, these poor deluded and corrupted young men now in our houses and streets, these tall and handsome sons of Odin, is a new god, a new idol, the Volk. The German Volk. They have been taught that the Volk shall one day reign over all the earth, just as you have been taught that Christ shall reign; that the earth shall be full of the knowledge of Him, as the waters cover the sea. This German Volk, they believe, has its living incarnation in their Leader. In little towns like ours all over Germany, on school walls and in shop windows, the portrait of this strange incarnation has replaced the "Ecce Homo" and the crucifix. Some of the children begin their day with "In the morning I salute the Führer 'Morgens, grusse Ich den Führer,'" and end it with "In the evening I thank him." They are even taught to repeat "The Führer gives us our daily bread" and to replace the Creed with "I believe in the Führer, I believe in Greater Germany." Oh, obey them when you must but show them also that your heart still belongs to your Church's faith. And God—*our* God —be with you in this, strengthening you.'

But of course there were German observers in that rapt congregation, and two mornings later Major Clauss, on instructions from O.C. Troops, went from his upper room in Sophie's chateau to the Presbytery in the Rue de l'Eglise behind the church. He passed beneath a metal cross over its gates. A woman of the congregation, who had come for an hour to help the Curé in his loneliness, opened to him and led him into the sitting-room. On seeing the Abbé sunk in a big easy chair almost as obese as himself, he clicked heels, saluted, begged him not to rise, and with a continuing courtesy told him that Colonel von Hoth, commanding the troops in Sainte-Marie, had asked him to explain that no public defamation of his soldiers could be tolerated, and certainly no implied derogation whatsoever of the Führer. As he mentioned this great name the young officer almost clicked his heels again.

'I see,' said the Abbé, and he struggled out of the chair so as to stand face to face with his visitor. A ponderous and untidy figure he made, in his stained and rumpled cassock, opposite the tall, spare young Major in trim green uniform. 'I see. And what, Herr Major, if I feel I cannot give any undertaking to refrain from speaking the truth as I see it?'

'Monsieur, I am sorry to have to say it'—yet again he almost clicked the heels—'but I am authorized to tell you that either you cease from all such derogation of the Occupying Authorities or—be expelled from this town.'

'I see.'

'You must understand, surely, that the Colonel finds all such attacks quite inadmissible.'

'Oh yes, I can understand that.'

'He doesn't want to hurry you in the consideration of this matter, or to take you at a disadvantage in any way. He authorizes me to say that you may have twenty-four hours to choose between giving him this necessary assurance and . . . being removed from Sainte-Marie.'

The Abbé bowed in sarcastic acknowledgment of these terms. 'From Sainte-Marie and into prison ?'

The Major's shoulders lifted and fell again, implying, 'That is not for me to say. I have no instructions about that. But . . . what else, Monsieur ?' Aloud he said, 'Perhaps you will permit me to call upon you tomorrow when this twenty-four hours will have elapsed ?'

'That will not be necessary, Herr Major. Please thank your Colonel for his courtesy, and accept my thanks for yours, but I do not need this twenty-four hours. I can give you my answer now.'

'Yes, Monsieur ?'

'Mais oui. In my church I have two masters only, God and my bishop. Such instructions as seem to me to come from God I can never, without sin, disobey or neglect. Those that come to me from my bishop I might conceivably, but only in the most desperate circumstances, disobey. But what is absolutely certain is that I can never take instructions as to what I shall preach, or not preach, from any military power whatsoever. That, I must tell you, I find quite inadmissible.'

Major Clauss, his face now rather white, bowed and went.

But at first the Germans did nothing. In these early days, seeking a rapprochement with France, they were anxious to create no martyrs. And the curé of a little town near the capital would be too public a martyr. The Abbé soon became conscious of this and felt his power increase. Felt, moreover, with a certain surprise, excitement and happiness, that he, though a lamentable sinner, had been instructed by God to use this power. On a Sunday, three weeks later, he preached to a crowded church what was, perhaps a more truthful and sincere sermon than any he had preached since the

77

early and ardent years of his ministry. Not for thirty years had any church been crowded like this to hear *him*, and he was touched and shamed. For twenty or thirty years he had been but a lazy pastor, visiting his people but seldom, and so failing to shepherd many into the church. A heavy man, weary and ageing, he had preferred the comfort of his great chair in a familiar room, and of the red wine in a shy, inconspicuous cupboard and of the books from his many shelves—not necessarily theological books, nor books that he would wish to be seen reading. And now, despite all this, the people of Sainte-Marie, the faithful, the lapsed, the unbelieving, all sat crowding his church to the walls. Touched and shamed, he told them the very truth of his heart, though aware that hostile ears were listening.

He said, 'Brethren, I have learned with shame in these days of our country's agony that, beyond any question, my love of my country has proved a far more powerful motive than my love of God. That is a sorry confession from a priest but I feel that I can at least be happy to think that it is God, in His infinite patience, who has shown me at least, with a kind of too-bright light, that my worship of my country can move me to far better things than my worship of Him. In His service, for many years, I have been slothful and negligent, seeking all the time a sensual ease. And I have been timid, seeking to evade trouble. In the service of my suffering country, on the other hand, I have suddenly felt myself ready for anything—yes, *anything*. I feel timid no more and capable at last of self-sacrifice. For her I am willing, even eager, to suffer, and, if I must, to die.

'Now I know that thoughts like these are astir in many of your hearts, or you would not have come here hungering for some counsel from me. They are good thoughts. Whenever I ask God to forgive me because my love of my countrymen is more potent than my love of Him I always seem to hear Him saying, "It is natural, my son. Your country is all around you. Your God is unseen. It is a lesser love but good. 'He that loveth not his brother whom he hath seen, how can he love God whom he hath not seen?' You need not be ashamed." So I say to you, Rejoice if this love is surging up in you, and let it urge you to whatever you feel to be the noblest deeds you can do. I think it likely that you will be called in days to come to kinds of holiness. If so, good. You will at least learn in your very blood what the highest holiness might be. You will learn what a love of God, were it as strong as this, might work in you.'

Oh, yes, the Germans were listening, but they could lay a finger on nothing punishable in this, and so could only meditate on the Curé of Sainte-Marie.

§

The parishioners of Sainte-Marie, both the faithful and the unfaithful, listened no less attentively and far more enthusiastically, though most of them, in the ensuing days, forgot to think of their acts as holiness. They were more inclined to think of them as a blend of malice and fun. The shopkeepers served the German soldiers in a silence as cold as the heart of their ice-boxes. The people on the pavements walked past them with eyes staring ahead as if they saw no foreigner in uniform anywhere. If a German entered the Café de la Forge the well-filled room went as silent as a hall of waxworks after closing time. The patronne served him as if serving a ghost invisible to all others and barely visible to her. He might give his order in French, trying to be matey, but he was answered in no language at all. Just served—with no one looking his way. Soon the German officers were calling Sainte-Marie 'la petite ville sans regard'.

Most willingly did Marie-Louise follow her shepherd's crook and bell, and without thought of holiness at all. She used her very clothes as a weapon. On her 'afternoons out' she wore an audacious hat as high as her contempt for the invader and as beribboned and colourful as would persuade him that there was no disheartenment in her—in short, as completely overwhelming as the fate she had in mind for him. She wore a short skirt as trim as anything in the old happy days, and went clicking noisily past the enemy (when leather became difficult to obtain) in chic wooden shoes with elegant glass heels. In a crowded train leaving Sainte-Marie station for Paris a German private, obeying his orders to show friendliness to the French people, offered her his seat; she stared through him as if she had seen nothing and heard nothing. The only time she spoke—or apparently saw—a German was when a young driver stopped his lorry in the Rue de Paris and asked her the way to the Mairie Square. Actually it was less than a hundred yards distant, but she looked up, waited, and then directed him, fluently and with precision, all the way to the cemetery.

Oh, very willing, Marie-Louise.

Like any gamin she did not hesitate, in safe moments, to chalk suitable *graffiti* on inviting walls, such as 'Vive Degolle' (so far she had only heard the General's name, not seen it spelt). She played her eager part in circulating the first clandestine newssheets. With a troop of her co-religionists she helped to bill-stick on licit and illicit places a poster which cried, 'Catholiques Français!' and, after recording the persecution of priests in Alsace and Lorraine—where thousands had been expelled for refusing to swear loyalty to the new German State there, and threatened with ten years forced labour in the stone quarries if they returned—concluded, 'A nous pour la liberté and l'indépendance de la France.' When September came, bringing a German broadcast: 'Very soon our soldiers will be marching home with the final victory in their hands, and they will tell you how they were the first for nine hundred years to tread the soil of England,' and September and October passed and with them the season for successful war, then Marie-Louise with other women, and some men, took by night, in a hat-box, a pot-de-chambre and tied it tight to one of the roofings in the market place, with the message below, 'Helmet offered to M. Hitler for the Invasion of England.'

The story was all over Sainte-Marie and visiting the country around before the Germans saw the helmet and got it down.

§

Sophie was one of the crowd in the church when the Abbé spoke of people being driven, in the coming days, to 'kinds of holiness'. She was there partly because Marie-Louise had told her excitedly that all Sainte-Marie was crowding to hear the Abbé's 'marvellous sermons', and Sophie never stayed away from anything that crowds were marvelling at; partly because she was living with fear in these days, and the fear was making her want to be a little nearer to God than at any time since Sir Hereward left for Gallipoli twenty-five years before. Already some English women had been carried away from Paris and interned in a barracks at Besançon; but not all; excuses had been found for some; and Sophie, who must ever insulate herself with cotton-wool comforts from the sharper pricks of fear, hoped that the Major in her house, who so often got linguistic help from Klem, would somehow save them all. Let Klem go on giving him all the help he could in translations and phrasings (no one spoke French and German like him).

The Abbé's sermon, besides lifting tears to her eyes and heightening her love for him, had made her long to do heroic things for the France (or, more accurately, the Paris) which she loved, but she was not driven to such daring acts as Marie-Louise's; France was not the native country in her blood. She was amused by Marie-Louise's deeds and in a way delighted with them, but at the same time terrified by them lest they brought down the wrath upon her house. From the first she had been ready to walk past German soldiers with her head high her breast out, her eyes unseeing, and her dress impressive—a 'grande dame' indeed though with the 'anglaise' laid well aside for the present—but she did nothing more positive than this until the huge posters appeared in the streets after the sickening naval 'incident' in the waters of Oran. There the British Fleet, to keep the French ships out of the German grip, had sunk or disabled them, and now the posters were shouting from walls everywhere that the British, after betraying their allies at Dunkirk, were busy sinking the French fleet and drowning French sailors. A picture on the posters showed a French warship ablaze and French sailors drowning in agony.

Then, for a while, the native blood rose in Sophie. 'It's lies!' she cried. 'They betrayed *us!* Lies!' and she went in the night with Marie-Louise and her friends to help them tear down these posters or scrawl 'Lies!' across them, her part being to keep watch while they did the work. She found herself accompanying them though fear walked with her all the time, stood at her side as she kept watch, and, the task accomplished, hurried her home at speed.

Home, she was proud of what she had done; was not the punishment for tearing down German posters deportment to Germany? And she had helped in it. Helped in it.

Jean had helped in this operation too, but Jean was more than usually quiet just now, listening mainly, and speaking few of her thoughts.

November, and students in Paris demonstrated against the meeting at Montoire of the leaders of France and Germany to arrange for greater collaboration between the two countries. The Gestapo arrested the students; many were executed, others sent to the salt mines, others imprisoned and tortured. November, and all France heard behind shuttered windows and closed doors, by courtesy of 'la bibici', that London, after fifty, sixty, seventy nights of bombing, still stood, unyielding, defiant, and more than ever determined to endure. The R.A.F., inspired by its triumph in the Battle of Britain, said the bibici, had inflicted such losses on the German bombers that it seemed probable they would in time have to abandon this blitz on London. Meanwhile London would take it.

Then a small leaflet, amateurishly printed and in dubious grammar, appeared on street walls, clumsily stuck over every German poster as if stuck there by men as they ran. It cried:

> Drive the Boches from France
> Crush this accursed race
> Frenchmen, arise

Tommies, aid us
GLOIRE à la R.A.F.
Soon we shall be delivered
Soon we shall have our revenge
Then we shall sing as in the past
VIVE LA FRANCE ET LA LIBERTE

Beneath the words was a crude picture of a Union Jack (quite inaccurate) and a Tricolor joined in partnership.

There was a new O.C. Troops in Sainte-Marie now, a Colonel Ranke, a far harsher and more impatient man than the courteous von Hoth; a man who took pride in announcing that all subversion would be ruthlessly crushed—favourite words of his, 'subversion', and 'ruthless' and 'crushed'. 'We shall show no mercy to disobedience.' He came in person with some of his officers to stare at this unco-operative leaflet. An adjutant translated parts of it that were not clear. Then Colonel Ranke went back to the German Provost's office and issued an offer of ten thousand francs to anyone who would give information that would lead to the apprehension of these 'anti-social and subversive' bill-stickers, and, with it, a punitive order that French flags were to hang no more in Sainte-Marie. This meant that the Tricolor which flew from the balcony of the Mairie must be hauled down.

Once again the Town Major came down Sophie's stairs, charged with the task of transmitting and explaining an O.C.'s order. The Mayor, Monsieur Philippe-Gabriel Galais, attended by his First and Second Deputies, and a few councillors of whom two were women, received him in the Mayor's Parlour. Major Clauss was no less courteous to Monsieur Galais, the host to all his troops, than to his own host and hostess in Sophie's chateau. He clicked, bowed, and said, 'I regret, Monsieur le Maire, to have to ask this of you, but such are the orders of the Colonel commanding the troops in your town.'

Monsieur Galais looked at his deputies, he looked at his councillors, he looked at his parquet floor, and then, rather suddenly, he said, 'Very well. I can only obey. I will take the flag down. But may I suggest that your loudspeakers in the town should summon our citizens to the Mairie Square at noon tomorrow so that I can take it down ceremoniously and demonstrate my obedience to your order?'

'But certainly, Monsieur le Maire,' said Major Clauss, relieved and touched by this co-operation. 'The Colonel will be obliged to you for that, I am sure. I thank you on his behalf. Good morning, sir.'

The click, the bow, and he went.

The Germans had fixed loudspeakers on suitable sites in the Mairie Square, the Market Place, the Place de la Forge, and the Avenue de la Gare, and in cafés and bistros, so that they could broadcast their news-bulletins and their propaganda with incidental music for the delight of the people. Gratified by the exemplary co-operation of the Mayor, they broadcast his summons. And, unheard, unsuspected, the bazaar whisper instructed the people what to do.

Ten minutes to noon, and all the shutters began to close in the Mairie Square, all blinds to come down, all shops to close their doors. The crowd assembled in the broad open space before the Mairie. The Mairie of this little town is a long cream-faced building, very French, under its steep mansard roof and with its small balus-traded balcony before the central french windows. From the balcony projects a flagstaff, and this morning a large Tricolor hung from it. Needless to say that Sophie was there in the crowd, and Marie-Louise; but today Klem and Jean were also there, to see what would happen. Eric, his great head higher than anyone else's, recognized them and threaded a way with difficulty towards them. He put a flat, fat hand on his breast and said, 'Sophie darling, but I'm terrified! Absolutely terrified. I've absolutely none of the blood of the martyrs in me, I should loathe the idea of being martyred, but I've just learned that, even though I never go to church or to any of my duties, I'm quite the most terrific Catholic ever. That's to say, terrific so long as I don't have to do anything about it.

What do you think I went and did? I'd got a wee bit annoyed with them for trying to tell our padre what he was to preach and not to preach—I mean, we can't have that—and when a frightful man, a typical German savage, came to my little 'pension' and asked, Was I Herr O'Healy, and, if so, I must report as an alien——'

Here the fear leapt high in Sophie, and she interrupted, 'They have come to you, have they?'

'Yes; yes.' Eric didn't want his story interrupted. 'Yes; this frightful man; I insisted I was Irish; I explained that the O'Healys were descended from the Irish kings; but it seems they know the difference between Ulster and Eire. Oh, dear, oh dear. They know I come from Belfast, so I couldn't come from Cork. This bestial type asked, Was I a Catholic; and it was then that the marvellous thing happened. Before I knew what was happening, I remembered my dear Abbé and said, "Yes, since my christening and with the grace of God until my death." Terrific, wasn't it? I simply heard myself saying it, I don't know where the words came from. The brute of a man looked a wee bit sour, and ever since then I've been in mortal dread of them coming for me——'

Again the uprush of fear in Sophie, speeding her heart, but this time she stayed quiet.

'—and, Sophie darling, I simply can't be arrested and go to prison. I should hate it. But they're making a set against the more enthusiastic Catholics like me, and they've got a special hold on me as an alien. I'm shaking with fear. In an awful state. Perhaps it won't be prison, but you know they're beginning to transport all males of military age to Germany for labour service. Could that include me, do you think? I mean, I've never had any use for labouring. Oh dear, it's worrying. Be an angel, lovey, and tell me they won't try any of this funny stuff with me.'

Sophie started to comfort him, not without a courageous banter, for her heart was still quickened. She was averring that he was much too big and fat for labour, when the church clock struck noon.

Then a common interest quelled all talk, stilled all movement;

and all eyes shot to the balcony. The Mayor came on to it in a formal frock coat as for a funeral. The Abbé followed him. The shallow balcony could hold no more with comfort, but the Mayor's four deputies could be seen in the room behind. Silence, unbroken, greeted Mayor and Curé. Monsieur Galais did not speak. He only drew down the flag from its mast slowly, unfurled it and waved it three times slowly above the people; then folded it small and kissed it. He handed it to the Abbé who kissed it too and, holding it in one hand, made the sign of the cross in benediction over it. Not a sound anywhere but the sobbing of women and the gulping of some men. The Abbé handed the folded flag to a deputy behind him, and it went out of sight.

Not one word had the Mayor spoken; he had shown the people in what way he obeyed their masters. All stood for a half-minute of silence, till Mayor and Curé turned and left the balcony.

§

Unable to point to disobedience in this scene, the Germans could do nothing against the Mayor. Nor was it easy to inculpate the Abbé. But the new O.C., furious at being tricked, stamped on the floor of his office and after much pacing and pondering, summoned the Abbé into his presence. When the Abbé appeared in the bare room, the Colonel tartly pointed to a wooden chair, but his visitor, bowing an acknowledgment, declined it, and stood before the Colonel with his fingers interlaced at his breast. Beginning to pace up and down, the Colonel said, 'Monsieur. You must divine what it is I have to say to you. Let us not waste time going into details. Quite simply it is this: either you desist from inciting the people to subversive activities or I shall take all necessary steps to stop you. I shall not hesitate to do so. You must know to what I am referring. Please remember I have the power to close your church.'

'You have the power, certainly.'

'I have, and unless you give me your promise here and now, I shall use it. What, please, is your answer?'

'Monsieur, your predecessor invited me to give an undertaking that I would counsel my people to nothing but collaboration with our enemies—if you will forgive that word; it is technically correct since there has been no treaty of peace as yet——'

'I accept it. Go on.'

'He said it must be collaboration or expulsion——'

'At present I do not go as far as that. I say only that I shall close your church because it is being used as a centre of subversion. I desire to be reasonable. But any more contumacy from you and I *shall* be forced to go further. I shall see if we cannot find a less recalcitrant priest to take your place in Sainte-Marie. Then I shall be pleased to open the church again. There are many clerics whose attitude to us is very different from yours.'

'I know there are, sir. Many of them.'

'They accept honourably the consequences of defeat. I should have no difficulty in replacing you.'

'I know it.'

'Very well then. Will you kindly promise that you will henceforward do nothing whatsoever to stir up dissidence and disaffection in this town?'

The Abbé stayed silent. He was thinking of two things. He was thinking of England and of holiness. He was thinking that it now looked as though England, with American help, might yet turn the issue of the war, and that then indeed she would need disaffection in the people of conquered France; and he was thinking that honesty was one of the 'kinds of holiness' he had preached. He no longer wanted to lie or dissemble before any man. So he said at last, 'Monsieur, I can only say to you what I said to your predecessor that I can give no undertaking but to act as my conscience directs me.'

'All right, Monsieur. And that clearly means that, as from noon tomorrow your church is closed.'

'As you will, Monsieur.'

Exasperated by this cold, indifferent attitude, the Colonel swung round from his pacing and stood opposite the Abbé; smart green uniform facing rumpled and shining black soutane; Army opposing Church; conqueror conquered. His eyes were angry as he said, 'Let me add a warning. Do not try us too far. We have imprisoned other priests if they have remained stubborn after we have given them every chance.'

'Monsieur, that threat doesn't seem to frighten me any more. Indeed I sometimes think that I should like to share the sufferings of my brethren. And not only my clerical brethren, sir. I feel I would like to suffer with the laity of France.'

'Sufferings? Nonsense. They bring them upon themselves. We have tried to treat the conquered French people with a generosity that surely has no parallel in history. If they show no gratitude and refuse all co-operation, we can change our methods, *and we shall*. Very good, Monsieur. I need hold you no more. We know where we stand.'

Next morning the iron bars and padlocks went on to the doors of the church, and the swastika flag drooped before the lintel of the central doorway.

§

A few weeks later a German soldier, very drunk, went rolling after a little girl returning from school to her cottage home. This was a cottage at the foot of one of the fields that sloped up to the forest, and only a winding dirt-track led to it. Half-way along the track the soldier, seeing the cottage, feared to lose his prey; he hurried to the child, clutched her, and with one hand sought to molest her little body adventurously. She screamed 'Maman, maman!' and her father, looking through his open door, saw what was happening. He snatched up a dung-fork with which he had just been spreading stable manure, and rushed towards the man, carrying the fork with both hands as a soldier carries his weapon in a bayonet charge. The soldier saw the spear-like tines of the fork coming furiously towards him, and he let the child go. With a drunk's fumbling fingers, he drew his pistol and fired straight into the father's body—what mattered a French labourer more or less? Then, sobered by the report and by the man's collapse on to the dirt-track, he ran out of sight, out of danger. The child flung herself, screaming and sobbing, on the prone, silent figure of her father. Soon her mother was standing above them both, throwing back her head and wailing for her dead man, with hands outspread to the sky.

This family, Pierre Dubosquet, his wife, two grown sons and one small daughter, were faithful parishioners of the Abbé; even the two sons, both of whom were now prisoners-of-war, used to come regularly to Mass. So now the mother's poignant request was that her Pierre should have a 'proper funeral' with a Mass in the church he had loved. 'Oh, please, please, Father. Surely they will let you do this for him.'

The Abbé took her request to Colonel Ranke. Surely, he submitted, the Colonel would allow the church to be used, at least for this service, since it was one of his soldiers who had shot down Pierre Dubosquet.

'No.' The answer was as smart as a click of German field-boots. 'We do not necessarily accept your account of what happened.'

'Madame Dubosquet saw it from the window. And the child Brigitte is not lying.'

'So far we have no evidence that it was one of our men.'

'Only the evidence of two witnesses. Mother and child. Madame Dubosquet and Brigitte Dubosquet.'

'Well, even if that is so, Monsieur, even if it is proved against one of my men, then by your own account this fellow Dubosquet was guilty of a capital crime, in that he took a weapon to one of our soldiers with intent to wound or murder him. A pitchfork or hay-fork or something when, as likely as not, the man had no intention of hurting the girl. I will not have a criminal elevated into a martyr. Our men are decent and well-behaved; we enforce this with the utmost strictness; and if it can be proved that one of them has misconducted himself, he will be severely punished. That is all I can promise you. As for the proven criminal, Dubosquet, well, it is perfectly possible, I am informed, to bury a man without a Mass.'

'That is your final answer, mon colonel?'

'Certainly.'

The Abbé went home to the Presbytery. Hands behind his back, he trod the worn carpet in his sitting-room for an hour; then went to the little oratory across the passage and, kneeling there, laid his purpose before God. Persuaded at length that his purpose could be used of God for France and her Church, he went out into the street and told it to one or two. One or two were enough. Faster than any telegraph, the bazaar whisper carried it to every home in Sainte-Marie. And to homes in villages around.

Two days later the hearse, an ancient black vehicle with high moulting plumes at each corner, stood on the dirt-track by the Dubosquets' cottage while many hundreds of the inhabitants of Sainte-Marie stood on the field that sloped up to the forest. With them were many who had come from the neighbouring villages in carts or on foot or on bicycles—these now the universal vehicle, since the Germans were commandeering the petrol. The coffin, massed with wreaths, slid into the hearse; no flag lay over it, for the Tricolor was banned, but Pierre Dubosquet's fellow-labourers had arranged blue, white, and red flowers, in broad strips together, to lie on its breast. The Abbé in his robes, waddling because of the width and weight of his belly, led the procession away from the cottage. Eight fellow-labourers walked as a guard of honour, four on each side of the hearse. These eight men, though unarmed, looked strangely threatening, their faces so grim and set; you could imagine them with sub-machine-guns in those empty hands one day. Behind the hearse, after Madame Dubosquet and her little daughter, Brigitte, came Monsieur Galais, the Mayor, his four deputies, his councillors, and his secretariat; then the hundreds of men and women in their mourning black, marching four abreast. Some of the men wore their medals of the last war, newly polished. Among the women was Marie-Louise in her black. Lastly came the pompiers of a neighbouring town in their uniforms and helmets. The procession, leaving the dirt-track went along the Rue de la Forêt, where Sophie, Klem and Jean stood watching at the corner of their little avenue, Sophie weeping. It went on to the Place de la Forge and the Rue de Paris, undisturbed by German or French police. Authority knew the mood of Sainte-Marie today. Better to let the boil discharge its pus and its core in the form of this demonstration through the streets and at the cemetery. The only escorts to flank and steward the long procession were powerful young men chosen from among the mourners. The German police, on orders, were staying out of sight; the French police had been told to employ all tact and much invisibility.

But the procession was not heading for the cemetery. Not yet. It was going to the church. The hearse halted before the central door, and the Abbé took out of it an axe and a clawed crowbar which had travelled among the flowers by the side of the dead man.

Men stepped forward to help him, but he raised a plump palm to stop them. 'No. Only me. Let no one else be incriminated. Please. Stay where you are.'

He went, not to the central doorway, but to the doorway on its left. Just as the central doorway carried above it the legend 'Aimez vous les uns les autres', so this smaller entrance, the one usually left unlocked all day, bore the words, 'Le pain que je donnerai, c'est ma chair.' Here, with the crowbar he, a big heavy man, powerful in his day, forced away bar and padlock. With axe and crowbar he forced apart the doors. He threw them wide—angrily, sadly—and, turning to the people, waved them continuously into the church, saying, 'Come.'

§

That afternoon they arrested him in the Presbytery behind the church, where he sat awaiting them with his breviary on his knees (for he had no lap) and a bag at his side filled with requisites for prison.

§

Then the temper of the town was such that they were determined to learn when and by what means he would be taken from

Sainte-Marie. This was not difficult. After six months of German Occupation the French had learned, with no small surprise and much grim-lipped humour, that German sentries, and not seldom more distinguished members of the vaunted German army, were easily suborned if the bribe was attractive enough. With other civilian prisoners the Abbé was held for several days, while letters wandered from Authority to Authority, in a lonely mansion among the first of the forest trees; and two of the German guards who stood with fixed bayonets outside the house, or sat in the guard-room by the door, proved reasonably corruptible in the presence of genial French citizens who spoke of four thousand francs. After all, what was there to do but answer a 'when?' and a 'how?' and a 'where?' Four thousand francs (some twenty pounds) was soon assembled in Sainte-Marie, and it opened up the secrets with far less noise than the Abbé opened up his church door.

The Germans were going to move the Abbé and the other prisoners to Paris and Fresnes on such a day, *by train and by daylight*.

'Bon.' The line from Sainte-Marie station to Paris, when it has passed the last of the houses, runs through orchards and level fields, and on its northern flank a footpath accompanies it for a mile or so, winding between the wired fence and ranks of pollarded limes. When the Abbé's train appeared round a bend, this narrow footpath held half the population of Sainte-Marie, all standing there to cheer him on his way to Paris and to Fresnes prison. As it went by them, the men stood at the salute, the women waved, and the girls threw kisses. There could be no French flags, but French girls had been equal to circumventing this ban. Many of them stood in trios, one wearing a blue scarf, the next a white, and the third a red. Marie-Louise, her sister, and Jean made up one of these successive trios; Jean wore a white scarf (by accident?) between the blue and the red of the young French women. Thus the Abbé Belfort and his fellow-prisoners, as their train ran on, saw, not only the salute of the men and the waves and kisses of the women, but, as it were, the Tricolor, which he had blessed in their presence and laid aside, still accompanying them on their way.

VIII

The Saint in the House

In all these months the young Major Clauss in Rennie's room and his orderly in Klem's workroom were hardly ever seen by the household. They came and they went with a quietness plainly inspired by the Major out of consideration for the feelings of the family. If the Major passed Sophie or Jean on the stairs he bowed and said nothing. If the orderly passed Marie-Louise in the garden emptying her kitchen refuse, he touched his cap in salute. A mild, kindly and most willing young man, he tried sometimes to break through the wall of Marie-Louise's silence and aversion, and among his ways of attempting this were the bringing of food scraps from his mess for Wallace and Bruce, and an ostentatious fondling of them whenever he met them. Indeed both Major and orderly never passed the dogs without patting their heads or stroking their ears, and the dogs were now disposed to collaborate most abominably with the enemy. When the Major sought help from Klem, or some small information from Sophie, they both answered him courteously; the young man's politeness bred this courtesy in response.

But in midwinter the orderly was seen to be going up and down the stairs alone, and nothing was heard of the Major; not even the rhythmic tramping of his feet and the creaking of his floor above the ceiling of the breakfast-room. Forty-eight hours of this, and

93

Sophie's curiosity could be contained no more; she spoke to the orderly on the stairs.

'Yes, Madame, Major Clauss is ill. But it need not derange you. I can look after him.' An incipient salute and he passed up the stairs to his officer.

A regimental medical officer, surprisingly young, and looking like a hospital student in his first year rather than a qualified practitioner, examined the patient in Rennie's room and came down to speak with Madame Burgermann. 'It is not serious, Madame—a small fever—but I will certainly move the Major to an army hospital if Madame wishes.'

But Sophie, moved to some compassion and a sudden unexpected liking for their so quiet and considerate guest, replied, 'Oh no, Monsieur. If it is not serious, let him stay. Do not disturb the poor young man.'

'But his meals, Madame?'

'Surely we can see to them. There is his batman to help. My maid will prepare whatsoever he needs and the batman can take the dishes up to him.'

'It is gracious of you, Madame.'

'Not at all. One is always ready to help those who are sick.'

So it came about that Marie-Louise made soup and light dishes for the alien invalid, saying as little as possible to the servant and keeping her eyes away from him. As the invalid improved, she found herself cutting up his meat or fish into small portions easily handled by a man with only one arm. But still not saying anything, nor looking the servant's way.

It was when Sophie came into the kitchen one evening and saw her cutting up these small portions that she was seized by an idea. It seemed a wonderful idea; it ministered like a healing potion to her chronic pain of fear.

Seven months had passed since the Germans entered Paris, and there were still British subjects at large in the capital and the Occupied Zone. Usually they were the old, or women with small children, or those who were useful to the Germans. The Major had long known that the Burgermanns were British subjects, but never had that dreaded knock come to the door of the chateau in some small, silent hour of a morning. Was it because Klem and she were considered 'old'? Klem sixty-four, she fifty-nine— Sophie was ready to be 'old' for the duration of the war and *vis-à-vis* the Germans, but worried, indignant, that they should call her old; at the thought of it she would go to her glass and study her face, this side and that, for wrinkles. Or was it Klem's mild help of the Major which was saving them? If so, let *her* be now of help to the poor young man. *She* would cut up his meat for him and take it to his sick bed where he lay all day alone and so quiet. She would even sit and talk with him a little.

She quickly eased her conscience about this fraternising with an enemy. From the moment he fell sick she was justified in ministering to him. That was almost international law. In all military hospitals a wounded enemy received the same treatment as the others. And had not she herself said to the M.O., 'One is always ready to help those who are sick'? Besides, this polite young man, so thoughtful for others, was quite different from the tough and brutal Germans. Also, all questions of nationality and war apart, Sophie coveted his thanks and praise and admiration when she appeared with his dishes, helped him to manage them with his one hand, and sat a little to talk with him.

So successful was she in earning his gratitude that she insisted on Klem adopting the same attitude. He must go and sit with him sometimes. 'Not only may it help to save us all, but it's your Christian duty, you heathen old man. Didn't the Samaritan do something like that to his enemy, or am I thinking of someone else? Go on and talk to him'—and she pushed him out of the breakfast-room and towards the tower staircase. He obeyed, saying, 'One minute you send me shopping for potatoes and the next you send me shopping for undue favours from the enemy. All right. Give me the bag.' And now quite often Klem was up in Rennie's old room, sitting in a chair by the old-fashioned brass bed, and talking amicably with a fellow German. It emerged that this Major Clauss, like his host, was a student of philosophy. He also was a Ph.D.

But what shocked Sophie was that Klem had no scruples whatever about dissembling before this occupying enemy. He just said 'All lies are fair in war' or 'One's freedom is worth a Mass', and went upstairs and pretended to be more or less in agreement with all the young man said. He hid all his revulsion from Nazism and all his loyalty to Britain, and came downstairs saying how much he was enjoying this double game. Sophie was deeply shocked. She had never believed that Klem, so mild and conscientious ('Klem is the honestest man I know') was ready to be such a liar.

Shocked and, in one part of her, glad.

Jean endorsed with joy her father's game and suggested that she too should be nurse to the young man and do some shamming before him.

'Well, I think it's all rather wicked,' said Sophie. 'But I suppose *he* knows best. There he is now, sitting up there and talking philosophy with a Nazi and pretending to agree with him.'

For the younger Ph.D. had organized his philosophy into a complete acceptance of the Nazi creed. Out of his masters and teachers, Fichte, Hegel, Herder, Klauss Wagner and others, he had built for himself a devotion to Nazism as complete as that of a saint to his religion. Happy in his faith, and in his consecration to it, ardent as the newest convert to any religion, he delighted to expound it fluently to an obviously interested and learned old man whom it would be a triumph to bring to the Light.

And as he expounded it, fervour brightening his eyes, as he declared excitedly, and with palpable truth, that he was ready to give up happiness, future, life to it, the idea came to Klem that this young man was, according to his strange and terrible lights, far more of a consecrated saint in his youth than ever their good, lost Abbé had been. Returning downstairs, Klem reported, 'I've had my bedside instruction. From the saint in his cell.'

§

'You see, Herr Doktor, we believe in the eternal values of Race and Blood. You were long ago naturalized as an Englishman, but *we* say—if you'll forgive me—that no German can do this. He cannot deny his Blood or his People. A German is everywhere a German whether he lives in Berlin or Paris or London. You have no free will in the matter, and to deny your Blood—forgive me again—is a treachery to the purposes of our German God for His German people. We believe our Führer has been raised up by God to teach us this. Your Race reclaims you, doctor.'

'Your German God, Herr Major? But who is he?'

'The age-old mystical spirit of our German people.'

'I see,' said Klem, who certainly didn't. 'And His purposes? What are they?'

'To redeem the world. Nothing less.'

'Redeem?' Even Klem, though wishing to hide his recoils, started back at this word. Then, drawing at his hooked Bavarian pipe, and fingering his heavy gold watch-chain, he said, 'But that was what the Jews thought.'

'Pah! The Jews! We have to redeem the world first from the Jews and then from itself. Why even Heine, himself a Jew, saw this. Don't you remember how he said, "I have often pondered over this universal mission of Germany as I strolled under the evergreen firs of my Fatherland"?'

'Yes, I remember. I remember it well. But . . . "redeeming worlds from themselves"—what does that mean? Forgive me in my turn if I say it sounds like so many words—empty words. What is the meaning in them, Herr Major? Do tell me. I am really most anxious to know.'

'There is great meaning in them. Look at the French. You are not French, Dr. Burgermann, nor is Madame, so may I speak my mind?'

'Yes, indeed. Go on.'

'Well, for years past this degenerate people have tried to keep us Germans, who are twice them in multitude, behind unnatural frontiers, so that they—*they*, if you please—can remain la Grande Nation. And what is the culture of this Grande Nation compared with ours? It's a culture of brothels and night-bars and nudist shows, with a literature that is mostly obscene and an art that is manifestly decadent. Is there a city in Europe which hasn't a quarter given over to filth and vice and calling itself a "Little Paris"? Which shows at once,' continued the Major, heating with the indignation of a righteous man, 'that their culture is a poisonous and infectious tumour discharging its pus all over the world. And the people! The people themselves! They are nothing but a mixture of all kinds. Look at their youth. They have lost all ardour and spirit of sacrifice. We wiped them up in twelve days.'

'And you're saying that you propose to take over the whole of Europe and order it on better lines? Is that it?' Klem continued to finger the watch-chain. 'It's very interesting.'

'Yes, that is it. Yes, sir: the whole of Europe from the Ukraine to the Ile-de-France. We've had enough of being encircled and enchained by these decadent nations. We're tired of being a great people with insufficient room—"Ein Volk ohne Raum". No, thank you! We believe the German Blood has called us to our duty. And that the German hour has struck.'

Klem, impatient with melodrama, kept his lips tight-closed over his pipe. He took off his rimless spectacles, breathed on their lenses, and polished them.

While the Major proceeded, forgetting that Klem wasn't French, 'But understand, Monsieur, it is our hope that a purified France will one day work with us as our partner and friend. The Western culture which was once Graeco-Roman will then be Franco-German.'

'And the other peoples?'

'The Eastern European races? They are inferior races and there is nothing to do but treat them as such. But I hope we shall be able to treat them with our German courtesy.'

'I see.' Klem said this with a half-smile, sure that this serious young man wouldn't suspect humour anywhere in the room. 'So much for France. And what of England?'

'England we think of as a cleaner country, its people sprung from a better stock—are they not our cousins?—but her Blood is shockingly adulterated and, moreover, she is tired and old. We are young. For years past she has taken the wrong road, embracing the causes of races inferior to her—the French and the Poles and the Jews. And because she has given herself over to money-scraping Jews her civilization is what? A paradise for cheating hucksters. No wonder her young men have always refused to be impressed into a national army. What have they got to fight for? No wonder they have gone soft.'

Klem felt like quoting 'Gloire à la R.A.F.', but wisely didn't.

'We might have gone soft too if our Führer had not been raised up to give us something to fight and die for, our Race, our Blood.'

But at this point Klem couldn't quite hold back from reminding him, 'The British are still fighting. Supposing they go on for years?'

Then it was the Major's turn to smile tolerantly. 'Herr Doktor, don't be absurd. It is winter now, but you can be sure that great armaments are being prepared to bring Britain to her knees. In the spring. You may remember that last spring, on April 9th, we invaded Denmark and Norway. We were in Copenhagen and Oslo the same afternoon. I suggest that much the same will apply to London.'

Klem, wisely turning from this topic, began, 'Monsieur, you are plainly an idealist——'

'I hope so, sir.'

'—Well, may I then ask you—for I am much interested—do you personally approve of . . .' he hesitated . . . 'of some of the ruthlessness which your forces have employed?' And he described that morning when the Stuka bombers flew back and forth, shooting down the refugees. 'These were civilians, Monsieur.'

'The answer is simple, I think.'

'And it is?'

'That ruthlessness is more merciful in the end. We aim to finish a war as quickly as possible for everyone's sake. Your English are doing much the same with their mass bombing of civilian homes. The only difference is that we succeed while they go on uselessly. You may remember we were in Paris the very next day, and your Marshal sued for terms three days later. Also, of course, it is part of our faith that if the Blood is to be strong it must not be afraid of shedding blood, whether our own or our enemy's. We Germans have learned that we have to be strong and hard. They took our Rhineland from us and our German Danzig; they drove a corridor between us and our brothers in Eastern Germany; do you suppose we'd ever have got Rhineland, Danzig, or corridor back if the Führer hadn't taught us to be strong and hard and, when necessary, ruthless? I think not. Twenty years and they were not back till we *took* them back. Heil Hitler who taught us ruthlessness. Total ruthlessness, when necessary.'

To hide his distaste Klem laughed as he asked, 'But that's hardly Christianity, is it?' the laugh suggesting that it didn't really matter much if it was Christianity or not.

'Is it not? I seem to remember that a highly moral Pope ordered the total massacre of the Albigenses for the health of the Church and that Martin Luther, in the Peasant's Revolt, didn't hesitate to tell their feudal lords to slay them all. But whether it's Christian practice or not is no longer of any relevance. We have done with Christianity, I am glad to say. It's an Eastern religion, a Jewish sect founded by a Jew, and its teaching turns men into weaklings. It has weakened and disabled our German men too long. What might they not have done if they'd been allowed to act in accordance with their own free German soul. The German believer has only one faith now, that his strength is of God and that he is part of a Great Whole indissolubly bound up with his own people by the divine links of the Blood.'

Hearing which, Klem felt that the only way to hold back from hot argument or hurtful satire was to go. He rose. 'I must not make you talk too much, Herr Major. It will tire you.'

'But no, it has been so pleasant, Monsieur. I thank you for coming. And Madame Burgermann has been so kind. May I hope you will come again? Not often, because you are busy, but it is very pleasant to see you.'

Klem did come again chiefly in compassion for him lying there, and Sophie, when he was up and about again, spoke to him on the stairs sometimes, not ungently; and soon the young man felt an affection for all in this household, the affection being the stronger because there were so few in this village who would look at him without a dumb but evident queasiness.

IX

The Trade

THE fervent arguments of the young zealot upstairs, so far from making a convert of his quiet listener, left an impression the exact opposite of what the young man hoped. In Klem, behind his silences and gentle smiles, there had risen like a tide a fuller realization of his horror at the terrible doctrines that could so corrupt the idealism, generosity and self-surrender of a devoted and brave young man. Though pretending to no religion, he now felt driven, by sheer recoil, not towards the dogmas of Christianity, but at least towards its practices, since these were the opposite of this 'poor young Clauss's dotty, evil-begotten, murderous nonsense'.

The arguments which he suppressed in that bedroom swelled within him, as he walked in the garden behind the hooked pipe or went shopping for Sophie with the string-bag. But for a long time he did nothing but think his thoughts. Three hundred thousand Jews murdered in conquered Poland by the hierophants of the young man's new religion! Three hundred thousand. . . . And what could *he* do? Nothing . . . nothing. . . .

It was in the second half of 1941 that he saw the notice on the walls of Sainte-Marie: 'Le nommé, Marcel Motte de Sainte-Marie a été condamné à mort pour aider l'enemi par recrutement en faveur de l'armée de l'ex-General de Gaulle. Il a été fusillé aujourd'hui'; and the sprays of flowers which had appeared beneath it. He had known Marcel, the eighteen-year-old son of Madame Motte, who ran Eric's pension-de-famille in the Rue du Maréchal Joffre. Then another notice on the walls, reporting that, in reprisal for the murder of a German soldier, ten French hostages had been executed in the Chateau of Vincennes. Ten! And, some weeks later yet, another announcing that unless the young men who had fled rather than be impressed into the Labour Corps returned before August 15th, their parents would be deported in their place. Sickening at 'all this pollution of the German name', he began to long to do something, if only a little, to expiate the sins of his people. Three hundred thousand. . . .

One evening in that autumn he divulged this longing to Sophie and Jean. They were sitting after a meagre supper (rationing was now more than a year old, and the sparse rations lessening) around the empty grate in the breakfast-room. Like other families in Sainte-Marie and indeed in all Occupied France, they were tending to shut themselves as much as possible within their house walls, largely to avoid people who might see them and speak dangerous things of them. The two dogs, Wallace and Bruce, lay near the cold fireplace, and one of them, Bruce, deprecating this unseemly cold, frequently got up and walked twice round the place where he would have been had he lain still; then lay down again with a yawning but philosophic acceptance.

And Klem said, 'I feel, quite simply, that one ought to do *something*. I mean, what are people *for*? I get the feeling that in a time like this all those of us who revolt against this degradation of our common humanity ought to begin to *do* something. Something to justify the existence of Man.'

'To justify the existence of Man?' Sophie repeated the words, bewildered.

'Yes, even if there's no God and no meaning or purpose anywhere in the world or in the stars or anywhere else.'

This was too difficult for Sophie, and not too pleasing. No, not at all. Jean kept silence.

And Klem explained further, 'All I do is to hang on to this

thought in case by any chance it *is* God. It's such a strange impera-
tive.'

This comforted Sophie a little, though she didn't fully understand it. At last she said, 'But what could you *do*—one poor lonely
individual? Or me? What could any of us do? Nothing.'

'Some people are doing something.'

'What are they doing?'

Klem found several answers to this, while Jean remained in her
silence, a curious smile beginning to form along her lips. One of
her long legs, crossed over the other, began to swing like a tall
young man's.

'Helping the boys who want to get to England and de Gaulle,'
said Klem. 'Helping escaped prisoners, whether French or British,
to get out of the country and fight again. Hiding British airmen
who've crashed, and helping to smuggle them back home. It must
be fine to do things like that. I'd like to. Oh, yes. To atone, as it
were.'

'No . . . no! It's too dangerous. Much too dangerous, Don't
talk nonsense, Klem. Besides, we're British; we don't have to
atone for the British, thank God.'

'I am German born. And I wasn't born for what they're doing
now.'

'Yes; German; and they know you're German—or were once—
and that makes it more impossible for you than for anybody to do
these things.'

'On the contrary, it makes it more possible. We might be able to
offer safer cover than most——'

'*No!*' cried Sophie, terrified at the direction of his thoughts.
'*No*, Klem, *no!*' She was seeing the notice outside the German
Provost's office: 'The General Officer Commanding-in-Chief,
German Garrison, warns all citizens that the penalty for harbouring
or aiding enemy personnel is death.' Her face was white. 'That
could mean death.'

'I know.' Absent-mindedly he took his pipe from his lips to
refill it. Remembering that it was empty, and that he had no

tobacco, he held it by the bowl between his lips again. Jean bent down to finger a dog's ear and hide her smile.

'And surely,' Sophie submitted, 'it would be shockingly dishonourable?'

'Absolutely,' he acknowledged cheerfully. 'On the face of it. But so is all bam-boozling of an enemy who's out to destroy you and all you stand for.'

Jean murmured, 'Of course,' apparently to the dogs.

'Well, I don't understand what's come over you of late.' Sophie could only shrug and add weakly, 'All I beg of you is, don't get us all killed.'

'I don't think you need worry, my dear. I'm afraid I'm not brave enough to do anything at all splendid. I just act the lying old humbug before my friend the saint upstairs.

'And you mustn't do anything else. Darling, you really mustn't —no, *please*.' She stretched forward an appealing hand to lay it on his knee. Her affection was opening out like a flower in the very warmth of her dismay. But, relieved by his assertion that he wasn't brave enough to do anything, she leaned back in her chair in some peace—only to be perturbed again, when he resumed, 'It's only for a night, as a rule, that one has to hide them. Just to help them on their way. We couldn't do it for more than a night. I suppose it'd really be better to do it somewhere well away from the house. In the forest, I sometimes think. But there: don't worry. I can't see myself doing anything, somehow. Perhaps Jean who's still young and vigorous and venturesome could do something.'

'No, no; she mustn't. It's playing with fire. It's playing with *death*.'

Jean spoke at last, the smile broadening, the leg still swinging. 'Jean *is* doing something.'

Both swung towards her. '*You?*'

'Yes. Me. Jean.'

'Jean . . . !' Sophie began.

'Mais oui. Jeanne. And Wallace and Bruce too. They're doing their little bit.'

'But Jean!' Klem, frightened too, said, 'God! How long have you been doing this?'

'Oh, for ages. I'm in the Trade,' she said, proud of the word.

'Trade?'

'Yes. That's what we call it. I've gone underground.'

Sophie could only beseech, 'Oh, do be careful; be careful,' while thinking, 'She's endangering the life of us all. Her father—well, that's her business—but I'm only her stepmother,' and striving to force away this unworthy thought.

Klem said, 'But, Jean dear! How did you start this?'

The grim, pleased smile compressed her lips again. Clearly she longed to tell them much, and was wondering if it would be right to tell. When she spoke it was with relish for the drama of it all. 'You may not know, my dears, but there is an English agent moving around in these parts. I've met him. A gent dropped from an aeroplane.'

'English? Who is he?'

'Who knows? We know nothing but his field name. He's a young man, quite good-looking. Rather a charmer, in fact. But we only know him as "Amos".'

'A Jew?'

'No. Couldn't be less of a Jew. Very tall and fair, and terribly slim—so slim you'd think he'd break. That's only his cover name. It seems there are quite a few of these boys round Paris and they've all taken names from the Minor Prophets. There's a Joel and a Micah, I'm told. You don't half know what's going on around here. The short names, you see, because there's no time for long ones. The War won't wait. Our Amos is helping us fine.'

'But in *what? In what?*' demanded Sophie, her eyes staring, her fingers beating on the chair-arm.

'Ought I to tell you, when it's all appallingly secret? But . . . if Dad's disposed to come in too . . .' She hesitated while she justified herself. 'Amos appeared about a month ago, and as I, like Dad, was impatient to be doing something, I was taken to meet him.'

'But by whom?'

'I'll leave you to guess.'

Sophie said at once, 'Marie-Louise,' like a child who wants to get her answer in first.

'Perhaps. And again perhaps not.' As well as delighting in the possession of her mysteries Jean was happy to be showing her conscience that she wasn't telling all.

'But, my dear,' pleaded her father, 'do you realize that if they find out what you're doing you could be shot or hanged?'

'I could indeed. What a pity.'

'Don't laugh. Listen. In Alsace they've already hanged women, claiming that they were German by birth and therefore far more guilty than any French or English women. Well. . .? You're the daughter of a German.'

'I know that. Can't be helped.'

'And it might not be only death. Often they torture first to make you speak.'

'I know. Oh, I know. God, I hope I shan't speak.'

'Oh, *please*,' begged Sophie, 'don't talk as if these things would happen.'

'I'm hoping they'll give me soon one of their cyanide tablets. I've asked for one. I don't trust myself under torture.'

'Give you *what?*' asked Sophie.

'A cyanide pill. It's tiny and easily hidden, and if you think they're going to torture you, you slip it into your mouth and bite.'

'And then?'

'That's the end. No need to betray anyone. They've lost you.'

'You mean *dead?*'

'Of course. Gosh, I'm praying they give me one.'

It was perhaps in this moment, more than in the moment when she saw the Stukas massacring the refugees, that Sophie realized the War and all that was happening in the world. It had come out of the streets and into her house. It was, so to say, seated comfortably in front of her. The only words with which she could express to herself this complete and stupefying realization were 'Oh, my God, my God, where are we getting to now?'

Klem, unable to talk further about the cyanide pill, asked, 'What sort of things are you doing?'

'At first I thought I'd never tell you, and not only because they were secret, but because I didn't want to frighten Sophie. But you needn't be frightened, Sophie. It's all much easier than you would believe. The Germans are fools in some ways, and chiefly in thinking they're so much cleverer than anyone else, when, as far as I can see, most Frenchmen can make rings round them. It's enormous fun humbugging them.'

'Don't be sure it's easy,' said Klem. 'They're offering enormous rewards for information.'

'Yes, and we know of no single person who has accepted their generous offers.'

Klem shook his head. 'The weak are always with us. What about the thousands who've accepted service under this present pro-German Government?'

'Yes, what about them? They're not the boys they were, Dad. At one time they were ready enough to hand us over to the Germans, but they're not so keen on getting us now. Now that Britain doesn't look like being beaten, and the Americans look like coming in, and the war isn't looking too sweet for Germany, they're remembering that if they've got our names, we've got theirs.'

'Oh dear,' Klem sighed. 'Well, well, tell us: what *do* you do?'

Appropriately, as he asked this, they heard the tread of booted feet in the room above. It was getting late, and Major Clauss must have returned. No one had heard him return, so quietly, in his courtesy, did he open doors and climb the tower stairs. Neither of the dogs had barked. They no longer troubled to bark when they scented this friendly guest or his lovable servant who came to them with food. Perhaps Bruce had heard something, for he rose wearily, walked round his vacated bed, and collapsed into recumbency again.

Klem's eyes sought the ceiling as if to hear the movements better.

'He goes to bed. What time is it? Not yet half-past ten. Such a well-disciplined and serious young man. Keeps the hours of a puritan. Go on, dear, What do you do?'

'You've already described much of it. We help escaped p.o.w.s to get back to England. We give them money and civilian clothes and forged papers. And tobacco, of course.'

'But where do you get all this?' Unconsciously, Klem took out his pipe and looked into its empty bowl.

'From England. Dropped from aeroplanes to Amos and Micah and the others. Mind you, we do some of the forging ourselves— the Art School is good at it—but we can't compete with London. *I'm* rather splendid at road maps. And soon I'm to be a guide.'

'A guide?'

'Yes. Just that. I'm to guide them through the forest to places where they can be hid or to homes and farms that'll take them in. I've found my own places in the forest where we'll hide them and feed them. Praise God for the forest. I shall take the food to them when I'm exercising Wallace and Bruce. They need their exercise, poor sweets, and they're delighted to think they're helping France.' Wallace's ears had moved at the sound of his name. 'Scots have always been pro-French. Think of Bonnie Prince Charlie. Or do I mean Mary Queen of Scots? Anyhow we have a cache of potatoes buried deep in the forest.'

'Potatoes?'

'Well . . . let's call that another cover name. Strictly, the potatoes are grenades and Lewis guns and a few thousand rounds of ammunition. And commando knives. Going to be useful later.'

Tramp . . . tramp . . . overhead.

Both Sophie and Klem were listening with a staring interest. Sophie muttered her dismay at times, while Klem sighed in a kind of humorous despair. Jean comforted them, 'Don't worry too much. It's very little I'm doing at present. All too few of the évadés seem to come this way. I wish there were more of them, so that I could really be doing something. At present I seem to be only dropping seditious leaflets in suitable places and distributing a Gaullist daily when it comes from England; but Gosh, it's fun: I've never enjoyed anything so much in my life.'

Tread . . . tread . . . above.

'I hope he sleeps well,' Jean continued. 'I wouldn't wish his sleep to be disturbed by any worry about *our* goings-on.' Sleep, my dear sir, sleep. Schlafen Sie wohl, mein Herr.'

And, looking at her, both of them saw that Jean, who used to be so self-enclosed, so plainly a secret and frustrated woman, was now different, her face filling out, her skin clean and freshly coloured, her eyes brightened and ready with mischief and fun.

§

Her father, though frightened by all this, could only tell her with truth that he was proud of her. Sophie echoed 'Yes'; but softly, because very much afraid: *her* fright was like terror, and she kept thinking within herself, 'What will she not bring down upon us? Upon my home. But why worry about that if it's death? Death for us all.'

Jean had heard from Marie-Louise of an organization of young Catholic women, banded together to help the Resistance in Sainte-Marie, and she had immediately said, 'Oh, can't I join? I'm not a Catholic, but my father was. Won't that do?'

And on Marie-Louise reporting to her associates that Mademoiselle at the house was a fire-eater, they had willingly conceded that if her father had been a Catholic she had a birth qualification to play on their side. She was as thrilled as any skipping, excited schoolgirl by this; she felt as she used to at school when she played with other children at belonging to a Secret Society. This was a real Secret Society. Never one more real and secret. For the punishment of membership could be death.

The first handbills which she circulated had only been typed and duplicated sheets. They reported the arrests, executions, or deportations of young Frenchmen, and the mass murdering of Jews in prison camps. Every time she dropped one in a likely place she felt a glow of pleasure as at 'something done'.

Later the leaflets came properly printed by the Underground presses in Saint-Denis and Paris. And about the same time her tasks became more dangerous because Sainte-Marie was now on one of the escape routes for prisoners-of-war who sought to reach 'L'Organization' in Paris. They had to be guided over the country from family to family who would hide them. They came through the Forêt de L'Isle-Adam to Méry-sur-Oise, and the guides met them at the far end of the Forêt de Sainte-Marie. And Jean was sometimes chosen as the guide because she lived close to the forest and had long been a familiar figure in its glades. The escapers, one or more, were told to wait for a tall Anglaise with two small black dogs. Recognizing her, they would give her the password and then follow her and the dogs through the trees. They followed from far off, just keeping her in view among the trees. Sometimes at the fringe of the forest they were taken from her by a goat-herd's daughter and then, perhaps, as they left her and her dogs, they blew her a kiss before following instead the goats with their tinkling bells.

Not too difficult at first, but, of a sudden, the Forêt de Sainte-Marie filled with menace. The Germans—how much did they know?—were patrolling the whole forest by day and by night with patrol cars mounting searchlights. And Jean was offered, though deprecatingly, the task of bringing by night an escaper through the forest, despite these cars and the searchlights. She accepted it with fear—and with excitement. The few motor roads ran north and north-west through the forest, and the patrol cars sauntered along them with their black-out slitted headlights gleaming like half-closed suspicious eyes. Ever and again they stopped and swayed their searchlights among the trees, slowly. Through this menace, footing a way in the forest deeps, Jean brought her man, and whenever she heard the soft throbbing of engines her heart throbbed with them. But she came on, shuffling, as taught, through dead leaves and brush. This shuffling would not disturb any roosting birds because it sounded only like friendly little animals slithering in starts below the leaves. Only a human sound—say a boot ringing on stones—might awake the birds, and their flurry bestir the enemy.

She suffered fear all the way, and at times a cold paralysing fright; yet she enjoyed the adventure, and offered to do the same again. She did it again, dressed as a man this time, her bobbed hair in a beret, her face blackened with soot from the breakfast-room chimney, and her body in old black trousers and jacket provided by a priest. Because she went thus in man's armour, and because they had learned that 'Jean' was Scotch for 'Jeanne' they gave her, with laughs, the cover name of 'Darc' (Jeanne Darc); and out of her hearing, the men called her 'The Pucelle', not without some obvious bawdry.

She feared and enjoyed it all: the secrecy, the excitement, the sense of being someone of importance. She felt sorry for the long years when she was no one; and sorry for all others who were not feeling this sense of importance and this pride in secrecy. The fear was a small price to pay for it all. Besides, was not her exhilaration a function of the fear? Was not the fear a drug even more potent than the exquisite secrecy?

But her most secret hour was still before her.

§

They were keeping a young British pilot in the heart of the forest. He had been shot down over Belgium while escorting bombers to the Ruhr. Captured quickly, he had been a prisoner-of-war for seven months in a Belgian camp. Escaping at last and finding the French Resistance, he had been brought by them down an Underground route: Saint-Omer, Abbeville, Beauvais, Chambly, to L'Isle-Adam, and the Forest of Sainte-Marie. Jean, learning that he was British—and, what was more, Scotch—begged for the task of taking supplies to him. Straining truth a little, she said she had a brother in the R.A.F. and that she was Scotch like this boy: was not his name McNair and her mother's McLeash? And, come to that, she said, were not both her dogs Scotch? Mr. McNair would like to see these two countrymen of his. She even went so far as to suggest that she would understand his Scotch better than anyone else, as if the Scots spoke some extraordinary corruption of English. Not too clear about these latter points, her masters concluded that there might be a wisdom in them beyond their ken. And they said, 'Ah well, yes. Let Darc do it.'

So Jean one day, 'exercising her dogs', strode deeper and deeper into the forest along paths that were narrow, secret and wet, the sun never finding them among the high crowding trees, and she came at length towards the brim of a cupped hollow in which tall, lank, leafless trunks stood closely congregated. In the thick of the forest there were many of these deep hollows to which no strangers were likely to discover the access. As she neared the place she called out, naturally and innocently, 'Wallace. Bruce. Wallace, come *here*, you little beast. Bruce, do you *hear?*' And promptly, breaking through undergrowth a man emerged from the trees that encircled the hollow, a man in a Frenchman's beret, blouse and slacks. Flying-Officer McNair. She saw that he was a tall boy, with fair hair long and unkempt and a fluff of golden beard about cheeks and chin. He could have passed for a young Viking had he not remained so thin and hollow-faced after his months in a prison camp.

Though she knew him for who he was, she spoke her password, not without a grin. 'Pardon, Monsieur, par où va-t-on à la Butte aux Boeufs?'

He grinned too. 'Suivez les poteaux télégraphiques.' Then, gaping at the tall, tweed-skirted Jean, he asked in English, 'Madame, excuse me, but who the hell are you? You're not a Frog.'

'We give nobody our true name, Monsieur.'

'Cut out that 'Monsieur'. I'm not a Frog either. Vic is my name. Vic McNair. Over to you. What's yours?'

'My *trade* name is Darc.'

'Dark?'

'D.A.R.C., and don't ask me why.'

'But you're English?'

'No, I'm not.'

'Nonsense, lady. No Frog ever said, "Wallace, come here, you little beast," as you did.' He imitated her, pitching his voice higher. '"Come here, you little beast." And calling a dog "Wallace". Did any Frenchy ever call a dog "Wallace"? Who are these bloody dogs anyway?'

'They're frae Bonnie Scotland. And so am I. At least ma mither was, so I've brought you a wee bite of food, Mr. McNair. And one or two wee comforts. With the compliments and thanks of all in France.'

'Scotch! My hat!'

'Aye. Wallace and Bruce, come here, and meet a countryman.'

'Och . . . lassie, but this is terrific!' He could not know the leap of pleasure in her at that word 'lassie', she who was fifteen years older than he. But before she could think of this he had seized both her hands and was dancing her round and singing, 'I luv a lassie, a bonnie Hie'land lassie, she's as puir as the lily in the dell.'

This of *her* . . . Jean! Tiring, she begged him to stop the dance— *and* the noise, reminding him there were Germans in France and it was necessary in this forest to move 'a pas de loup'. So he dropped her and danced a Highland fling, with one hand on a hip and the other in the air—'Yee-*ipp*!' seizing her hand after a spell and twisting her round under his arm—'Yoi! Yoi!'—while the dogs, wholly sympathetic, did their own form of Highland fling around them both and emitted barks as gaily as he. 'Yee-ipp!' . . . 'Yoi! Yoi!' You could almost see a pipe-major accompanying him and beating a toe to the rhythm, under the trees.

Breathless, he paused, stood still, and said, 'But why the hell aren't you interned?'

'Not all the British are interned. And France is no longer at war with Germany.'

'My God, England is. And Scotland too, believe you me. Vic McNair is. The jolly old R.A.F. is. Like Holy Smoke it is.'

'Yes, praise God.'

'And Germany's at war with England. Just you go over there

and see. London's half flat. Lady, why aren't you interned? Repeat: why . . . the . . . hell aren't you interned? Are you getting me loud and clear? Over to you.'

'Perhaps my papa is a collaborator. Over to you.'

'Could be, but I don't believe it somehow. *You* don't come from a house of collaborators. Oh, no, lady. There's mystery here.'

'I'm not telling anything.'

'Okay, beloved. As you will. I'm all for security, so let us sit down and gobble this food. "Careless talk costs lives". Saucisson, by God! And home-baked bread! And fags—English fags! Honey, where's the smoked salmon? Where's the caviare? And the phiz? What, no bubbly for poor Vic McNair? And this is France! Never mind. Young woman, I love you. Sit here, sit here, and watch me eat.'

Young woman. . . .

While they sat, she asked him if he knew her 'brother' in the R.A.F.

'The R.A.F.'s a big show,' he laughed, with his mouth full. 'About as big as India. What's the laddie's name?'

'Ah, I can tell you that, because he's not really my brother; only my stepmother's son. Rennie Quentin. He was accepted for aircrew, but whether he ever flew we don't know. Last we heard of him, he was disgusted at being employed as a wireless operator on the ground. We hope now that he never got into the air, but we've heard nothing since before Paris fell. He may not even be alive.'

'Quentin? No, I don't know any Quentin. He's probably in Bomber Command. I say, I'm afraid I must look God-dam awful to you.' He had turned the talk to himself, a more interesting member of the R.A.F. than anyone's brother. 'The Frogs gave me everything I needed at Saint-Omer, *except* the razor. I got a shave at Abbeville and then forgot to ask for one. It looks sus'pish to the Krauts, a beard like this. Will you be coming tomorrow?'

'Yes. Yes, indeed. You're my chore, just now, Mr. McNair.'

'Good. Oh, good. Then bring a razor like a noble girl. And scissors. Scissors to trim me 'air.'

Girl. . . .

When at last, after talking and talking, she rose to go, he caught her hand and, still sitting there, begged her to stay. He was so bloody lonely, he said. So she stayed a little longer and when again she rose, he rose too and picked up her hand to thank her. He kept her hand, looking into her eyes; and in *his* eyes, wistful almost as a dog's, she saw what he wanted. Something that she had lost all hope of seeing in a man's eyes. But this was a man from prison, a young man and strong, who'd been woman-hungry too long. She smiled, and he drew her against him and kissed her with hunger. 'I love a lassie, a bonnie, bonnie lassie, she's as puir as the lily in the dell.' His hand stroked her arm, felt for one of her breasts and rested there; then sought to touch her thigh. But here she shook her head, though not unkindly; not without a smile. 'No . . . .No, Vic. . . . Please. . . . Vic. . . .' And she went from him, striding homeward with the leaping dogs, never so exultantly.

All that night she tossed with the memory of it and with the new hot desire the memory kindled. Next day she left the dogs behind and went to him with her hair carefully tended, her face made as beautiful as might be, and her body scented. He quickly took the food from her, quickly laid it down, and drew her to him so as to repeat the kisses of yesterday. And this time, in the great quiet of the forest, in their brief remoteness from all men, in this covert screened by a thousand trees, she let him have his way. She told herself that it was not wrong to reward him for all he had suffered, but she knew that this was far from the whole reason for her surrender. She was wanting to know what she had never yet known.

She lay beneath him on the crisp dead leaves and breaking twigs; and many times more than once during the silence of the long afternoon, in his vigour and hunger, he gave her what she had longed to know. Between whiles she lay looking up at the high green fan-tracery between them and the sky, or looking up into his face and smiling, which stirred his passion again.

Later she was cutting and trimming his hair for him as a wife or a mistress might.

Next day they took Vic McNair from the forest and put him on the road for England. Never in all likelihood would she see him again. A brief entry into her life was over.

X

Over Beauvais and After

FLIGHT-SERGEANT QUENTIN, in his wireless operator's seat behind
the pilot's, peered down through the perspex whenever the aircraft, banking, gave him a glimpse of France beneath. He was
hoping to see in the moonlight the lofty choir of Beauvais Cathedral
rising above its brood of lower buildings. He was remembering a
long ride on Uncle Klem's cycle, when he toured all the sights
along the Beauvais–Paris road: the church and ramparts of Beaumont-sur-Oise, then Chambly and Puiseux and Méru, and for the
final prize the Cathedral of Beauvais, loftiest in Europe, 'Wonder
of the Middle Ages'. Because of these memories this trip had excited
him. Why, Beauvais was only thirty miles from Sainte-Marie,
from that little chateau under the forest. The Huns had laid out
an airfield in the flat country near the town for some merry bombing of England, and tonight they were to get the acknowledgments
from England.

But even in this bright moonlight he could see little on the turn
but drifting clouds.

'Alan. What's our height?' he asked of the pilot through the
intercom, no other way being possible against the engines' din.

Alan looked at his altimeter. 'Under five thousand feet, cock.
Going down a bit. Bugger this moon. To hell with it.'

'Quite,' Rennie agreed.

'And, Dicky'—Alan was speaking to the navigator in the nose—

'get shut of your blasted bombs as soon as you can, and I'm for home.'

'Okay,' said Dicky. His voice sounded breathless. It tripped. 'Oke-ay. Good idea.'

This was but a small bomber with a crew of three, Alan, the pilot; Dicky the navigator; and Rennie, the wop.

Alan had hardly bayed the moon when a searchlight flooded the cockpit with light. 'Oh, *shit!*' he exclaimed. 'We must be sitting pretty in this. Hope you're as pleased as I am.'

'Delighted,' said Rennie.

'Always wanted to shine in Society.'

Rennie answered in the same mode, but his voice stumbled. 'Yes, always had a fancy to be a star . . . a star in my profession.' (He joking, I joking, so that neither may know what the other's heart and bowels are doing.)

More searchlights joined the one so happily embracing their frail home in the sky.

'Now we're for it,' said Alan.

'Undoubtedly.'

Flak. The shells hammered beneath and about them in flashes of yellow and red. If one burst near they heard the sound of it like the slam of a door. Alan swung out of the beams, and the bursting shells lit the cockpit. The aircraft swayed, danced, bucketed in the blast.

'Damn and damn. Any holes in her, Rennie?' She pitched and packages slid down the floor. 'I heard a rattling.'

'Can't see any, Alan.'

'All the same . . . I think we took a peppering.'

'Could be.'

'I'm hit! I've been hit!' Dicky's voice. In some pain but also, it seemed, in some pride.

'Hell! Badly, Dicky?'

'Not too bad. Leg. Don't worry.'

'Can you do the bombs?'

'Sure. Sure. Like hell I can.'

'Good lad. Shan't be long. Then——'

But then came a sickening yellow flash on the port wing and an explosion. The engine on the wing roared and rocked and trembled like a jungle creature shot. It began to trail fire like a comet's tail.

'Port engine's alight.' Alan cut off petrol and ignition and pressed the fire button. 'Bloody hell.'

Rennie wanted to say 'Certainly' or 'Quite', but his voice wouldn't obey.

The fuselage filled with smoke. It stank of burning oil, burning metal, and explosive. Rennie's eyes smarted and stung; once or twice he thought he must suffocate but intermittently a draught through the machine brought a cold clear wine of relief.

And then the starboard engine began to complain and tremble. Hit too. But not afire. Not afire yet.

'Have to go down, chaps. Rather go down in my own time. Do my best.'

'Okay, skipper.'

Rennie signalled, 'S.O.S. . . . S.O.S. . . . S.O.S. . . . V,' and his aircraft's call-sign, 'F.7B.', adding in plain language, 'We're making a crash-landing.' Suddenly he seemed chiefly conscious of the ground; so unremittingly conscious of the firm earth that he was thinking of it, seeing it, almost feeling its breath, its pressure, as he reached to fix Alan's safety-straps for him.

'Fraid there'll be no height for jumping, Rennie. We're low now. Got to be a belly-landing. How're things with you, Dicky?'

'Not too bad. Bleeding a bit.'

'Bet you are. Give us time and we'll help you. Only a minute.'

'Okay, skipper.'

'Let the bombs go. Jettison them safe, since France is supposed to be a friendly country. Wish we could've given 'em to Jerry. Never mind.' As all things enlarged beneath them, hedges, fields, trees, he laughed, 'Well, we're alive now, but where we'll be in half a minute I don't know. Do my best.'

The bombs went, and the aircraft leapt as it lost them.

Belted and braced so as to meet the impact of the landing, they

sat, each with his own thought, 'Is this It? . . . Fire? . . . Explosion?
. . . Agony? . . . *It?*'

Wheels up, flaps down, Alan brought the machine, tail low,
on to a hedgeless field. The tail unit tore off; the propellers buckled
as they touched the ground; the port wing, meeting some obstruc-
tion, was ripped away; everything loose in the fuselage shot towards the nose; but the machine skidding on through an uphurled
cloud of dusty earth, sliced along the field . . . and stopped.

Rennie, stunned by impact and onrush, shaking, deaf, managed
to stammer out, 'Splendid, Alan.'

'Yes. Might have been worse. Out, Rennie. I'll help Dicky.'

'I'll help too.'

'No, *out*, chum. Don't argue. Get out.'

Rennie clambered out through the escape hatch over the cockpit.
On the ground, eyes blinking, ears thrumming, he heard Alan
talking to Dicky. Then Alan reappeared.

'Rennie.'

'Yes, Alan?'

'Scram, old boy. This is going to be a difficult business with
Dicky. I'll stay with him.'

'Let me help too. I'll——'

'Shut up! I said *I'd* stay with him. But we shall both be for it.
Bound to get us. But they're not getting more than I can help.'

'No, Alan. Look——'

'Scram. You say you speak their lingo rather better than they
do. So hop it, quickly. My orders. No argument, buddy, *please*.
Find the bloody Resistance. Go *on*. Quickly. Engine's a bloody
beacon to all the Huns in France. See you again some day.'

§

Where? Rennie ran across the field towards a thicket of trees
on a low hill, chiefly because these would give him temporary
cover. From the crown of the hill he saw a huddle of farm buildings across further fields: a low grey house with a squat tower
in one corner, and barns and byres mustered around it. Its lonely

position in the depth of the fields offered hope of security, and he ran down from this holt towards it. He went with more hope in him than fear; he had learned in England how the name of the R.A.F. stood so high in France that there was pride among the farmers and peasants who could say that they had hidden an R.A.F. man for days. The more the days, the prouder the boast. To have helped an allied airman was now, as it were, a special and coveted decoration. Coming into the midden-scented yard, he saw a sliver of light beneath a black-out curtain. Someone then was awake, having heard, perhaps, the roar and tear of his crashing machine. 'Chance it,' he thought. 'Chance your arm. If they hand me over, well, I'm no worse off than Alan and Dicky.'

He knocked gently on the farmhouse door. Silence. Then steps. The door opened a very little way. To a weather-beaten old face just distinguishable in a dark hall, he said, 'Pardon, Monsieur. Je suis un aviateur anglais,' and he pointed to a flickering glow away over the fields. Alan must have got Dicky out and thrown the incendiary into the plane. 'Anglais.'

'Venez.' A rough crooked hand pulled him in. 'Vite.' The door shut.

The farmer, a small round hump-backed man, never saying much, took him to a back room where he could sleep and pointed to the window by which he could escape, if the Boches came hunting him. In the morning the farmer found an old suit of his son's, who was still a prisoner-of-war, and a beret of his own, and sent Rennie to work in the orchard, saying, 'Your French, Monsieur, mais c'est magnifique! Voilà. You are my son.' That was all. He said no more.

The Germans came, at least to the extent of throwing a cordon round the area and beginning to search the farms, but before they reached this house the farmer had made contact with 'Ceux de la Résistance' in Beauvais and driven Rennie there in his tumbril, speaking not at all except for an occasional objurgation to the horse. He put Rennie down outside the old Ursuline Convent and, raising his hand in goodwill, drove on. Half a minute later a young Frenchman with a slight limp emerged from a street corner, halted abruptly as if astonished to see him there, and came quickly forward with arched eyebrows and uplifted hands that said plainly, 'Well, well, well, fancy seeing *you* in Beauvais. My *dear* fellow!'

§

A heart-leap started Sophie awake. Her eyes swung to the black-out curtain through the sides of which the moonlight peered. *Had* something struck the window? A bird's beak? But did birds fly long after midnight? Would the sound come again? Or was it part of a dream? Klem lay sleeping at her side, undisturbed. She closed her eyes to sleep again.

But . . . the briefest of rings—never so brief a ring—on the front-door bell. Oh, heavens, could it be they? *No!* Oh, please God, no. But . . . it was said they came at night or early in the morning. And they had already taken Eric—why, nobody knew, for they had left him in peace in his 'pension de famille' for nearly three years. Poor harmless Eric—possibly they had taken him because he'd been a friend of Marcel, whom they shot long ago. And now, if so many of the French went to their beds dreading a knock on the door before the hours of sleep were over, how much more a British subject who had so far escaped internment? Was this It? But that sound on the window . . . And the bell fixed to the garden gate, why had its tongue not spoken? That ring at the door: it had seemed a reluctant ring; a ring that only half wanted to be heard. Marie-Louise apparently had not heard it, nor the Germans upstairs. And—think—the dogs had not barked. Jean was still out on one of her foolhardy ventures——

Jean! Ah, yes, it was Jean. The relief! Jean without her key. Who else would throw a pebble at their bedroom window? And that was why her dogs had not barked.

Better go down to her quickly. Those upstairs mustn't know that a member of the household was out like this long hours after curfew.

Sophie slipped from Klem's side, drew on her pink peignoir and soft satin slippers, and tip-toed down.

She opened the door softly and only a little way, much as the Beauvais farmer had done. By the light of the sinking moon she saw on her little stepped porch a tall figure—but not in grey or black uniform, thank God; not Gestapo or Milice; a man in a beret and loose, worn, ill-fitting garments. Some working man; obviously not a gentleman. There was a dark bundle on the step at his side.

'Bonsoir, Madame. Mille pardons, mais——'

'Oh!' The voice was like a light; it showed her who he was; it showed the grin on his face and even some of the mischief in his eyes.

'Je suis un aviateur anglais, Madame. Un évadé, tu comprends. Vive la France.'

'Rennie! Rennie! Oh, my dearest! Rennie! Where have you come from? Hush. We have two of *them* upstairs.'

'Fritzes?'

'Yes. Permanently, it seems. Tsh. . . . Where have you come from? Oh, but how *wonderful!* Where from?'

'Through the forest. From Villiers-Adam.'

'Alone?'

'Yes, rather! I told them I needed no guide to Sainte-Marie. And I knew where I'd hide tonight. They're gradely lads, the boys of the Underground. They found out for me that you were all still here. And did I come quickly along on a visit?' He was speaking excitedly because he was standing on the threshold of this house. 'Did I decide to call?'

'Oh, my darling, but this is wonderful—just come inside and speak softly—we didn't even know if you were alive. I've worried terribly, terribly, about you. And to think that I came down all in a quaver, fearing you might be *they*. But where are you going to? Oh, *do* be careful, my sweet.'

'I hide till early in the morning the day after tomorrow when I meet a certain Monsieur Paillasse of "Ceux de la Libération".

It's like this: the day after tomorrow two men meet by the fountain in the Place de la Forge, and start up a hell of an argument over a copy of *Paris-Soir*. One of them is wearing a blue smock but actually he's the quite distinguished Monsieur Paillasse from Enghien. They argue till I come. I ask them what the hell it's all about, and they look at me suspiciously and after a time tell me—damned ungraciously. Then they go off along the Beauvais road and I follow behind. Where they part there'll be a lorry waiting for Monsieur Paillasse to take him, smock and all, to Paris, and Flight Sergeant Quentin with him. Just like that.'

She was delighted with this lovely story. 'Oh, darling, I can't get over you standing there, and all these wonderful things happening to you. Where do you go after Paris?'

'All the way to Spain, I hope. That's the idea.'

'*Spain?*'

'Yes, and I tell you what I want, Auntie dear. Those old walking boots of mine. These are Raf boots, and the only thing I'm afraid of the Fritzes seeing. No one from Beauvais to here had boots big enough for me.' He spoke with a young man's pride in his height.

'Of course I'll get you your boots, my darling. Stay here and I'll get them. Oh, *Rennie*. Do be careful, my precious. Where are you going to hide?'

'Here, of course.'

'Oh!' It was a gasp of dismay. 'Oh, *no!* No, Rennie darling.'

'No?' He echoed the word, bewildered by it. The one word he'd never expected to hear.

'No, my sweet, *please*. We have the Germans in the house and——'

'But I'd *hide*. Anywhere. Anywhere.'

'Yes, but——'

'And it's only for one more night after this. Only for a little more than twenty-four hours. Just two nights. Others have taken me in.'

'Yes, but—it's so much more difficult for us than for most,

because of Uncle Klem—Uncle Klem being officially a British citizen and all that. They've taken Eric O'Healy. Poor Eric. They came and took him away in the small hours one morning, and not just to intern him but because he'd said something rude and flippant about Hitler. No one knows where he is or what's happened to him—' but he was not ready to hear about Eric; he was hardly aware who Eric was. 'I never know whether or not they'll come for us.'

'I'd be hidden. That was all I meant.'

'Yes, but my darling, my sweetest, I'm never sure that the house isn't under observation. And we've got these Germans. The orderly—he's nice enough but he goes all over the house now. And the Major upstairs—he's an absolutely fanatical Nazi and I can't think what he'd do, if he suspected anything. We're only here on sufferance, you see. And if——'

'I see.'

'And there's a German headquarters now in the old chateau. A German general's. The place is crowded with Germans. We were bombed two nights ago, and before that too. You can't imagine what it was like.'

'I dare say I could.'

'We're having dreadful times in France just now.'

'Ours haven't been too rosy.'

'Oh, you know I'd do anything to help you if I could. But it's death for harbouring—you know it's death, don't you?'

'Oh, yes, I know that.'

The door was still partly open, and as he picked up his burden and walked towards it, she said, 'It'd be worse for us than for anyone. You *must* see that. You do see that, don't you?'

'I see.'

'I'll get you those boots. I know where they are. Oh, I'm glad to be able to do *something* to help you. Just wait, dearest.'

'Don't trouble about the boots.' He went through the door and out on to the threshold. 'I quite understand, *Mother*. Don't trouble about me any more. I remember Sir Hereward said you were never to be troubled.'

'*Mother.*' He had said 'Mother', and the word stopped her at the door. And 'Sir Hereward . . .' Stricken speechless, she saw him go down her steps, along the gravel path in the dimming moonlight, and out of her gate.

§

She could not speak; she could not call, '*Rennie.* Oh Rennie, come *back*'; and he was gone. Nor did she quite know, even though shattered with pain that she wanted him back, for she recoiled from facing the embarrassment of that word, 'Mother'. And those words, 'Sir Hereward. . . .' But—oh *no*, she couldn't let him go like this, and he mustn't, whatever the shame for her. She ran to the garden gate. He was nowhere in the avenue. She ran out in the pink peignoir and satin slippers to the corner of the avenue and looked down the long road to the Place de la Forge. No figure could she see in that blacked-out road, barely lit by the moon. Turning, she looked up the hill towards the forest. Yes, someone climbing the slope obliquely—a tall figure—but she was still unable to call to it, because of the embarrassment—and because of the distance—and now he was gone into the trees.

Lost. 'Don't worry about me any more.' Did that mean that he'd never come near her again? 'Mother'. Then he had known all along. 'Sir Hereward.' Known all through the years and said nothing. But he had come happily to her for shelter, and she had turned him away. Told him to go.

Not in all the sixty years of her life till now, at this corner in the darkness of a midnight, had she known such pain. It was a sickness of shame, disorder, disablement, torment.

His love was lost for ever, and she could not bear the loss. He must be feeling only contempt for her, and she who liked only comfort found contempt a torturing hair-shirt. And this hair-shirt could never be removed now; she must wear it for ever; nothing could undo what she had done; there would be no healing for her pain *ever*; no real peace evermore. Probably she would never see him again: he would die hating her, and she had wanted to be loved by him more than by anyone else. 'Oh, come *back*, Rennie. *Please* come back to me, Rennie.' She said it to the forest above. Safe enough to say it now, because he could not hear.

He must be somewhere there in the darkness among the trees. Lying there to sleep in the cold night since his mother had denied her roof to him. 'Oh God, save him; keep him alive. What have I done? What have I done?'

An aeroplane hummed through the night, high overhead. If only it would drop a bomb and kill her. Then she would be done with this pain, done with the memory. Oh, she'd be glad to be killed, so that she could have no more pain.

And yet . . . in the midst of all this suffering, this shame, a tiny part of her was glad that he had not hidden in her house and put her in danger of death; glad too that she had not had to look into his eyes after he'd said 'Mother'.

Shocked that she could still feel this, she saw, as never before, how much of her suffering, even now, was no more than a self-centred desire not to suffer. Oh, but surely there was a little, there was *some*, that was better than this. Standing there, shivering in the night, she tried to remember times when she'd denied herself so as to make him happy. Not many could she recall. Many? Hardly one.

'Oh, God. . . .' Chilled, shivering, she turned and staggered back, almost drunkenly, to her little chateau from which she had just turned a danger away. Her closing of its door was all the pain again because it was a closing of it on Rennie out there. She staggered up the stairs to the bedroom. Klem was still asleep. Strange that these last few minutes which had overthrown her life and gutted it, as if they had tossed their bomb into the heart of a house, had not touched his sleep. So quietly, on such soft feet, had the fearful incident passed by.

Shivering, she got into the bed at his side. 'Klem. Klem.' She turned and lay prone, her face in the pillow.

He woke. 'Did you speak, dear?'

'Klem . . . oh, *Klem*. . . .' Sobbing, with her face hardly out of the pillow, she told him all. 'I am awful. I am awful. I am utterly wicked.'

He stroked the back of her head to comfort her. 'Perhaps it will not be so bad, my pet. He will come again one day. And he will understand.'

'Oh no, he will be killed. God will do that to punish me. I shall never see him again. Never be able to say I'm sorry. Oh, if only he'd come back . . . come back. . . . But he won't. He's hating me and he always will. Klem, I'm feeling now as if I could give my life to save him. And yet I did nothing to help him only a few minutes ago. I just sent him out to die.'

XI

The Ferry

RENNIE spent the rest of that night in the forest, lying on a bed that seemed made, less of leaf-mould than of small stones. He could not sleep for the cold and the stones, and he lay nursing his wrong, caressing his indignation, justifying self-pity. He might want to think of it as pain but somewhere in him was a struggling wisdom which saw that it was more nearly pleasure. While loving her in a way, even if it was a lamed and limited way, he had always enjoyed his resentments against her, and when had he been given a resentment like this? Let him drink of it deep. Only a few nights ago an old mute farmer who'd never seen his face before had taken him into shelter and said, 'You are my son.' His mother had bidden him go. 'Oh no, my dearest. Go. Go.' Probably he would never see her again—never in his life would he seek her out again—but he wished that she could somehow learn that an old farmer, a poor man and a stranger, had said, 'You are my son.'

'My dearest. . . .' 'This is wonderful. . . .' 'I've worried terribly, terribly, about you. . . .' 'I'm so glad to be able to do something to help you. . . .' 'Yes, but my darling, my sweetest. . . .' Words. Never anything but pretty words. Never anything to hurt herself.

'Sir Hereward said I was never to be troubled.'

Sometimes in the small hours an irrational fear started that he might freeze to death, and he got up and, walking among the trees, pictured days after the war when he might meet her at some party, and he would look at her and turn away. Or appealing letters would come from her and he would throw them unopened on the fire. Perhaps Jean or Klem would come to make peace between them; to whom he would say, 'I bear no malice, but she killed something in me that night. She told me to go. I have gone.'

'Very fine. Very dignified,' he told himself in a moment of sense. 'But no malice? There's a big fool i' the forest, Rennie, old boy, if you think there'd be no malice in that.'

All next day he had to linger among the trees because he was not to meet his guide till early tomorrow. He stayed hungry because he did not dare to go down the slope and into the village to buy food. Not a shop in Sainte-Marie where he might not be recognized as the 'beau jeune homme' who would stay so often with Monsieur and Madame Burgermann. Probably most of the patronnes, with their gay scandal-loving French eyes, had long ago referred to him as 'Monsieur le bâtard de Madame.'

But as evening darkened in the forest he decided that he could not endure another ice-cold night on a fakir's bed of stones. After that quick welcome at the Beauvais farm he would again risk asking for cover in some lonely house. So he came to the forest's edge and, after deliberately keeping his eyes away from a little cone-capped tower behind a screen of firs, he walked along a beaten footway above the pastures that tilted down to the village. Soon, at the foot of a field, he saw a cottage with a dirt-track winding towards it. It was the cottage of the widowed Madame Dubosquet whose husband had been shot by a German when he was rushing to protect his daughter with a dung fork at the ready. Rennie could not know this; he only saw that the cottage stood alone at the field's foot and might suit him well.

He waited till the darkness was fully down and all the village was blacked-out and quiet; then descended the slope and walked along the dirt-track to the cottage door.

The door was open a few inches, moving and creaking in the night breeze. Peeping round it, he saw a seam of light under a distant door. Even as he peeped a woman came out of that lighted room, possibly to latch the door which was gently slamming. By the thrown light of the room he saw that she was in a long stiff black dress and that her black hair was drawn sternly from the central parting to a chignon at the back.

'Madame,' he began.

At the sound of a voice out there in the night, her hand rushed to her startled heart. 'Oh!—oh, how you frightened me. What do you want? Who are you?'

'Madame, je suis un Anglais . . . un évadé.'

'*Comment?*'

'I've been all night and all day in the forest.'

Her brows had drawn together in an effort to see him better. 'Vous êtes vraiment anglais?'

'Mais oui. Un aviateur anglais.'

One of her hands picked up his and drew him into the passage, while the other instantly shut the door. 'Oh, mon pauvre, but you are cold. Come in and get warm. I will light a fire for you. I have none at the moment—coal is difficult to get—but I'll manage it. We have a little coal. I light one for you.'

'No, Madame. I must not put you to any expense.'

'Allons donc! What have you not spent for us?'

'I will just hide somewhere. It's only for a few hours. I meet good friends in the morning. I know the danger for you and the penalty.'

'Oh, *that*. That is nothing, Monsieur. Have you not risked death for us? Any true Frenchwoman would do this for you. And *me*—why, certainly. They killed my man for me out there on the path, and they keep my sons prisoners in Germany so that now my daughter Brigitte and I have to do all the work. . . . It was one of them, a filthy swine, who attempted the pudor of my little Brigitte and then shot my man dead when he ran out to protect her. I hope the Americans come soon and drive the pigs out of our country. I am for the Americans—and for you English too. Je suis de coeur avec vous. So you will let me do what little I can for you.'

'It is very good of you.'

'Perhaps you are hungry?'

'Well, I'm afraid I've eaten nothing since yesterday morning.'

She turned at once towards the lighted room. 'Come in here. Come in and sit down. Par ici, Monsieur.' The room proved to be a kitchen surprisingly large for so small a cottage. 'Tiens, Brigitte! Un anglais who fights for you. A soldier of the R.A.F.' At the mighty word 'R.A.F.' a girl of about fourteen years, short, and baby-faced, but buxom as a woman of twenty, jumped up from the side of the cold stove where she'd been sewing. 'Brigitte is living for the day when the Americans come——'

'*And* the English, Madame. We're coming too.'

'But of course, the good English. You who fight so bravely. Brigitte prays for the day every morning and at Mass. Upstairs in the attic we have our little poste de T.S.F. and we listen together to the bibici for news of when they're coming. Brigitte learns her English at the school and we know that when the bibici talks some nonsense sentences, it is really giving its messages to your agents over here. Two days ago it said something about two bullocks and twenty ewes going to some fair——'

'Stamford Fair!' Rennie instantly interrupted, guessing an allusion to Mr. Justice Shallow, when Falstaff came recruiting.

'Yes, yes. Some name like that. And Brigitte thought it must mean that they were coming soon. I must warn you that she is now nearly fifteen and has ideas about marrying an R.A.F. officer when you are all here.'

'I am but a sergeant, Madame.'

'I don't think she'd turn up her nose at a sergeant, if he was R.A.F.—oh, but *no*—so Monsieur, watch out; take guard. Get Monsieur a chair, Brigitte. Then go and get some coal.'

'No, Madame. I don't need—— You must not——'

'Ça va bien, Ça va bien. We have our little supply of coal. There is a coal yard by the station, and they give some to Brigitte if she stands there long enough with a basket in her hand, because she is pretty and plump. That's what you men are, you see. She gets a lot that way. Men! Mon Dieu! Mon Dieu! Once there was a time when they would look at me more than once and whistle, but not now. Old and ugly now. No coal for me. Ah well, c'est la vie, quoi?' As she said this in the new light of the room, she looked at him, came closer, and peered at his face from under a a creasing brow. 'Monsieur, but I have seen you before, is it not? Votre visage m'est familier. Oui?'

Then he told her how he used to be a schoolmaster in England and come every holiday to Sainte-Marie because he had relatives here—never mind where—and please never to speak of this.

'I would do nothing to endanger any English people anywhere,' she said.

And as she got frying-pans and eggs and cooked him an omelette with 'pommes frites', she told him all about the shooting of Pierre, her husband, and the procession to the church and the Abbé's smashing open of the church door so that the poor murdered Pierre might have the funeral he would have wished. 'They talk to this day in Sainte-Marie about the funeral of Pierre Dubosquet,' she said, slicing the omelette smartly out of the pan.

'I knew the Abbé Belfort well,' said Rennie. 'Where is he now?'

'Ah, Monsieur, who knows? They took him away, the swine. He is starved and dead, perhaps. He was too fat, surely, to survive in a prison camp. Not one of *theirs*. His heart would never stand it. No, we think he is dead. And Brigitte loved him. He drank a little, we believe, but he was good to the children. And he was good to Pierre that day.'

She set before him the omelette, the potatoes, a jug of acorn coffee and a dish of coarse grey bread. Also a bottle of red wine. Meanwhile the fire burned high beside him.

When he had eaten and drunk—voraciously, which pleased her— she said, 'Now you are tired. One cannot sleep in a forest. That is a bestiality. You shall have my younger son's bed, and Brigitte shall call you in the morning, while I make you a petit déjeuner, hein?'

'Madame, you are wonderful.'

'No, it is those who still fight for France who are wonderful. Such things as this are all that we poor people can do . . . pour vous rem'—but here she arrested a gulp and lowered her face to busy herself with the crockery on the table and hide tears which had sprung—'pour vous remercier de ce que vous avez fait pour la France.'

In the morning Brigitte called him while it was still dark, and Madame Dubosquet had acorn coffee, slices of bread, and ersatz jam waiting for him in the kitchen. She had also her younger son's boots, because Rennie had told her about his R.A.F. boots. 'My son is big like you,' she said proudly. 'Very big.'

In the hall before he went she kissed his cheek, and he at once saluted her in the same way. Far less respectfully he picked up Brigitte and hugged and tossed her, much as he used to toss Marie-Louise towards her ceiling—but thinking, 'Crikey, this Dubosquet child's much heavier than Marie-Louise.' In his pocket he had the escape money given him at Beauvais, and for one moment he thought of offering Madame Dubosquet some payment for lodging and board; but his courtesy saved him. Instead he said, 'I'll bring these boots back to you one day when it is all over and your son will be home again and have need of them. And it could be that I shall have come back to marry Brigitte. See that she is faithful to me.'

§

Only twice in the long journey home did Rennie have to act as captain of his own escape, deciding by himself what risks to take. Once was when he left the burning plane and ran to the Beauvais farmhouse; the other time was when, rejected with loving words from his mother's house, he sought the Dubosquet's cottage at the foot of the hill. After that, after he had seen two men arguing hotly by the fountain in Sainte-Marie over a copy of the *Paris-Soir*, and had asked them what all the heat was about, he was in the care of 'contacts' and guides who conveyed him from covert to covert, or from one 'safe house' to the next, all the way from Paris to the Spanish frontier.

This was '43 and all the French Underground, comprising 'Ceux de la Résistance', 'Ceux de la Libération', the 'Front National' and the 'Franc-Tireurs et Partisans', was more or less co-ordinated, organized, instructed, and fed from England. Also, oddly enough, the secret journey was easier now since the Germans, in November of the previous year, had marched into the Unoccupied Zone after the British and Americans had marched into French North Africa. Before this, the business of getting escapers over the border between Occupied and Unoccupied Zones of France, or the 'Ferry' as it was called, was sternly guarded by motorized patrols, concrete pill-boxes, and sentries, sentries everywhere. But now the so-called 'Unoccupied Zone' was little more than a name. France was one; and the 'Ferry' was the whole long journey from the point of escape to the frontier of Spain. Hitherto the Unoccupied Zone, not having felt the hard German heel like its sister Zone to the north, had been apathetic about organizing pockets of resistance and helping Allied escapers at the risk of death. Not now. The Underground was now pullulating (if that is not too great a contradiction in terms, since the last thing it sought to do was to sprout above ground) all over Southern France, from the Saône and the Loire to the Pyrenees.

Sometimes Rennie's guides had been young women like Jean and Marie-Louise; once his contact was a Vichy French policeman whose official business was to round up all underground 'traitors'; once, more strangely still, the contact was one of the Milice, or newly organized French Gestapo, working for the Germans; this collaborator met Rennie in silence but with surely the biggest wink Rennie had ever seen in France; again—and this he would never forget—his guide was an old fat nun waddling along with her eyes on her feet, each arm asleep in the opposite sleeve, and her lips never once parted for speech. Perhaps, he thought, it was her hour of silent meditation and retreat from the world. It was only when she lifted her eyes and looked straight at the 'safe house', bowing, so to say, towards it, that she accorded Rennie the beginnings of a smile and explained, 'One is French, Monsieur. God guard you.'

'Thank you, sister,' he said, not sure if he ought to speak to her in this time of her holy silence. 'God bless you too.'

But she made no reply; she just waddled on, safe again in a retreat from the world.

In small Citroën cars, in costly limousines, in crowded trains with false identity cards, ration cards and food coupons, all exquisitely forged in London, in third-class compartments disguised as a peasant in blouse and sabots; in a first-class compartment smartly dressed in a Swiss gentleman's natty grey suit (with papers to match)—stage by stage, often with long waits between them, he was conveyed to Port Vendres near the frontier and then led by the 'passeurs'—who did the job either for big money or for love—over the mountains into Spain.

At Figueras station in Spain a fat little white-haired round-bellied man said in excellent French, 'Welcome to Spain, gentlemen. We are all very glad to see you'; and after explaining that he was a commercial traveller returning to a branch of his house in Toulouse (but who knew who was talking truth?) thrust wads of bank-notes into Rennie's hands (into the hands, that is, of the natty Swiss gentleman) and into the hands of two other escapers who were now joined up with him (two remarkably well-dressed friends). These notes, said the business man from Toulouse, would be plenty to pay for their journey to Barcelona, Madrid, Cordova and La Linea, 'from which, my excellent Swiss nationals, you will be able to see your Rock of Gibraltar. And, perhaps, if you are delayed there some time, you can start to learn some English. It is largely spoken there. Bonne chance, mes enfants.'

As soon as he was gone Rennie flipped through the bank-notes. Here in his hand was the best part of a hundred pounds.

At La Linea they got out of the train, walked a little way and then saw the Rock rising high out of a sun-flushed haze that must be shrouding the town on its flank; the Rock, sudden and dark and huge, a grey, rather frightening shape against the clear blue Mediterranean sky.

They passed through the Spanish guards who looked at their papers doubtfully, and shrugged and grimaced, but thereupon stamped them sullenly and, as it were, helplessly, guessing, Rennie thought, exactly who and what they were. They passed through, and their feet were on the British Empire.

At a small match-boarded office to which they were directed to report they went and stood before a clerk who was sitting knees-crossed behind a table, in khaki shirts and shorts. The wooden table seemed far too small for the disorderly crush of papers sliding about its top. Other paper-piles lay cradled in wire baskets around the elegant, fawn-stockinged legs of the clerk. He was a man in his forties, already grey; after a time he looked up at them and asked, 'Who in hell are you?'

Then, before Rennie or either of the others could answer him, he swayed round to a younger clerk at a table behind and announced wearily, 'More of these bloody escaped prisoners.'

The clerk behind protested even more wearily. 'Christ! Not again.'

'I'm afraid so. . . . Well. . . .' Accepting the inevitable, the senior clerk sighed and repeated, 'Who in hell are you?'

Rennie explained that he was Monsieur Frantz Zimmermann, merchant, of Zürich, Switzerland, and showed him his papers to prove this, together with his business card and photographs of his fat wife at home, his two fat, fair daughters, and his place of business in Zürich.

'Oh, call all that off,' begged the clerk. 'Sick to death of it. Besides, I'm sure we've had a Monsieur Zimmermann through before. You've not been through before?'

'Not that I can recall.'

'Well, it was a name very like it. Who in hell are you *really*?'

Rennie told him, and the clerk half-turned again to his colleague behind. 'Christ! Another bloody sergeant of the R.A.F.'

'Good *God!*' sighed the other man, as one who was touching

despair. 'Well, there's a troopship putting in tomorrow. Perhaps they can go by that.'

'Is there? Thank God. Okay, Sarge. Got your name. I'm sorry you can't stop, but glad to have seen you. Thank you for calling and all that. Now *you* two sods?'

In such fashion, by courtesy of the Underground Ferry, was a flight-sergeant returned from Beauvais to Base in England.

XII

The Privacy of Sophie

RENNIE, leaving France behind, had left Sophie awake to a new face of Reality—the reality of herself. That morning after he had gone down her steps with the words 'I understand, Mother' she had risen from her bed to daylight and to sights of herself bewilderingly clear and in focus, as when a short-sighted person wears distance glasses for the first time. 'Oh, awful, awful!' So wrapped up in herself that she had sent him away—out into the night, perhaps to die. 'Go, darling; don't endanger me; go and, if there's nothing else for it, die.'

From that day she began a long wholly private fight with herself. 'I must, I *will*, achieve a little unselfishness and a little *real* love.' She told no one of this continuing fight, not even Klem; it was what she did with her privacy; it was something that she discussed with herself as she sat at the table in the breakfast-room before her sewing-machine or beside her basket of darning wools; or when in her bedroom she sat before the poudreuse with all the bottles and jars of cosmetics which had now lost nine-tenths of their charm. None the less, however laid waste this dressing-table might be, she would still bathe her face sadly in olive oil—no face cream being obtainable—to smooth out the lines and wrinkles. Bathe it and think about her sorrow and her desire to be good, This struggle to conquer the hateful parts of herself forced her to avert her eyes no longer from truths about the war and about this, her household. And the terrifying question, now that she dared to look straight at it, was 'How many of us will be alive when the war ends?'

Look straight at it; look it in the eyes. There's Jean with her 'trade'; and the penalty for that is death. There is Marie-Louise plying the same trade, Heaven knows when and where and how, for she tells me little. There is Klem, speaking fair to Major Clauss but abetting both Jean and Marie-Louise in the tricks of their trade; Klem cheating the Germans daily. I cannot stop them doing these things—and I no longer want to stop them, now that I want to be better. I must no longer want to, I suppose—but what then?

Sooner or later the Gestapo or the Milice would uncover all the 'treachery' which was issuing from this house. Never had she imagined, when with much delight she bought this pretty little chateau amid its firs and equipped and garnished it with beautiful things, that it would become a little headquarters of rebellion, from which 'traitors' fared forth by night because their deeds were dark. The Germans had been careless enough during the first two years of the Occupation when the war was going well enough for them; but not now; not in '43 when the whole climate of the war had changed, and it was they who must fear an invasion from England by Americans and British, aided by uprisings of the French everywhere. Now they were stopping at nothing. Only a few days ago they had shot Farmer Georges Lemontey and his wife and son because they had harboured an American agent dropped by parachute. The wife as well as the men. And the Milice had to their account the deaths of many women who were little more than the wives of 'traitors'. No safety any more in being a woman—but think of others, think of *others*, not only of yourself. Klem . . . Jean . . . Marie-Louise.

Yes, death might come to this house at any moment. For all. And soon. Even very soon.

One day, in her misery of remorse, she who could seldom keep anything wholly to herself told Marie-Louise all about Monsieur

Rennie at the door—but nothing, of course, about his being her son. All, however, about her remorse and shame. And her fear.

Fear of Death. To aid in self-conquest what power so strong as Death? Death coming close so that you almost feel his breath? Often in her privacy, as she sewed in the breakfast-room or washed her hair over the basin or cleaned her Sèvres vases with a mixture of soapy water and ammonia she would be pleased with some small triumph in her struggle and would think, 'Oh, perhaps if I am unselfish and loving to others he will come back before it is too late. God will make it that he comes back. Come back and I will tell you that I was just frightened that night but that I am braver now. I *will* be brave. I *will*. Like Jean.' And as her eyes followed her needle, or she bit her thread, or wiped her washed hair, she would say to herself, 'How pleased I was when they used to call me "la grande dame anglaise" as I walked to the station all dressed up for Paris. But a real grande dame anglaise wouldn't have hesitated about helping an English boy even at the risk of her life. Jean, that gawky, unkempt, sexless girl, has been the real great English lady. I must be brave like her. I *will* be.'

In bed, as she lay by Klem's side, she would repeat these vows over and over again. 'I *will* achieve a little unselfishness and love while there is still time. I *will* be brave like Jean.' Over and over again. Lying awake, she would remember, and strain her thoughts over, words which this man asleep at her side had used that night when they had first heard of Jean's activities. 'What are people *for*? . . . I feel that those of us who revolt against all this degradation of our humanity have got to *do* something. . . . Something to justify the existence of man. . . .' At last all that was truth in her cried 'Yes' to these words; and 'Yes' again. And she saw how much they demanded. They insisted that she honoured these new vows. They asked nothing less than daily attempts to overthrow a life-long character. 'Oh, well. . . . What are people *for*? . . . If I must, I must; and I *will*. A little unselfishness. . . . Justify the existence of man. . . . Brave like Jean. . . .'

But all too often in the daytime she fell back into egotisms, and impatiences and irritabilities; she seemed incapable of a real considerateness for Klem and Jean; incapable of not worrying them with her own worries and pains instead of suffering silently and alone; and then, disappointed, discouraged, sickened, she would sigh and tell herself, 'Oh well, I must just pick up and go on. That's the only thing to do. Pick up and go on. Pick up and go on.' Over and over again.

Seldom a meal but she was demonstrating to herself her new power of self-conquest by practising a little more of it.

Food was scanty now. The farmers of Normandy, who usually supplied France with so much of her food now saw their fields violated by Allied bombs or despoiled by German tanks. Much of their fair green land was now swamp or glistening lakes. Many of their cattle, pasturing where they might, had been blown to pieces by the mines laid over wide areas to receive the invading Allies. Nor could the railways bring food into Paris as regularly as in the first years of war: the Underground and the Maquis, the France-Tireurs and Partisans, were doing their work too well, sabotaging tracks and trains while British and Americans bombed the junctions. And even if the trains could have passed with the old regularity, the coal to drive them was getting scarcer. And so the rations sank lower. A few ounces of butter, sugar, fat and oil, and only a few more of meat, were the lot of each person each month.

Let the excuses for this be what they might, Marie-Louise would not listen to them. She persuaded, and daily declared, that these were unreasonable rations. And that, so far as might be, she was not putting up with them. It was simply not enough for Monsieur. Nor for Madame and Mademoiselle. Mademoiselle was doing good work for France, and they should give her rations that were reasonable. They should build up her strength instead of starving her. She was almost a soldier of France, and a good deal better one than some one could mention. 'Et moi aussi.'

So Marie-Louise, with a high bold hat on her head and a fashionable umbrella along her arm, would patter off in her painted wooden shoes to—well, to conjure up food from somewhere. Le Marché Noir? Perhaps. It could be. A crime? But nonsense! One must have food. And Monsieur was sick of potatoes. (Potatoes had been fairly plentiful since the Germans began ravishing Russia). Potatoes stuffed, potatoes grilled, potato soup, potato salad—there was a limit to the ways one could dress potatoes. 'Calories? I care nothing about calories, Madame, I don't know what they are.'

Marie-Louise had an ancient bicycle in the shed—everyone in France had some sort of bicycle now—and sometimes she was seen from the breakfast-room window wheeling it through the garden into the avenue. She mounted and was away. Let her go. Better to ask nothing. Though, almost certainly, she was going to some cottage in the country where she could buy, illegally, a chicken or cheese or eggs. Her work with the Resistance had sent her to many a farmer who would hide an escaper in barn or attic and—well, it was nice to visit old friends on a Sunday and exchange presents, hers a small gift of money, theirs a piece of meat or a dozen eggs.

Then, without a word said to Madame, who had long learned—yea, even in pre-war days—not to interfere with any bustling in the kitchen, Marie-Louise would come up to the breakfast-room and lay on the table a little savoury-smelling dish.

'But, Marie-Louise!' Sophie would exclaim. 'What is this?'

'A little something extra for Monsieur. And for Madame and Mademoiselle.'

'Marie-Louise,' Klem would say. 'You are wonderful. And wicked.'

'Mais non, Monsieur. One cannot eat potatoes for ever. It is not reasonable.'

Her little dishes cooked in wine (of which there was no scarcity) were tempting with their savoury smell to anyone who was always hungry now, and then it was that Sophie forced herself to do her drill in unselfishness. She remembered what her dear Abbé had said in his pulpit long ago about being driven by fear and love to 'kinds of holiness', and she wondered if her action now, though small, was worthy of this name. She gave the best of the dish, and the most of it, to Klem and Jean, drawing no attention to her nobility, as in old days she would certainly have done, lest a single word destroyed the virtue and turned it into selfishness again.

And whenever she managed to keep the virtue unspotted, she thought, 'Perhaps if I am good like this, he will come back and I shall be able to take him in and hide him instead of driving him away. Hide him and feed him, giving my food to him.'

Seldom did her mind drift far from this lodestone thought. Any minute of day or night she would be drawn back to it and, after thinking of him as a fat smiling baby in her arms during the first two years of his life, after remembering him as a tall, ever-vivacious young man rolling with the delighted dogs on the garden lawn —then charging back at them, himself on all-fours and barking as vigorously as they—after all such memories she would hear behind her lips the prayer, 'Oh God, *God*, send him back to me one day. One day, *please*. Give me power to be good. Help me to deserve this. Help me to be brave and unselfish like Jean.'

XIII

The Privacy of Jean

JEAN was now an agent-de-liaison between 'Jodelle', the second-in-command of the Underground in the district of Sainte-Marie, and a new British agent operating in the district of L'Isle-Adam. This agent who went by the name of 'Biron' had been dropped 'blind' under the last moon down into the Puy-de-Dôme miles away, and had come north to his field of work around L'Isle-Adam. He was now hiding in 'safe houses'—in Mériel or Villiers-Adam, or Montsoult or Nesles-la-Vallée—'in fact', as he said, being a parson's son and knowing his Bible well, 'in all the parts of Libya about Cyrene.'

Jean carried messages from Jodelle to him and brought back his in return, or she brought the money for Sainte-Marie dropped to him by parachute, or perhaps she carried his coded reports to secret radio-operators for transmission to London. She had been given this job of serving Biron because Underground work was getting more and more precarious as the certainty of invasion deepened, and, though Biron's French was considered perfect in England, they decided in France that all talk with him about risky plans had best be in English.

By arrangement she would meet him, now in a street in Villiers-Adam where she appeared to be searching the shops for food, now on the station platform at Méry-sur-Oise where she appeared to be waiting for a train, now in the churchyard of Taverny where, on encountering another wanderer among the graves, she took him into the church to show him the thirteenth-century work and to mention some twentieth-century work too.

But later they met in the forest. It was she who had persuaded him to come and find her in the forest. Though she was still excited and flattered by her hazardous tasks, and called them, without lying, 'fun', she was never free from fears—even terrors—and she felt safest when the tall trees were standing around her, thousands deep. Moreover she had a privacy like Sophie's in which she thought the thoughts and fought the fights that could be spoken of to none. In her, as in Sophie, there was now a realization, full and very strange, that she might have only months or weeks— even days or hours—to live; and, having loved her forest always, she had a mind to enjoy its long sun-streaked paths and shadowy, sprinkled depths as long as her stars allowed this to her. Live for Now only. There may be only Now.

There was no love-in-the-forest or desire-under-the-chestnut-trees between these two, as there had been when the boy, Vic McNair, stayed hidden in the hollow. There had been one or two others whom Jean had met in the forest and rewarded with her body for their sufferings or their service—and not for their sakes only—but this boy was not to be one of them. She was forty next year and she saw at once that she had no appeal for Biron who was but twenty-three, newly married, and more than ever in love with his wife now that they were apart. Rather did she feel motherly towards him with his untidy head of dark hair and his raptures about the wife. When they had exchanged their messages they would stay seated among the trees while he talked and talked about his 'Chrissy' and the baby she was expecting.

One afternoon they sat within the old proud gates of a garden long dead. Or, rather, they sat behind the tall brick piers of a long-lost gateway that had once stood by a road through the forest. This old abandoned road could be distinguished still by its ribbon of artificial levelling and by the splendid light green of the thick-pile carpet that a hundred years and more had worked over the old stone metalling. The mansion to which the jungle-hidden drive had once proudly swept existed no more; you could hardly find, if you followed the drive's dim tracks, one mossy fragment of its walls or the sunken brickwork of a single cellar.

Jean loved these haunted places behind the twin forgotten piers. She liked to imagine the fine equipages that once came up this buried drive, and the young girls—in poke bonnets and bunched dresses, perhaps—who walked out through the gates with shy and awkward gallants at their sides.

And now she sat at Biron's side with her long legs under her and her fingers fiddling with the dead leaves or snapping the twigs, while he lay back with hands behind his head and said, apparently to the highest branches above him, 'It's rather wonderful, you must say, having a baby coming.'

'Absolutely wonderful,' she agreed, smiling inwardly at a remark which was at once so naïvely new and a million years old. How often had it been said or thought before in this old ruined garden or along that old weed-conquered drive. But in what different, what unforeseen, what unlikely conditions now. Surely death rather than birth was hovering nearest to these two who spoke now.

'It makes one hope one'll get back all right,' he mused aloud. 'The kid should appear early next year. Gosh, it's wonderful.'

'*You'll* get back all right.' This was more a piece of motherly comfort than a statement of anything she could easily believe.

'Yes, but . . . will I? I wish I felt the least bit sure of it.' Obviously, with the conceit of his twenty-three years, he didn't want any underestimation of the danger in which he stood. 'I'd have you know there's a price on my head. Two million francs, dear lady; no less.'

'Indeed I know it.' So proud he was of it!

'Yes, I believe I'm Enemy No. 1 around here, and I sincerely hope I am. That's rather the point of the exercise. I've had to shift my headquarters—' fine word for some small upper chamber in which he slept—'from village to village about six times. They come combing the whole village for Monsieur Biron. It's fun, this special-agent lark, I don't mind telling you. I reckon I'm already finished in about six villages. But so far I've managed to elude some of their most highly skilled agents, and I intend to go on doing so. I do so terribly want to get back to Chrissy and the kid one day.'

'I think you will. London's learnt a lot in the last two years and they manage these things much better now.'

'You're telling *me*! They're getting real smart. They gave me three different identities. *Three*! If one of them gets blown, I have two other cartes d'identité, with different photographs of me, and different life-stories. I'd show them to you, only I never carry more than one at a time. I'd be finished if I was found with two.'

It was all so new and exciting to him that he imagined he was telling her something it would thrill her to know—she who had been working with London's special agents for nearly two years. Irritated, she had a desire to bruise his self-satisfaction by telling him not to 'teach his grandmother', but she repelled it for his young sake and said only, 'Yes, I've heard of things like that. It must be comforting. Help you to believe you'll get home all right. Back to Chrissy and the baby.'

'Well . . . yes . . . but'— once again he wasn't going to have his dangers depreciated—'but the fact remains that the majority of us get caught. And that's the end. As a p.o.w. you're not shot; as a spy—it's a prompt and unpleasant meeting with a firing squad in the prison yard or the market square.'

'Not always. I know of several who were caught and are still in Fresnes or in some concentration camp.'

'Yes, being tortured. To make 'em talk.'

'Maybe.' She played for some time with the dry leaves, crumpling them to powder in one hand and tossing the dust of them away. 'Did they give you a pill?'

'Of course they did. We all get them. That's why I generally wear this old waistcoat; the thing's in a breast-pocket and instantly accessible. A pretty little thing. Have you ever seen one?'

'I've had one for nearly two years now.'

'*Have* you?' His surprise, almost indignation, was offensive, but she let it pass. He was so young, so proud.

'And shall you use yours,' she asked, 'if the worst happens?'

'I don't think so. Sometimes I fancy I'll throw it away. What I believe, or like to believe, is that there's something in one, ever so deep down, which torture can't get at. So many thousands seem to have proved this all through history—I was reading History at Oxford when this jolly old business started—priests and martyrs and what-have-you—they've all stood up to torture. I believe I could.'

'I wish *I* felt like that.'

'Besides, you see—what I think might save me would be my desire to get back to Chrissy and the kid and all.'

'Yes, that'd help.'

'Help like hell,' he mused, still lying back with hands joined behind his head. 'And I feel in my bones somehow that I'm destined to get back to them one day.'

In the silence that followed this, Jean, playing with the leaves and twigs, was thinking, 'Is this child, for all his tough talk and braggartry, the proper metal for his terrible occupation now?' Wasn't the metal soft in its centre and frangible? How many security vows was he bending, if not breaking, in all this patter to her? On the soil of France, as she knew, he was ordered to have no name or existence except that in his cover story—or in one of his three cover stories. In England he had not been allowed to say one brief word about his mission or destination in France, and for sure he had been delighted to display this stern secrecy. But now— far away from the stern colonels at home—alone in a forest with a sympathetic woman at his side . . .

At Special Operations Executive in London the sieve through which volunteers were screened was said to have the finest mesh of any, and yet sometimes one of these pliant morsels filtered through. Seldom, but to the danger of all when he came.

'How did you come to get this job?' she asked.

Pleased to be able to brag a little more, he answered, 'Well, first, I'm bi-lingual, because my dad was attached to the English Church in Paris and we lived at Passy; secondly—' here he hesitated, not wanting the bragging to sound like bragging—'I did earn quite a reputation for—well, bravery, I suppose—in' the retreat to Dunkirk. Yes, I was given the M.C.'

'Splendid!'

'Oh, but it was nothing really. So when, after the fall of France I heard of this Special Operations lark, I volunteered, and after a hell of a long wait I was accepted and transferred to S.O.E., the Old Firm in Baker Street. S.O.E.: the Stately 'Ome of England.'

'The training's pretty stiff, I suppose, for such a responsible job, and the rules very strict?'

'You bet! Responsible job? I'll say it *is*. D'you know, I have to report on the strength and quality of the Maquis for miles around; I have to arrange for all the moon-drops of arms and ammo and supplies, choosing my landing grounds; I have to know all about every new weapon so as to instruct the Froggies over here; and, of course, I have to name all the targets for the saboteurs as London radios them to me. It used to be all rather higgledy-piggledy and amateurish; now not a pylon goes down or a railway goes up till I give the word.'

'You must feel the responsibility of it all rather terribly. You must have to move very carefully. And quietly.'

'Oh, yes. Yes, yes.' But it didn't seem a point of the first interest to him. He went on: 'If I'm picked up—and I don't fancy I shall be, somehow—and if they don't shoot me on the spot, I have my hopes of getting out of jug all right.'

'Escaping?'

'Well, you could call it that. But what I fancy will happen is this.' And now followed his biggest brag of the afternoon. 'If London hears they've pinched me, it'll move heaven and earth to get me out. What they do is to moon-drop a few million francs to the right person, and he knows where to place them. A few million francs, properly placed, opens the doors.'

Jean had heard of this method being worked successfully with one or two of the most famous agents in France. She looked down on this boy lying at ease by her side: a youth of twenty-three, brave and silly, who believed—or at least wanted her to believe— he was worth a few million francs to Britain at war.

§

Jean was right. His very bravery made him reckless. The Gestapo knew all about him. 'Get Biron' was the word among them. Get him alive. He knows where the caches of arms are, and the names of the Maquis, and where they hide in the woods, and who are the leaders of the Secret Army. Pull in this Biron, please. Heil Hitler.

And soon one of his safe houses was blown.

There was a boy in Ecouen, only seventeen years old, with his hair usually in his eyes, who longed for a part in the Resistance. He begged for it from the local commandant. 'Please let me do something, Monsieur.'

'But, mon gars . . . mon petit gars . . . if you're caught you'll be shot.'

'Yes, Monsieur.'

'And that isn't all, Auguste. Before they tie you to a post and shoot you, they'll torture you till you tell them all you know. And you mustn't tell them. Not, at least, for forty-eight hours. During that forty-eight hours we shall learn that you've been picked up and have time to clear everything and everybody out of sight. You'll have to take the torture for forty-eight hours.'

'Yes, Monsieur.'

'Perhaps after that you can talk just a little, because everything to do with you will be as if it had never been.'

'Yes, Monsieur.'

'There was a time when you might have had one chance in forty of being spared the full treatment, but hardly now when they're expecting the Invasion any moment, any place. The old Boche is fairly on fire now, everywhere.'

'I understand that, Monsieur.'

'Very well, Auguste. You seem a good boy, but your name is no longer Auguste. It is . . .' He pulled his lower lip while he considered. He was a man fond of his books, and as a hundred names paraded before him one stepped out and stood in front of the foremost rank: Victor Hugo. He saluted it. 'Your name is Hugo. Like Victor Hugo, you know. And may you indeed be a victor. Good-bye, Hugo. Not a word about Auguste to anyone. Try to be Hugo even in the presence of your dear mama. Thank you, Hugo.'

How delighted was Auguste to be Hugo. To have a cover name in a Secret service. For his first task he was given one of the simplest: to take messages on his bicycle to the cottage of a loyal old widow in Boissy-la-Chapelle on the north of the forest. Her husband, a sergeant, had been killed in '15 at Neuve Chapelle, and she held it her duty, in his honour, to help the boys of today who were fighting for France. Hugo's messages, verbal or in cypher, were for delivery by her to Biron, who sometimes slept in her cottage.

And the boy had only done this secret business twice with excitement and joy when he was betrayed to the Gestapo by a double agent.

They picked him up in a street in Ecouen, forced him handcuffed into a small car, and took him, slapping and cuffing him all the way, to Gestapo Headquarters in Saint-Denis.

There they thrust him in front of an interrogator seated at a table in a small bare office: a lean emaciated man with a face so hollowed beneath the cheek-bones that it looked like that of a monk—or saint—who practised the severest asceticism and mortifications in his cell. To him one of Hugo's captors proudly introduced his prize. 'Hugo. Son vrai nom Auguste Mathieu.'

'Fetch Walther and Hans,' was all the monk replied.

The captors went out, and soon two men entered. Huge, heavy-shouldered, sour-faced men in careless mufti. Palpably men picked for the strength in their arms and hands. One held a leather-bound riding whip which showed in torn places its bone of flexible steel. They clicked to attention, saluted, and said, 'Heil Hitler.'

'Heil Hitler,' acknowledged the interrogator. 'Hands behind his back, Walther.'

The one with the whip unmanacled Hugo's hands, which were hanging in front of him, and re-manacled them behind his back. It was a warm summer day and the boy was in nothing but trousers and open shirt.

'Good. . . . Where do you go with your messages?'

'I will not say.'

'Walther . . . Hans . . .' said the questioner.

These two beat their great fists into his face, swung them against the sides of his head so that he fell, dragged him to his feet again by his shirt which ripped as he came, held him erect, and bashed at his eyes, nose, and chin.

'Where, please, do you go with these messages?'

'I do not say. I . . . I mustn't . . . I——'

'Walther.'

Walther with the whip came to the left of him and slashed at his bared chest. 'Oh!' cried the boy and Walther slashed again.

'Will you say now?'

Silence. And then . . . 'No.'

The other man, Hans, not waiting for an order, swung new blows at the side of his head and kicked him savagely on a buttock. And spat in his face.

The questioner waited placidly till Hans had finished; then asked, 'We know you go to a house in Boissy. Does Biron come there?'

'How should I know?'

'Give him a little more, Hans. Then perhaps he'll know.'

The beatings again.

'Well, sonny, does Biron come to the house? This is only the beginning. We have other ways of persuading people to speak the truth. These are just elementary ways. We can do much better than this. Does he come to this house in Boissy?'

'I tell you I don't know.' (Hold out if you can for as long as you can, so that they can hear you are arrested and escape. But not forty-eight hours; oh, please, not forty-eight hours.) 'How can I tell you if I don't know?'

'We'll show you how.'

Again; and a cry, 'Oh, don't! Don't! How can I know what goes on in the house?'

'Because you know what is said in your messages, clown. Where is the house, and is Biron ever mentioned?'

'The messages are in cipher. I don't know what they mean.'

'Oh, no, they're not. Not all. And they are meant for Biron, aren't they?'

Silence.

'I can't waste time like this. Continue, Hans.'

Hans produced a leather cosh from his pocket.

'Oh . . . no . . . please. . . .'

'Well, are you going to tell us? Is Biron ever mentioned in the house?'

Still silent. (The time is passing. But oh, not one of the forty-eight hours has gone yet.)

The questioner stayed silent too. All he did was to turn his eyes up to Hans and lift an index finger.

Hans stepped forward. Hugo was standing with legs apart, as he was almost compelled to do with hands locked behind him and balance unsteady. Hans swung the cosh with all possible force against the boy's testicles.

The boy collapsed to the floor in agony and rolled and rolled there. They dragged him to his feet.

'Well, Hugo?'

Hans held the cosh uplifted.

Hugo's head hung forward because of the agony. Slowly his eyes lifted to the cosh—in terror. He could not take it. He was too young, too new. (I have lasted for a little. A little. But not enough. Perhaps I can gain time for them.)

'You have met Biron, eh, Hugo? *Have* you?'

'Oh, yes. . . .' And again: 'Yes. . . .'

'Well, go on.'

He mentioned the widow's house but denied knowing her name. He told them of two messages. 'But I don't know who they were for.'

'Hugo, don't lie. You delivered a message for Biron today. We know you did.'

'I don't know that I did.'

'What do you mean?'

'It was written on the top of a *Paris-Presse*. I don't know what it meant.'

'What did it say?'

'Something about giving some alms to——'

'Yes, to . . .?'

'To "le mendiant avec un chien".'

'And who is this "beggar with a dog"?'

'I don't know. How should I know? I don't.'

'All right, sonny. This was delivered today?'

'Yes. This morning.'

'To the old lady?'

'Y–yes. . . . But I don't suppose she knows who—'

'Tell them to fetch her,' he said to the men. 'To get her at once. They must find her and bring her as she is. There's no time to lose.'

'Heil Hitler,' said the men, and went.

'Please . . . she doesn't know anything,' the boy begged. 'She's just a simple old lady. She doesn't know anything . . . *please*, she doesn't. . . .'

'We shall see. We shall soon see.'

It was some sixteen kilometres to Boissy-la-Chapelle. If they found the widow at home they'd be back within the hour. The questioner left Hugo standing handcuffed there while he wrote at his table or leaned his chair back to think, knocking his pencil on his teeth. Between whiles he examined his nails. After about half an hour he touched a bell. A clerk came in. To him he dictated a report in low, rapid German.

Steps and voices outside. Two of the four men who had seized

Hugo entered, holding between them, by armpits and wrists, the little trembling, beseeching widow. Between these two tall young Germans she looked small even for a Frenchwoman, and lined and old. Older than she was, for her eyes were protruding with fright and her mouth falling open.

'I . . . I . . . oh, please,' she was begging. 'No. . . .'

Then she saw Hugo there and screamed, '*No . . . No.* . . .' His bruised face, purple and yellow, was so swollen that his eyes looked at her through slits. Blood lay in clotting trickles from his broken lips and loosened teeth. A cut down the side of his head had not opened enough to bleed but was long and ugly. The ripped shirt showed the slanted weals on his chest.

'Oh, the pauvre. . . .'

He tried to smile at her.

'Give her a chair,' said the questioner. 'It's all right Madame. You have only to tell us the things he refused to tell us.'

'Oh. . . .' She was still staring at Hugo.

'Yes, he was not helpful, Madame. Sit down. You will help us better, I am sure.'

She sat, trembling; and the two men stood on either side of her.

'Do you know where you are?'

'It . . . it is the Gestapo?'

'It is, Madame.' He nodded, and enunciated carefully so that the words might do their work, 'The Geheime Staatspolizei, Madame. Madame, where is Biron? This young terrorist and traitor here has confessed that you know.'

Hugo made a move as if to deny this, but she was no longer looking at him.

'Oh, I do not know where he is now. Please, I don't. He has stayed with me, yes. Imprison me for that if you must, but, oh, don't torture me.'

'Madame, death is the punishment for what you have done, harbouring an English spy.'

'I know I know. Shoot me if you must, but don't torture me.'

'Yes, death is the punishment, but who knows? If you help us now, we may help you. We don't want to hurt old people—unnecessarily. We are not savages. Now be reasonable. You might even be spared to go home—who knows? I might even promise you that no harm will come to your young friend here. You may be able to save his life. But not this English Schweinhund's. We do not spare him. Come, Madame. No one need ever know that you have told us.'

'But, Monsieur, I do not know where he is. Truly I do not.'

'A message was delivered to you this morning by this lump of Communist trash here. He has told us so. It instructed Biron to give some charity or other to the beggar with a dog. You see we know all. Who, please, is this beggar with a dog?'

'I don't know. I don't know what the words meant.'

'They mean one of his contacts, of course. You gave him the message?'

'Y–yes. . . .'

'When?'

She hesitated. Oh, she would like to do her best, but if the boy Hugo was too young to accept all, she was too old. And perhaps it would do no harm if she answered *this* question. 'When? It . . . it was a little while before these gentlemen came.'

'Gott!' The questioner speeded up his questions. 'What did he do then?'

'He burned the paper.'

'What else?'

'He went out.'

'Now Madame: we have put a cordon round your house, so we shall know if you lie. *Did he say he would come back to you tonight?*'

No answer at first. She would so like to be able to suffer rather than give away a pleasant young man who had laughed and joked with her and was risking death for France like Etienne, her husband, years ago.

'Be quick. You need not be afraid of giving him away because he *won't* come back. You can stake your life on that. He will know that his courier here has been caught and he'll certainly keep away from your house. I only ask you, did he *say* he would come back?'

'Yes . . . he did. . . .'

'Thank you. And where does he usually meet his contacts when he stays with you? Quick, please.'

'I don't know. Truly I don't.'

'If he goes to and fro from your house is it not possible that he's meeting someone in the forest?'

'Perhaps. I don't know.'

'Have you seen him with any of his liaison agents? *Have* you?'

'No. Never.'

'Do you *know* anything about them?'

'I know nothing. One hears talk, that is all.' (Say something so that he doesn't torture me. Something that can't mean much.) 'They say that one is a woman.'

'Short, tall, fat, thin, young, old?'

'I do not know. I do not know. Fairly young, I suppose, since they joke about it.'

The questioner rose. She shuddered back from him. 'Madame, I cannot wait. The truth, please. Does he usually go into the forest when he stays with you? Perhaps to meet this woman?'

No answer.

He came closer, and she cried, 'Oh *no* . . . *no*, please. Yes, he does . . . sometimes. But whether to meet a woman, or anybody else, I don't know.'

'Be quick.' This he had said in a lowered voice to the clerk. 'The patrols.'

The man understood and went.

'But Monsieur,' the old woman begged. 'I don't know what he does there. I don't know that he meets anyone there.' (Oh God, protect him. The forest is big. He is clever. And surely he will not go to the forest if he knows that Hugo is arrested. Oh God, let him know, let him know. Save him. Save him.)

XIV

The Forest

MEANWHILE the beggar with the dog (though neither Wallace nor Bruce was with her now) sat by Biron's side in a deep of the forest where the trees were close—but not the closest, since these would be the first places in which Germans might search. Their covert at the moment was a shallow, light-spattered dome whose walls and roof were formed by embracing shrubs of sycamore and thorn. Biron had given his charity to the beggar: a share of twenty million francs dropped by parachute to the Reception Committee waiting under the moon and under the blinks of the aeroplane. These alms were now in the beggar's blouse, ready for transmission to Jodelle.

And happy in the vast silence of the forest, the silence that cared nothing for the remote humans and their deeds, Jean and Biron sat talking of England and his Chrissy, and of their hopes and plans for 'après la guerre'. The soft evening air, warm as milk from the udder, stroked brows and cheeks and bade them continue these dreams for future days. Biron, sitting there in a labourer's blue overalls and an old worn beret, said he fully intended to acquire a pub in some Cornish fishing village, where he would be the jovial landlord to 'some fine old crusted characters caked in salt' and have his own yacht down in the bay. This idea shocked his 'old man', an Evangelical parson active in the Church of England Temperance Society.

'And he's not only a teetotaller but very much the gentleman. He says pub-keeping is no job for the son of a gentleman. But I can't help that. I'm a natural mixer without any class-consciousness at all. I like people of all classes, and on the whole prefer the lower classes to my own. I always got on like billy-oh with the lads of my platoon. And then I want the sailing and the fishing; but my biggest dream of all is to go out with the lifeboat. Through a helluva sea to a wreck! Gosh, there's only one thing more exciting than watching a rescue; it's being a part of it. And you?' he asked, thinking it was time she had a chance to speak.

Jean only asked, did he see much of the R.A.F.

'Oh, yes, yes. Lord, yes,' he said, not being one to admit any ignorance easily.

'You haven't by any chance come across a Flight-Sergeant Rennie Quentin?'

'Who's he? A relation?'

'No. And you know I mustn't say any more.' She laughed and was suddenly glad of the security rules that forbade her to say any more, because she saw that he had jumped to the idea that Rennie was her lover. And though her meeting with this boy was but a transient wartime encounter, and he was but young, vain, and self-occupied, she liked him to think she had a lover.

Of course he knew nothing of a Flight-Sergeant Quentin, so he turned to asking her what she proposed to do when 'this silly old chemozzle is over.'

'That rather depends on who wins,' she said.

'Oh, *we* win. And *soon*, I don't mind telling you. By God, I could tell you a few things if I were allowed to. You see, my work here involves my knowing a helluva lot. No harm in telling you one thing, because old Fritz knows it as well as I do: the moment we set foot on a French beach all France rises. The Front National, the Francs-Tireurs and Partisans, the Maquis, the whole damned Secret Army—all rise. It's been part of my work to see to this, as Fritz undoubtedly knows. Even your little Sainte-Marie will come to the boil. Like fun it will!'

'*I* know something about that,' Jean reminded him. 'And I hope to have a small part in it.'

The sun was going down.

'Suppose I must be breezing off,' he said. 'I must get back to my old dear in her cottage. She always thinks I've been arrested if I'm late back, and worries her head off. She's got rather fond of me, I don't mind telling you.'

'I must get back with this too.' Jean touched the alms in her blouse. 'I shall be glad to be rid of it. Never handled so much money before.'

'Haven't the Krauts ever tumbled you?'

'Should I be here if they had?'

'No, but I mean: how is it they haven't?'

'Because I've been one of the sights of the forest too long. For years everyone's seen me wandering with my dogs in different parts of the forest. Probably I'm considered a little mad. But, however that may be, we hold that women make better couriers than men.' She was lifting bog-myrtle leaves from beneath her and holding them to her nose for their fine pungent smell. 'There is nothing remarkable about women wandering about in the day-time with their dogs or their children or their shopping. The Huns expect them to be doing this; they expect men to be at work. I love the smell of bog-myrtle. Besides, even now, few huge big he-man Germans can really believe that women are any good for anything but humble tasks in the home, or for gossiping with anyone they meet. Women should keep to their——'

It was then that she heard the soft beating of the patrol vehicles. Many an alarm in the past had taught her to catch their sound at once. Unlike other cars speeding innocently across the forest, they travelled slowly, so that the straining eyes of their crews, or the fidgety beams of their searchlights, might sweep the vistas between the trees. Sometimes they halted while their men prospected in the veiled deeps, and their engines turned over gently.

Jean's hand was on Biron's. 'Listen. . . . Hear anything?'

'Nom de Dieu!' came from Biron.

She did not speak for a little. Her hand said all. At last, her heart beating faster than these soft engines, she whispered, 'They will go by. Let them go by.'

But they halted, engines rotating.

'They often do that,' she whispered. 'They'll go on.'

But the engines stopped. Her fingers left his hand and flew to her mouth. And stayed there.

'They've stopped,' he said. 'What does that mean?'

'They're hunting deeper. What do we do?'

'Don't move. Freeze. That's what we do in No-man's-land when the Very lights go up. Keep still.'

But fright was now possessing Jean like a devil inside her, for she felt certain, all reasoning suspended, that the hunters were coming this way. She craved to move—to be moving—away.

'Why are they hunting here?' he asked, and even *his* whisper now limped. 'What could they know? They can't know anything.'

'Unless you've told someone about this rendezvous, and he's shot his tongue out.'

'I've told no one. I'm not an idiot.'

'Hugo, did he know?'

'Certainly not. The old dear knows that I come into the forest. But she'd never shoot her mouth out. Mind you, they've been looking for me for a long time past. They don't love *me*.' Even so near to death he bragged. 'There's a huge price on my head, and I'm blowed if I trust every Frog in my circuit, when there's money for the taking. They've got too damned big, these circuits.'

She was hardly listening, for she thought she heard steps. And she was waiting to hear dogs.

He too perhaps. For he said, 'I used to hunt with the Quorn when I stayed with a friend in Leicestershire, and I loved it. Now I'm the hunted animal, and it's rather fun too.'

Not to Jean. Death? This could be death because she had long decided that she couldn't endure under torture. Nowadays she always wore a white or cream shirt-blouse with a small flapped pocket over the left breast. In this pocket it lay. Alone. Reached in a second. With one finger she now felt for the tiny protrusion of it. Even if she did endure, she guessed what they might do: they might torture her father before her eyes, and so make her speak. And she mustn't speak. Hugo? Hugo's knowledge was small because he was so new, but if she gave away names and safe houses and command posts a hundred might die.

Death? Now? In moments? She looked through the windows of their leafy covert at the forest. This forest which she had loved, was it to be the last of the world she would see? Was it going to give her to the enemy? 'General Forêt turned traitor'? Father seen no more . . . Sophie . . . Rennie . . . the breakfast-room in the chateau. . . . So strange it seemed. . . .

The fright in her head was like a too-bright light in a room. She heard herself say to the man at her side, 'If they find us, what do we do? Quick; what do we do? Submit?'

He did not answer.

'It'll be torture.'

His lip was drawn down beneath his teeth. 'I know one thing: *I* shan't talk whatever they do to me. My God, no! There's too bloody much depending on my silence. I swear I won't talk.'

'The barking of dogs? . . . Did you hear it?'

'Yes. Yes, I thought so.'

She turned and looked at him. She did not doubt that he was brave with a young man's foolhardiness, and that he wanted to believe he wouldn't talk—but his face was pale as he stared at disaster, and she knew that, however he might protest, he had his doubts of himself. And in that moment, with a shaking, a terror, a strange empty bewilderment, and yet with a small exultation, she fell in love with the idea of doing a good thing. If one had to die, good to die knowing in the last moment that one had done a good thing.

'You go,' she said. 'Go quickly. I'll stay around here for a little. Don't mind me: you're much more important than I am. If they come this way they'll only find me, and I've no reason to suppose they're looking for a woman. I'll lie to them about having seen two men going the opposite way from you.'

'But those dogs? They seem to have dogs.'

'Maybe I'll draw them off. And I daresay I shall be all right. It's you they're after; not me.'

'Can you hear them any more?'

'Not now. But their engines haven't started.'

'No.'

'They haven't gone on. Biron, they . . . they're——'

'They're probably beating the wood in extended order, and it'd need a devil of a lot to cover a thousand acres of it. How many damned police are there in these patrols?'

'Not many.'

'Maybe we can both get away. You're right. I'd best leave you.'

This was neither cowardice nor desertion, but duty. It was the law of the Underground that the safety of all must not be endangered by chivalry to one. Anyone caught must become to the rest of them as one who had never been. Leave him. He was expended. Wipe away every trace of him, wipe away, if possible, the memory of him, lest any unnecessary quixotism tear the tender filaments of their vast spider's web. Security of the whole circuit before all.

Jean had been taught this harsh, grand law and had accepted it. 'Yes, go,' she said. 'I'll stay and see what happens. I'll play the aggrieved and innocent woman if I have to. . . . But, oh, Biron, I could wish I had my dogs with me.'

He went with a friendly grin (though still pale) and a 'Good-bye, ducks. Good luck.'

'Good luck.'

She stayed in the covert for a little, with her hands pressing on the ground, ready to help her rise—save when they left the ground to touch again that tiny protrusion on the pocket of her blouse. The palms pressing the rough earth sweated on it. Extended order.

And the forest large. Perhaps the men beating it were now far away, and all would yet be well. The relief in this thought was a small ecstasy. To live. To live after all. But the dogs? And those distant motors didn't beat again. Thinking this, she felt driven to move quickly. Not to be found here lying in what looked like a hiding-place. She rose, broke out of the thicket, and walked through the trees towards Sainte-Marie, but not innocently. Softly, fearfully, rapidly.

And she had not gone far before she heard barking as of a single dog not far off. Then reason failed, and nothing but terror drove her as she hurried too quickly, too noisily, the opposite way, through a brush of bracken and sycamore.

'*Halt!*' It was cried in German.

Sense lost, she only hurried on. She had forgotten all about the money in her blouse, thinking only of that other thing in it.

'*Halt!*' again. '*Halt!*' A German outraged by disobedience to a German. And the very fury in his voice made her break into a run like a threatened child.

Bullets sang towards her. They impinged on tree-trunks, ripped through undergrowth, spat on the earth. Were they firing low so as to take their prey alive? For interrogation, for torture, for torture before death?

Faster she ran, her breath now pants and gasps. Voices following the bullets; more than one; many. In her panic she didn't even know the small pleasure of thinking that perhaps she was drawing the hunt away from Biron. And the bullets tore into the flesh of her thigh and the bone of her knee. She pitched forward, and the steps came crashing through the scrub towards her, the leashed police dogs snarling spitefully as they dragged their masters to their quarry— just as Wallace and Bruce in their excitement used to drag her homeward through the trees.

'No, I'd never have been able to stand it.' She fumbled for the tablet in her blouse. Here it was. Take it. Now. So abrupt this action seemed. So slap-dash. So frightening. So *blind*. But she was thinking something like 'Good-bye, all. Good-bye, Dad. Life over? Really

over? Strange—but I'm glad to be doing this if it'll save the others';
thinking even that perhaps her life was justified because she'd done
something good with it. She lifted her eyes for a last look at the
forest; found herself saying, 'Oh God . . . if Thou art . . . forgive
me all'; then put the tablet on her tongue, closed her lips over
it and, after waiting one second in amazement and wonder, bit.

A spasm and contraction of her long body, a moan still-born,
and she lay dead, when the men broke from their extended order
and converged upon her, their sub-machine-guns pointing down at
her.

XV

They Come at Last

It was later, and the day was darkening, when the tongue of the little bell fixed to the trellised gate of Sophie's garden spoke loudly and irritably, as if the gate had been pushed with violence. Sophie, driven always by curiosity to a window when that bell sounded, jumped up from the breakfast-room table where, as so often, she was at work with her sewing-machine on an adornment, and, rushed to the window, rushed quicker than ever this evening because Wallace and Bruce had leapt up too and were barking continuously, as if strange scents angered them. She saw a uniformed German officer, four men of the Gestapo in their civilian clothes, and two of the S.S. in their black uniforms, all coming along the brief drive to her steps. And oh, others of the S.S. were standing along the avenue and entering the garden to cordon the house. These were young men, hardly more than seventeen or eighteen and looking all the younger for their black uniforms and peaked caps, cocked sideways in imitation of their officers. The skull and crossbones on their caps and lapels made them look like schoolboys playing a game and all dressed up for it.

Four small Citroën cars waited in the avenue.

'Klem! Oh, Klem!' Sophie cried. 'Oh, look! They've come.' These two syllables uncovered her thoughts for three years past, and more. 'Klem! They're all round the house. Oh, God. . . .'

Klem who'd been in the bedroom behind, brushing a suit, was

now at her side, looking. He said nothing. But he noticed that the officer had but one arm.

'Klem, what does it mean?'

'It means what you said. They've come.'

'Come? For us?'

'Yes.'

'For *all*?'

'So I imagine.'

An imperious slam of the little brass knocker, the ship in full sail, which Sophie'd brought with such pleasure from Bruges. Like the forest, that little trinket too had turned traitor. This was the knock of the secret police which she'd always expected to hear in the dawn. They came so often in the dawn to catch their prey in their beds.

'I will go down to them,' said Klem.

'Oh, Klem, what does it mean?'

'Marie-Louise, don't go,' he called from the stair-top. 'It's them.'

He opened the door, and the officer standing on the threshold was Major Clauss, the Town Major. It was months since they had seen him, for he had long ago left Rennie's room upstairs for new Officers' Quarters which the Germans had established in the Hôtel de la Forêt, a deserted chateau within the forest fringe.

'Herr Doktor,' he began. He did not bow, he did not salute with his only arm, clicking his heels, he only snapped out like a pistol shot, 'These men are here to arrest you, your wife, and your servant.'

('Oh, no . . . no. . . .' A low cry from the top of the stairs.)

'In God's name, why, Herr Major?'

'Because we have a short way with traitors. We generously left you free because you were of German nationality, and you used our generosity to work against us. We are not such fools as to imagine you do not know all about your daughter's activities.'

'My daughter? What has my daughter done?' For the moment Klem was more apprehensive about Jean than aware of what awaited himself. 'Come in. Tell me.'

The Major, the four Gestapo men in their civilian clothes, and the two S.S. men in their black uniforms stepped into the hall. From the kitchen door Marie-Louise stepped into it too.

'My daughter, you say? Where is she?'

'Her body is in a cell in the temporary prison at Féricy.'

'Her *body*? "Body" did you say?'

('Oh . . .' from the top of the stairs. And had Rennie been caught and killed like this too? Was this her punishment?')

'Ja. But she was not killed by us. Shots in the leg do not kill anyone. She must have swallowed her lethal pill before we could get to her. We know all about these lethal pills which the English issue to their agents.'

'My daughter is dead?'

'Ja. By her own hand. But she would have died in any case. She was acting as a courier for the brutal terrorist they call Biron. A million francs were found on her body, undoubtedly given to her by this bandit for the terrorists and saboteurs here.

'I know nothing of this. . . . Please . . . may I sit down?' He staggered towards the door of the salon. Now that their late lodgers were gone from the house Sophie had dressed her salon in beauty again, even though it was seldom or never used. Only Klem played the piano there sometimes in the quiet of an evening. It was used however for this business now. 'Please come in here. I must sit down. Jean. So Jean is dead. . . .'

They all followed him and stood about him as he sank on the brink of the beautiful chaise-longue. Marie-Louise came as far as the doorway. Sophie hastened down the stairs. It was, after all, her room, and she the hostess. Her face was white with dismay, but in the moments since hearing those words 'arrest you, your wife, and your servant' she had remembered her secret desire to be brave and to practise unselfishness. She summoned them to her aid now, and they helped her thrust the terror a little way aside. With dignity, her head high, her breast thrust forward, a 'grande dame anglaise' for the moment, she demanded, 'May I know what all this means? This is my house.'

The Major bowed to her, automatically clicking heels and lifting his one hand in salute. 'Madame, I am very sorry. This is Madame Burgermann,' he said to the men. And to her, 'It was to see if I could be of any help to you that I came along with the Unter-offizier here. I had not forgotten many kindnesses from you and your servant in the past. You are English, and what you and your daughter have done is perhaps understandable. We National Socialists do not despise bravery in our enemies.'

A loud angry voice from the doorway. 'She was *not* her daughter. And Madame has done nothing. She has never done a thing to help your enemies.'

The Major looked at the servant in the door, and turned away. 'With your husband, Madame, I have no such sympathy. I regard him as a traitor to his blood. And anything more contemptible than that I cannot imagine.'

Klem's lips set tight at these words; anger turned his blue German eyes to steel. 'Oh, *do* you?' he said, his voice low, but not so low as to hide the sneer.

'Ja.' Now anger flared in the Major's eyes too. 'I remember, Madame, his courtesies to me with loathing, now that I know them for the contemptible perfidy they were. There is no place in the new Reich for double-faced traitors. I myself would willingly shoot him here in this room, did I not know that he was reserved for a death less dignified.' Could this man with the furious eyes be their quiet and considerate German guest who had wished to give them no trouble? 'Let him know we shall stamp out all traitors as we stamp on worms. They shall be exterminated with the ut-most ruthlessness for they are creatures without a shred of honour. These are the Führer's orders. As the trustee and protector of our German blood, he is determined to purge it of all poisonous matter, He has himself proclaimed that if he did anything less he would himself be guilty of treachery to the Volk.'

'Heil Hitler,' said Klem. His nostrils were dilated with a sneer.

For this insult the Major drove his fist into Klem's face, nearly knocking him to the floor. One of the Gestapo men, following this lead, dragged him from the chaise-longue and smashed his fist into his eyes. Another pummelled him and spat on him, while an S.S. man felt for the Lüger pistol on his belt.

'Stop it! Stop it!' cried Sophie and, her courage being uppermost, she flung herself at his side and her arms around him.

'I believe he's a filthy Jew,' said the man who had touched his Lüger pistol.

'He's *not* a Jew,' cried Marie-Louise.

'I'm not a Jew, but I would not be ashamed to be one. I should be proud.'

For this shocking heresy they began to beat him again, while Sophie struggled to stop them, and Marie-Louise begged, '*Non, non!*' from the door.

'That will do.' The Major bade the men desist. 'He will be properly punished for his treason elsewhere, and you can be witnesses that he jeered at the Führer. Understand, sir, that no true Germans, as distinct from loathsome traitors like you, will listen to any word against our beloved Führer. An insult to him is an insult to the whole German people and therefore an insult to each one of us, as I think these men have made clear to you.'

Pleased by this tribute, one of the men justified it further by instantly saying, 'Heil Hitler.' Others, thinking this a good idea. followed his example. 'Heil Hitler.'

'We believe that our God has raised up the Führer to be the representatives of us all without exception, and the very soul of the German people. For us Germans he is the source of all right, all law, and all power, and therefore we regard any sneer at him as blasphemy.'

'Am I, perhaps, in a lunatic asylum?' asked Klem.

Sophie, still holding on to him, was astounded at his bold defiance; that he who had always seemed so mild and passive could turn to fire like this. She saw that it was anger at the words 'traitor to the German blood', and an ever-heating contempt, which had raised the latent hero in him to his feet. Also the memory of Jean. Was not Jean lying dead in one of their prison cells?

She aspired to be bold too, but she dared not speak as he had done. She only declared what she longed to declare by holding tight to him.

The Major had to draw her away from him, but he did it gently. 'Madame, your husband asked for this treatment. I do not blame these men. They acted as loyal Germans. We true Germans do not deal in mercy when we have a proven traitor in our hands. We administer instant and overwhelming justice. That is German discipline as we understand it.'

'And has it never occurred to you, my poor young fool,' asked Klem gazing into his face even though he was trembling, partly with fury, partly with the fear which had now risen again to stand side by side with the courage, 'that I as a German born may think it's you and these poor deluded louts here—yes, and your crazy leader—who are the traitors to the German blood in me? Let me tell you that I am proud of all that my daughter has done, and that I knew all about it and blessed it. And now these good gentlemen can be your witnesses that I said this. Would they like more evidence? Very well, I give you it. I say "A bas Hitler!" Now take me. I am ready to die for a Germany I believe in. You may not understand but I like to think my daughter died for it, and I am very ready to go with her.'

The Major stood listening only; such words were driving speech from him.

But words continued to come from Klem. 'I can die happy, Monsieur, knowing that your Hitler has lost his war and that his next home is the refuse pit. The wheels turn, my dear sir. Only wait; I shall not see the end, but you will, and so will some of these poor children here.' He turned his face towards Sophie. 'Vive la France.' Then, deliberately, before them all, he lifted two fingers in the V sign to the women, and smiled.

This defiance was unspeakable, and the defied had no speech. All the Major could do was to say, 'Take him away. He will pay for this. Take him. Handcuff him.'

A Gestapo man seized his hands and forced the handcuffs on to him roughly, glad to express by savage action the wrath that had found no vent in words. Klem offered no resistance; he only smiled.

'Madame, you must be ready to come too. We will not handcuff you. I do not believe you are to blame as much as he, and I will do all I can for you. It is even possible you will be given back your liberty. But you must have known what this man and his daughter were doing and you must learn that those who countenance such things do so at the risk of their lives.'

'I will come, I will come, I will come,' cried Sophie, hysteria giving her speech. And she ran towards the handcuffed Klem and put her arm about his shoulders. 'Darling, I will go with you. Yes, yes, *yes.* . . .'

'Listen.' Marie-Louise's voice from the doorway. 'She has done nothing. She even turned her son away when he came seeking shelter after his aeroplane had crashed. She turned him from her door because it was against your law.'

Klem looked at them. 'That is so,' he said.

Son? Then Marie-Louise knew that he was her son, though never had she admitted this to her. But what mattered such knowledge now? 'Yes, I did,' she cried loudly, 'and I wish with all my heart I had not done so; I wish, I wish I had taken him in'; and she fell to sobbing hysterically. 'You can take me away with my husband. Let me go with him.'

The Major turned to the men. 'Look,' he said. 'We will leave the women. They were both of them good to me when I was in this house, and I do not for a moment believe that they are anything like as guilty as this man. We have no evidence against them, and they are neither of them Germans as he is. The woman terrorist was not her daughter, and if it's true she turned her son away, she behaved correctly. Let that speak for her. The servant—she is nothing.' Obviously he was anxious to save them, and must pile up the excuses for doing so, lest his men thought him weak for a good German. 'Madame, I hope I can secure that we shall trouble you no more so long as you have no further association with the terrorists. But you will certainly be watched carefully.

Bear in mind that even the little you may have done is punishable by death. We have not hesitated on many occasions to put a whole household to death because they'd harboured a traitor in their midst. Come, men. Bring him away. I think one will be enough.'

'Two, sir,' corrected Klem.

'What do you mean?'

'My daughter, sir.'

The Major turned towards the door. 'She killed herself rather than face her judgment.'

'Thank God for that. Sophie, I'm afraid this is all; but I think I have expected it for a long time. Good-bye, my sweet. I have loved you.'

'Klem!...'

'It is odd, but I'm not unhappy. This had to come. I have been expecting it. Sixty-eight is perhaps not too early to die, and at least I shall have seen the beginnings of victory before the end. Some of these poor lads will die at twenty or only know defeat. And Marie-Louise, thank you for all. Take care of Madame.'

'Oh, I will, I will.'

'Thank you; good-bye, my dear.'

'*Monsieur.... Monsieur....*'

'I am glad you are there, Marie-Louise. I must go....'

'Klem.... Klem, my darling!'

'Lead on, gentlemen.' Klem, between two Gestapo men, was now almost in command of the company. 'Let us go. This sort of thing is best done quickly. Herr Major, may I go quickly? You have that in you, I have seen, which would not wish to torture women too long. Allow me to go wherever you wish to take me.'

'Take him,' commanded the Major, not displeased to be considered an humanitarian. 'For *their* sakes. Not for his.'

'Klem!' Sophie ran to follow him, grasping at him. 'No, it can't be! It can't be!' she cried in what was perhaps the last statement of her refusal ever to accept harsh things. They held her away, and he, at the door, lifted the two handcuffed hands so as to blow her a kiss with one of them.

'*No!* I'll go too, I'll go too, I'll go too!' she screamed madly and tore towards him, as she saw them leading him away. But Marie-Louise put a hand on her arm and stayed her; and she stayed, gasping, for in truth she was not wholly ready to go. She stood gaping at what was happening, at the unimaginable, the unbelievable. As their feet sounded on the steps she cried 'Oh . . . oh . . .' and ran to the window, to see him going along the path through a darkening night, as Rennie had gone. When they opened the gate, and its little tongued bell sounded for him going through, and she was alone in her unused and useless salon, she sank and rocked on the chaise-longue. 'Klem . . . Klem. . . . No, no, no. . . .'

Marie-Louise came and gathered the rocking woman against her breast, saying nothing but stroking her hair.

XVI

The Approach of André

BEHIND the barely lit nose of the great Halifax bomber, where the half-darkness seemed half-brother to the heavy roaring of the engines—and to the heavy heat too—André Chamier sat for'ard of the unopened hole in the floor. He sat in his cumbersome parachuter's overalls and harness, with rubber helmet on his head, pads on his knees, and spongy spine-pad at his tail. Inside the bulking overalls his suit was of a neat French cut though somewhat old; such a suit as any bourgeois of Paris might wear to his office. His shoes, rather worn, were also of a French shape and had indeed been bought long ago from a shop in the Boul' Mich'.

Crouching near him because so tall, stood Tony Hislop, the dispatcher, more talkative and ready with jokes, since he had only to open up the hole and tell André when to jump into empty space— or into eternity, did anything go wrong. Or was he, André wondered, dealing in jokes because he was hardly less taut with nerves than André himself? Usually these air-drops were steely, tight-lipped operations, dark, chilly, and lightened only seldom by a comic remark.

At present the hole was closed over by two half-doors.

'Open it soon,' promised Tony, yelling against the din and providing an encouraging smile. 'Any moment now. Guess we're nearly over the dropping zone.'

'Good,' said André. But it was doubtful if Tony heard.

Making an adjustment of André's harness, Tony bellowed, 'Yes, time, gentlemen, soon. Last drinks.'

'One for the road,' André responded, pretending jollity too.

The time was an hour and forty minutes after midnight.

On the other side of the hole a young and new assistant dispatcher sat there to learn his mystery, with André for the rabbit in the instructive experiment. The Assistant Executioner, André called him.

André's papers in a breast pocket of his jacket, his Carte d'Identité and his Fiche de Demobilisation from the Armée de l'Air, told his story. The identity card explained that his name was André Chamier, his profession a schoolmaster, his nationality French by birth, and his birthday March 3rd, 1913. The demobilization form added that his rank had been sergeant; his address 'avant les hostilités' 19a Rue Monsieur le Prince, Paris 6e; and his 'situation de famille' a 'célibataire'. In these last moments André was thinking—thinking hard—about the past thirty-one years of his life so sparsely touched upon in these papers. He thought of his father, Joseph Chamier, that successful lawyer, and of his dear mother (née Corbière), and of their handsome appartement in the Boulevard Malesherbes. He thought of his boyhood at the Lycée Condorcet and tried to remember the names of the teachers there in his time. He tried also to recall the names of his colleagues at the school in the Avenue du Maine to which, after the unhappily early death of his father, he had gone as a young teacher. Many of these names he repeated to himself as if he never wanted to forget them, as if it was necessary to remember them in case he—but Tony was unbolting the hole. He was turning back one hatch after the other. The night wind gushed in, driving from around them a close, over-heated air.

'We're just there,' Tony bawled cheerfully. 'Just coming to Hyde Park Corner. We let you jump off the bus without waiting for it to stop.'

'Good of you.'

''S'matter of fact, we never do stop,' he explained pleasantly.

'No . . .?' But André was looking through this opened window in the floor, his mind a sick medley of dizziness and interest; breath-catching dizziness and pure topographical interest. There below him were field and forest and farm with a long, serpentine, willow-fringed stream shining beneath the April moon. A bird's-eye picture unrolled beneath him, grey and white and beautiful, of the Ile de France lying in pastoral peace. Over fields and hedges, road-ways and roofs, ran the silent shadow of the bomber. Occasionally a white cloud veiled the picture for a second and travelled quickly behind them.

Then he saw the lights. The pocket torches of the Reception Committee, spaced apart and turned upward to the sky, followed the plane round as it wheeled. They formed a triangle, their apex pointing into the wind. One lamp was flashing the signal letter E.

'Them's they,' said Tony.

'Good,' stuttered André.

Above the hole a red signal, switched on by the bomb-aimer, came alight. André's eyes strained upward at the dispatcher.

'Action Stations!' bellowed Tony. 'We're going down to five hundred feet.'

Instantly André flung his legs through the hole and pressed his hands on its brink, eyes still on Tony. He strengthened himself with, 'Courage, mon vieux, courage! Oh, que tu es courageux!'

Tony's hand was uplifted; it was descending slowly. 'Win the war for us,' he was shouting as he bent towards André. 'Liberate Paris for me, please. I love Paris. Love to your gang of delinquents down there.' The green light appeared. Down came Tony's hand as he screamed, '*Go!*'

'Courage, mon vieux.' And Flight-Lieutenant Rennie Quentin, who had left this name and personality on the airfield in England when he stepped into the Halifax as André Chamier, let himself fall into the slipstream which immediately swept him away under the belly of the plane. Clear of the stream, he went floating down, swinging, swaying, and whirling quite pleasantly. It was an exhilaration. It was merriment. It was wine, making glad the heart of man.

All those identity papers of André Chamier, the demobilized sergeant, had been made in London with every detail perfect including the stampings of the Police Nationale. So too his forged food coupons, forged ration tickets, and a convincing order to report to a centre d'accueil in Paris. All that cover story of his father, the good lawyer, and his dear mother (née Corbière), and of his undistinguished career at the Lycée Condorcet together with the names of his teachers there, had been taught to Rennie with patience and perseverance by an English lady in S.O.E. whose talents were those of a lady novelist—and a historical novelist at that—with a creative fount as unfailing as the widow's remarkable cruse in the Second Book of the Kings. Ahead of André—or perhaps that word is inapt since they were all now below his feet—went the containers swaying below their parachutes and bearing gifts of weapons and ammo, especially 'weapons for Paris', towards the winking lights of the brigands below. After him would come the packages bearing many other useful gifts, but especially tobacco and cigarettes. Always cigarettes. And down with André, lodged in his head, a-quiver in his heart, came the knowledge of his mission: to act as weapons instructor to the Armée Secrète; to direct the sabotage of railways, telephones and factories; to form guerilla companies ready to rise on London's order in every village of his area, and to advise, supply and prepare the Maquis for the coming Day.

He was replacing Biron. Biron had been exfiltrated home by a Lysander pick-up after his whole area had been blown by the capture of two couriers, one a boy known as Hugo, the other some woman called Darc. What had happened to these two was not known in London; it was assumed that they were prisoners or dead. All that London knew was that the old widow of Boissy-la-Chapelle had been allowed to return home, probably because the poor old dear had talked. Anyhow Biron must be recalled and another agent exchanged for him. First, after a deliberate lapse of several weeks, they had sent one with the field name of Kinsman, but he had been arrested within a few hours of the parachutage, and shot. Now, after another deliberate interval, they were sending André.

Once Rennie had volunteered for service as a special agent his acceptance was a certainty. His French was perfect and he knew Biron's country, north of Paris, far better than anyone in S.O.E. Further, he had made many friendly contacts and learned of many hide-outs between Beauvais and Paris during his escapes after the Beauvais crash. That he would volunteer for the service had been certain too. A longing for excitement and adventure had sent him into Air Force and aircrew; this was a longing he had never hidden. But hidden within him, because unavowable, was another longing; a longing for fame and medals, the George Cross, perhaps, or at least an M.C.; and maybe a Croix de Guerre. These he was ready to seek even within inches of the torture chamber and the execution yard. More than ever now he craved such distinctions so as to impress a mother who had turned him away.

He had chosen his own cover name of André because of his admiration for the young French poet, André Chénier, guillotined in the Revolution. But they had not allowed him to keep the name Chénier, compromising instead with Chamier. As André Chamier he dropped clumsily and with all his ambitions on to the soil of France and was towed along it like a field-harrow by his parachute. Above him the Halifax, dipping its wing in a farewell to him and a salute to the Reception Committee, wheeled round for England again.

§

Seldom a better drop—not that the droppee had touched down becomingly; his landing would have raised vituperation from his trainers in England. But his body, however awkwardly, had struck the earth of France in a field less than two hundred yards from the bomb-aimer's pin-point. It was a large acreage of pasture whose few cows had gambolled away from the sudden low roar in the sky; and here Rennie rose from his momentary and undignified crouching for his work in the 'field' of France. The roar dwindled into the night, and the cows came slowly back to have a look at this figure disengaging himself on their land from a quarrelsome parachute. 'Go away,' said Rennie in French, since they were French cows, but apparently they decided that he was a friendly visitor, or they didn't understand his French, for they now stood their ground and moo'd to be milked.

Rennie could do nothing more with them for the present, because one of the Reception Committee, a short but splendidly fat man, whose girth was only an inch or so less than the Abbé Belfort's, was running towards him at a notably gay pace considering the weight of flesh he was bringing in front of him and the purple-grape tinctures of his round, merry face. One could detect this deep colouring even though the face was roughly blackened for these stealthy manoeuvres in the night. He wore only trousers, shirt, and a leather jacket which had no more chance of meeting over that protension of stomach than had the top buttons of his trousers. He came alone because the other men were all rushing towards the forty containers whose weapons within interested them more than the British officer. Or they were hurrying to the packages which had been dropped to them immediately after Rennie, and contained cigarettes.

The big belly and the purpled face came opposite Rennie where he stood removing his overalls and waving to the cows to 'hop it', or, alternatively, to 'shut up'.

'André?' It was inquired with the friendliest of smiles.

'Yes, Monsieur, and I wish you would stop those bloody cows from signalling to all the German patrols around. Perhaps if you would lie down and milk them——'

'Shoo! Shoo away!' commanded the fat man, waving the back of a hand at the cows, who retreated a little way and seemed gradually to accept that it was after midnight and no hour for milking. 'Welcome, André. I am Le Petit; yes, the Chief Bandit, ha, ha, ha.'

'Le *Petit*, did you say, M'sieur?' asked Rennie, with an involuntary dip of his eyes to that stomach.

'Oui.' With both hands he stroked the whole hemisphere—not without pride—along its equator. 'Le Petit. The Little One. But I am a great bandit. Oh, but, Jesu Christ! I should have asked you for the password. You may not really be André. You may be somebody I ought to kill. M'sieur, the password, please.'

'L'Angleterre est une nation de boutiquiers.'

'So it is. So it is. How true. The Emperor was right. But what shopkeepers! Look at this magnificent mail-order delivery now. What have you brought us, André? Brens?'

'Yes.'

'Piats?'

'Yes.'

'Rifles, of course?'

'Plenty.'

'A few incendiaries? Just a few?' he begged.

'More than a few.'

'Bombs, bombs, bombs?'

'Yes, indeed.'

'The good God forbid that I should worry you, André, but—some phosphorous bombs?'

'Some phosphorous grenades, yes. A wicked weapon.'

'But useful, André. Useful.'

'No doubt.' Rennie was now folding up the overalls and parachute for burial with the packages in a secret place already provided. 'Are there no Germans around? Don't we hurry?'

'No. No Germans near here. No danger. If any come, we assassinate them. No hurry. And bazookas M'sieur?'

'Some light 2·36 bazookas, yes.'

'I am the most ennuyeux of men—I know it—but—much explosive?'

'Much.'

'Money?'

'Quite a little.' Rennie grinned promisingly. 'Twenty-five million. Enough?' And he thought with relish of a hundred thousand francs of his own, in a pocket.

'Aha!' Le Petit seized Rennie's shoulders and kissed him. 'We liberate France, you and I and my bandits. We burn them out, the swine. Smoke them out. And then we massacre the collaborators. Especially Monsieur Paul Bluteau and Madame his wife, and his two filthy daughters. They sleep with the Boches. With horrible Boches by the cartload.'

'Oh, no, not massacre.'

'Oh, but certainly, M'sieur. We massacre lice, no? La belle France needs a deal of delousing. Oh, yes, we have our little plans for Madame and her filthy daughters. Directly you——' he leaned forward, lifted a warning finger and whispered, 'They are coming?'

Rennie understood. 'Security' forbade him even to suggest the day and the hour when the invasion armies would appear, or the place, but he thought it safe to grin significantly and offer the tiny embryo of a nod.

'When, when?'

Rennie shook his head and was silent.

'Soon? Not wait till all the Boches are killed by the Russians, no? Soon?'

'Perhaps.' But if ever 'perhaps' was another version of 'Soon enough', this was it. Had he not long been dreading that he'd never get to France before the day? So great a day, under the sun.

'Ah, little André knows, but he mustn't say anything to Le Petit. I quite understand.'

'Little André knows damned little.'

'He knows they're coming. Aha! Victoire!' His hand was on high. 'Vive les Américains.'

'*And* les Anglais,' Rennie objected.

'Oh, yes. But yes! Les Anglais. God save the King. But how is poor London? Is there anything left of it?'

'Quite a little here and there.'

'And how is Monsieur Shurshill?'

'In good health, thank you. He sent you his kind regards.'

'Ah, vive l'Angleterre. She it is who save us all. But perhaps a little slowly. And what shall Le Petit do after the victoire? Become a poor shopkeeper again? It will be sad. This is the only life. André, we need your help. These desperadoes of mine are the stupidest of men. So am I. We have the fire in our bellies—' he patted his own belly as if to say that in that roomy stove a great furnace was aglow—'but we have so little in our silly heads. You will teach us. You will teach us how to use the bazookas on the dirty Boche tanks and to blow them up to heaven and out of France. And, André—a thousand pardons—but . . . there will be more arms-drops, no? A thousand pardons.'

'There will be more.'

'Ah, good, good. I have found some of the most beautiful fields for your drop-sites. Much better than this beastly exhibition of cow-pats. Lovely level fields north of Domont and between Pontoise and Beaumont-sur-Oise. There you drop us plenty, plenty more. They want them in Paris. Colonel Rol who's in command of the Paris region is a good man but impatient. He——'

'Rol?'

'Yes, Rol. Even as I am Le Petit. Not even I know his real name.' He winked. 'I tell not even you. But the good Rol wants all your new weapons; he's been plaguing me about them for weeks. He wants you too; he's going to work you hard teaching all his unscrupulous young men how to use them. Piats on the German trains, no? Come, we take you to a good friend and give you food. And wine. And listen: *tea!* Madame has been buying tea in the Marché Noir for years—years!—and all for the tommees when they come. See? Tipperary. Long vay. You are arrived in front of them. Like the cuckoo who tells us it'll soon be summer. Come, mon enfant, I will take you. Never mind that parachute. My ruffians will look after that.' He gathered Rennie by the elbow and led him proudly towards the Reception Committee.

§

As soon as his tasks allowed, Rennie was hurrying on a pleasant morning through the forest of Sainte-Marie so as to look down from its fringe at the tower of the little chateau. What had happened there in the last two years? Was it possible they were still there, Sophie and Klem, Jean and Marie-Louise? Was the house even standing? Last year there had been bombings of Sainte-Marie because of the general's headquarters in the old chateau. How could he find out all about them? Ever avoiding embarrassment, he had no intention of approaching the house; his idea was only to come and look long at it, and think his thoughts, and go away. Perhaps—another idea came to him as he walked—he would show himself with delight and laughter to Mme Dubosquet and Brigitte in their cottage at the end of the dirt track and ask them guardedly about residents in Sainte-Marie; perhaps he would say to Brigitte, who must be about sixteen now, 'You see, Brigitte, ma chérie? I said I'd come back to marry you,' and kiss her vigorously, and fling her up in the air, as it had been his habit to do with Marie-Louise.

He arrived at the forest fringe and looked down the green slope. There were all the roofs of little Sainte-Marie and the steeple of its church. And there, above a small garden of firs, a cone-capped tower and two gable-peaks. An intact, untroubled roof—but who lived beneath it now? He sat himself below the trees that he might stare at that roof and at memories. Like Biron before him he was in the blue overalls of a French labourer, with a worn black beret on his head. But this peasant's overalls were faded into a smoky-blue by much rain and washing and sun. His hands clasped one knee, and at his side lay a short-necked potato hoe.

He sat there long with his thoughts, sometimes taking up the hoe to beat it rhythmically on the ground. Time was in plenty on his hands because so much of his field-work at present was like that of a nocturnal animal seeking its prey in the dark; and there were no happier places in which to lie hid during daylight than these forests to the north and west of Paris. 'André, mon garcon, tu es content. Pourquoi? Parce qu'il fait beau, mon ami.'

And then, as he sat there, he saw a woman coming slowly and, it seemed, sadly up the road from Sainte-Marie. Two lively dogs accompanied her. *Jean's dogs surely?* Two black and fussing Scotch terriers with tails on high and noses restlessly researching. Then who—she was too short for Jean, too thin for Sophie, too tall for Marie-Louise. Some stranger? But, gracious saints!—it was—could it really be?—yes, it was Sophie. But Sophie thin. So *thin*. Shrunken. By lack of food, perhaps. And walking so sadly, with bent head and a stoop instead of eagerly and self-admiringly, with the old breast-high carriage and a stately hat for her crest. So thin, but still dressed with care, and her ruined face studiously tended. Certainly she must be sixty-four now, but whoever expected to see her as a little old lady, wizened, but making the best of herself? Never till this moment had it occurred to him to think of his Aunt Sophie as 'small'. Resentments against this small bowed woman began to waste a little away.

She was coming nearer and he heard her voice, sad and impatient, 'Wallace—*Wallace*, come here.'

His heart pounded with doubt what to do. Almost inevitably she must notice him because there was no one else in sight between village and forest. Should he rise quickly and hide among the trees? But some compulsive hesitation stopped this, and now it was too late to move; it would only draw attention to him. Now, if she kept to the road, she must pass him barely forty yards away. Heart protesting, he bent his head that she might not see his features, and played with the hoe, beating it on the ground between his legs, as a resting man will beat with his walking stick.

The side of his eye showed her now on the forest path but, instead of walking on into the trees she turned round, as they had so often done together, to look back at that little roof-tree and at the distant Tour Eiffel, a wraith in the sunbright mist of morning.

And there they were: forty yards between them, she standing, he seated, and both looking towards Sainte-Marie and Paris.

And the dogs bounded towards him and sniffed at his legs. Whether they recognized him he could not say, but it seemed they did; they looked at him, barked at him, and Bruce leapt up at him.

'*Come* here, Bruce,' ordered Sophie. 'Wallace, come here.'

Rennie kept his head low, and the dogs did not come to her, so she came towards them. 'Bruce, come *away*. Wallace, come *here*.'

§

Sophie was angry with them for barking at and worrying that peasant with the hoe. Probably he was resting here after some work in the forest. He seemed slight and young; how was it they hadn't taken him for labour in Germany? A demobilized prisoner-of-war, perhaps invalided home. But Frédé was still held in some prison camp. Held, she supposed, as one of many hostages by these terrible Germans. Oh, Klem . . . Klem, why are more of them not like you? That day—that awful evening when they took you away. Darling, they didn't torture you before they . . . She couldn't say the next words, though she had learned how the sentence should have finished. Before they hanged you?

'There was no one like Klem. I lost Rennie because of my selfishness; I don't even know if he's alive; maybe I sent him to his death. He was my son, and I suppose God punished me for this wickedness by letting them come and take Klem. Klem is dead and lost to me; alive or dead, Rennie is lost to me, and I am for ever alone now; old and alone.' She was not self-critical enough to discourage these thoughts as self-pity. 'Come, Bruce. *And* Wallace! What on earth is the matter with you both? Come back. I am sorry, Monsieur. I don't know why they are behaving like this. They don't usually run after and trouble——'

'It's all right, darling.' The blue-clad peasant was looking up at her. 'I like to think they recognized me.'

'Rennie! . . . *Rennie!*'

'No "Rennie", please. André. One André Chamier, son of old Jo Chamier who had that handsome appartement in the Boulevard Malesherbes. You'd have loved it. Pity the old boy died so young. But just for today I've definitely come down in the world. A jobbing gardener . . . I think. Just for this visit to Sainte-Marie.'

'But Rennie—oh my dear——'

'André, please; not Rennie.'

'What are you doing here? Oh, you're alive! And I was that moment thinking you might be dead. That very moment. How did you get here?'

'Dropped from the sky, lady. Literally. Drifting down by parachute.'

'My *dear*. But wasn't that terrible?'

'No. Rather fun. I'm a special agent now. But please know nothing about me. I only came to take a peep at the house and go away. Don't mention me to Klem or Jean——'

'Klem is dead. So is Jean.'

'Klem is *dead*?' He could not speak. One was so used to death by now—bret *Klem!* He could dredge up no words. He could only think: Uncle Klem dead: then all forgiveness for her now. That settles it. And what relief to have done with anger. Only gentleness now. 'Do you mean . . . ?'

'Yes. Jean too. Jean was shot in the forest after she'd been getting money for the Resistance from one of your people. A man who called himself Biron.'

'Good God. . . . Good God, was *she* the woman? Our Jean? Was she called Darc?'

'I don't know about that. "Darc"—no, I never heard that. All I can do now is to look after her dogs for her.'

'We know they captured a woman. Then it was our Jean! Our *Jean.*'

'She was running from them and they shot her, and she took her tablet of poison before they could get to her.' (Rennie's hand went instinctively to the flap of his breast pocket and touched something.) 'Can you imagine it? Then they came and took Klem away. Oh, I hope they killed him quickly. But he defied them, you see, and scoffed at them, and they dragged him away. Oh, do you think they tortured him?'

'Even so, my dear, perhaps he didn't suffer too much. I've heard from one of our lads who was tortured before we rescued him that it's bearable if you know you're doing right. And the dear old Deutscher would have known that.'

'They let me stay. And why? Because Marie-Louise told them that I'd turned you away rather than disobey them. I was saved by the wickedest thing I've ever done in my life. Rennie—or whatever it is I have to call you—you do know that I've hardly had one moment's happiness since that—that last time. How could I have been so awful?'

He rose at once (the dogs leaping up at him) and said, 'My dear, that was nothing. Forget all about it.' He kissed her cheek and said, 'Mother darling.' And if one of these two was happy, it was he. Such relief, such ease, to be back to gaiety and forgiveness, and done with loneliness.

She had broken into sobbing against his shoulder, while he gently patted her back. 'Oh, Rennie, how is it you can be so good when I am so awful?'

'"Good", my dear? Don't make me laugh. Sometimes I think I'm hopeless. A sour beast. Caring for nothing but myself and my fame.'

'Oh, I'm so glad you've come,' she sobbed. 'Ever since that night I've dreamed of your coming again, and how I'd of course take you in, even if they killed me for it. I've tried to be less awful and selfish, so that God would let you come back. And look: here you are. Here you *are*. But I've been so terribly afraid I'd never see you again. Oh, God is good.'

'Sit down, Mama. There's no one in sight between us and Paris. Tell me all about everything. My poor dear Uncle Klem.'

She sat at his side rather stiffly, with one of her hands pressing on the ground between them; and the dogs played around them on the grass. Occasionally he laid his own hand encouragingly on hers as she told him how for months now she'd lived in the house with only Marie-Louise for friend and companion, and with little desire to go on living, unless——

'Unless what, please?'

'I've had my dreams of living in England after all these horrors are over . . . somewhere near you. Not to be a nuisance to you, of course——'

His hand pressed on hers. 'And that's what we're going to do.'

'—but to see something of you sometimes.'

'Perhaps we'll even live together. And even if I marry, I'll promise to live close by. But are you really ready to leave your precious chateau?'

'Leave it? My dear, every time I come out I feel that I never want to go back into it again. I used to keep the door of the salon shut so as to preserve all the furniture; now I keep it shut because I cannot bear to see the room. Or its furniture. We were all in there, Klem and me and the terrible men, when they took him away. In handcuffs like a common criminal. They kept me back from following him, and all he could do was to blow a kiss to me with his poor handcuffed hand.'

These words so broke her down that the tears dragged her head forward. 'Why didn't I fight them and scratch their eyes out and let them take me too and kill me too. I cried out that I'd go too, but I didn't really mean it; the terror was too much for me; and I just let them put me on one side. He was magnificent. He was like someone suddenly inspired. I was terrible. I just let him go as I let you go. To die.' Rennie kept his pressure on her hand till the tears should be stanched. But then she said, after wiping her eyes, 'You simply can't *imagine* what it was like,' and he felt a touch of the old irritation and a desire to say boastfully, 'My dear, may I remind you I've been fighting a war for nearly five years?' but he kept quiet, since she was unhappy, and all was to be forgiveness now.

After a little silence, while with the small lacy handkerchief she patted her nose, and continued to think of herself rather than of *his* part in the war, she asked, 'Darling, how long have you known that I was your mother?'

'Since I was about twelve.'

'Oh, *no*, dear.'

'Well, say eleven.'

'Is it possible? I suppose I always half knew you must know, but I'd never let myself think of it. Oh dear, what fools we are. And you knew that Sir Hereward was your father?'

'Say at thirteen.'

'But did Granny ever tell you anything?'

'Never a word. But she let fall a lot about Sir Hereward in Paris and then about you in Paris. A talkative old lady, not very cautious in her talk. She didn't understand "security".'

'And did you never ask her who your parents were?'

'Certainly not.'

'But why?'

Smiling, he picked up her hand. 'Because I'm extraordinarily like my mother and always take evasive action when I see anything the least bit uncomfortable looming up.'

'Do you bear any malice against your father?'

'No. As I remember telling Jean once, I've lived with a dream that he'd have loved me a lot, and I'd have loved him. And I tell you what: one day you and I are going together to find his grave on Gallipoli.'

'Oh, you're so sweet. But Rennie, my precious, just fancy you and me sitting here like this. I can't get over it. It seems incredible. Marie-Louise'll be so——'

'Darling, you're incorrigible. Not a word to Marie-Louise. Not a word to any living soul. Please, I mean this. All that you have done is to meet a poor sweaty labourer in the forest. Say a word to anyone, and you may ruin all my work.'

But this did not stop him from telling her some things about his work, things which he chose to feel justified in telling her because they must already be known to the Germans. But really he told her because he wanted to impress her. Just as Biron had sat beside Jean in the forest and bragged of his tasks, so Rennie now with Sophie. And Rennie felt a far greater need to impress this mother who from the beginning had defaulted in her duty to him than ever Biron could have felt towards a woman met in the forest for a day.

Justify this talk as he might, his conscience nagged at him, and he pleaded, 'Promise you'll tell no one. I don't think I've told you anything that it's not safe to say. I'm not giving away any secrets, but . . . for the Lord's sake don't tell anyone about me.'

'Of course I won't tell anyone.'

'Not a soul. Promise.'

'Of course I promise. Not a soul.'

And he didn't believe her. He was certain this easy-gossiping mother would be driven, sooner or later, to tell Marie-Louise that she'd actually met Monsieur Rennie in the forest, and that he was doing such and such. But Marie-Louise could probably be trusted. She was of the Underground. This he had just learnt from Sophie who had told him, with complete and untroubled improbity, all about Marie-Louise's work with the Resistance. So Marie-Louise was of the Underground. Then she would know its laws.

'Darling, you will take care of yourself, won't you,' Sophie said, thinking of all he had told her. 'Don't let them do anything to you. Oh, I don't like it. Shall I see you soon again?'

'Good gracious, no. You don't want the Gestapo discovering who I am and burning your house down. And half the village down too. I'll see you again when I've got the British and American armies all round me.'

'And are they really coming?'

'Of course. The whole world knows that.'

'Soon? Will it be soon?'

'Beloved, I know nothing. And you know nothing. And no one knows nothing—except, I suppose, the P.M. and the G.O.C.s and the High Admirals and the Air Marshals. And now I must go and do my bit to help them in whatever they have in mind. Today, for instance, I go to my guerilleros in Paris—'

'Your *what?*'

'My cloak-and-dagger boys in Paris, and I teach them all manner of unspeakably dirty fighting with all manner of filthy weapons.

Unarmed combat too,' he added, still showing off a little, 'which is just about the dirtiest game in the business.'

He rose, bent his head and kissed her forehead. Her hand found his and tried to keep it, but gently he drew it away. Her last words as he went were, 'Do take care of yourself, my sweetest'—words like a touch on the elbow of a parting guest. 'Don't do anything dangerous.'

He turned and smiled at 'dangerous' a little sadly. In a kind of laughing despair of her.

XVII

The Breach of Festung Europa

'OH, *Madame!*' Marie-Louise was breathlessly climbing the stairs to the breakfast-room where Sophie sat at her sewing-machine, stitching sadly a new blouse for herself. Her self-decoration was almost her only remaining interest; she would admit it, quoting Klem who used to say, 'Sophie, you'll feel your ruling passion strong in death.

'Oh, Madame! They've come!' In the room, panting before Sophie, Marie-Louise could only repeat, 'They've come.'

'They?' In her excitement Marie-Louise had forgotten who, for the last five years, had been meant by 'They'.

'Oui. Les Américains et les Anglais.' The dogs caught her excitement and leaped and barked. 'They're on the beaches, he said. It's the Débarquement des Alliés. At last. Down, Bruce! *Down*, Wallace. They've landed.'

'But where? Where?'

'Normandy. On beaches all the way from Cherbourg to le Havre.'

'How do you know this?'

'The bibici, Madame. The announcer of the bibici said they'd come in four thousand ships.'

Not an ear in France, during these last weeks, but had been listening to the B.B.C.; not though the penalties for this crime could be anything from long imprisonment to deportation to

Germany with confiscation of all goods; not though the posters on the walls everywhere announced these penalties and tabled the sentences which had already been passed on 'radio criminals'; not though the controlled Paris newspapers proclaimed that the B.B.C. was 'an instrument of Jews and plutocrats' and 'a monster hissing out its lying propaganda'. The ears of France listened. They listened from receivers in cachettes under their stairs, on top shelves behind books, under mounds of junk in the attics, and away in the quiet of the forest. Sainte-Marie like all the rest listened, not only to the B.B.C.'s 'Les Français Parlent aux Français' but to the news in English at all hours, and great was the stature of those who understood English; great their secret pride as they relayed the news to all standers-by. Marie-Louise, at noon this morning, had been one of the standers-by in the attic above the épicier's, when Monsieur Dupré, the charcutier, once a waiter in Brighton, was the delighted and admired trumpet-relay for the B.B.C.'s tremendous story.

'He said there were four thousand big ships in the Baie de la Seine, Madame, and thousands of smaller ones. And they landed on a hundred and sixty miles of coast which, Monsieur Dupré says, is more than two thousand five hundred kilometres. They not only came in ships but from the air by parachutes and gliders. He said it was the biggest débarquement from the air that the world has ever seen. And they played the Marseillaise, Madame, and we all kissed Monsieur Dupré, and he kissed us, and then we all kissed each other. And we all cried.'

'I don't wonder, Marie-Louise.'

'Yes, poor Monsieur Dupré was crying as he translated some of it to us. Quite often he couldn't go on at all for crying, and we were afraid we were missing something. It was he who pointed out that it was the sixth of June; June 6th; almost exactly the anniversary of the day they started their attack against Paris. He said it was the Day of Judgment, and that's what it is, Madame. Le Jour du Jugement. Judgment for Monsieur. Judgment for poor dear Mademoiselle. For Monsieur le Curé and Monsieur Eric.' Marie-Louise was crying again, now and fumbling for her handkerchief. 'Oh, Madame, do you think it means my Frédé will be back soon? M. Dupré says the Germans can't possibly stand up against the Americans and English on one side of them and the Russians on the other. He says they're finished, and it's only a matter of time before they go. And we know he's right. Any day now the word is coming for the F.F.I. to rise in Paris. The F.F.I. in Sainte-Marie rise at the same time. We're all of us just waiting. Then perhaps you will see Monsieur Rennie again.'

We? Yes, Marie-Louise accounted herself a part of the Forces Français de l'Intérieur, in which all bodies of the Resistance had lately been combined. And 'Monsieur Rennie'? Yes, she had met André once with the Resistance in Sainte-Marie and had nearly 'died of the meeting', so heart-stopping was her surprise and excitement. He of course had picked her off the ground and, holding her small body tight against his, a foot from the ground, kissed and kissed her, saying, 'Yum . . . yum . . . never tell Frédé,' and then kissed her again. 'Let me go, M'sieur; let me down. I feel rather sick; it's so strange, so merveilleux.' But, loyal to her oath, she had told none of this to Madame, though longing to do so, aching to do so. It was a triumph on which she prided herself, that she had not done so; not even when Madame told her all about her own meeting with Monsieur Rennie on the forest fringe.

Marie-Louise went down to her kitchen, heart shaking, limbs unsteady. Sophie turned again to her sewing-machine. 'Yes,' she thought, as she swung its wheel abstractedly, 'a victory will give Frédé back to Marie-Louise but not Klem to me. These wars do not give my lovers back to me. Hereward remains in his grave on Gallipoli, and Klem—I shall never know where. But there is still Rennie. And he did say "Perhaps we'll live together" and "Even if I marry I promise I'll live close by". Oh God, grant that he's still safe. All is so happy between us now. Keep him safe till the end. Let *him* be left to me.'

§

'Listen. Listen, Madame.' The two women, standing under the firs of the garden that same night, heard a distant palpitation as of many hundred guns. They heard—or, rather, felt—the thudding of bombs; the earth beneath their feet recorded shocks. Never before, not even when the enemy was approaching Paris, had there been such distant thunders as these, rolling there in the north-west, such assaults upon the earth's face; such shudderings in the ground and in the night air. Were these the guns along the Normandy coast which had breached the walls of Festung Europa? Could one hear guns that were four hundred miles away? No; more likely they were the bombs and guns of aeroplanes, shattering communications between the capital and the coast; arresting the approach of reinforcements. But whatever the magnificent vibration and drumming might be, it could be thought of as a joyous and continuing salute to those who had stormed the walls or overleapt them, bounding through the sky from English fields onto plains in Cotentin and Calvados. It was said that the Führer had ordered the annihilation of the enemy on the bridgeheads before this night was over. 'Every available German unit is to be diverted at once to the points of penetration. The beach-heads must be cleared up not later than tonight.'

Poor man. It was already near to midnight, and this tremendous shaking of the earth could only mean the footfalls of these new visitors to France. When the footfalls were so heavy that these two women's hearts shuddered as well as the ground beneath them and the air around them, Marie-Louise sprang up and down on her toes with joy. Her tears slid down, and she bit on all her lower lip. 'Oh, Madame!'

§

While the battle stormed around and within the coast-walls of Festung Europa, and gradually the penetration by the invaders deepened, most notable was the change in the bearing of the

Germans as they sat in the cafés of Sainte-Marie, or bought goods in its shops, or walked its streets. And, oh yes, most notably different when the Americans swung suddenly south-east and east and north-east in a broad right-hook whose obvious goal was the whole of the lower Seine and all these parts around Paris. If their aim is the encirclement of Paris, how then? Shall we not all be cut off? Could not the whole country between capital and coast be one great prison camp for us, and we be the prisoners of these French who have one or two reasons for not loving us? All Sainte-Marie waited with ears addressed, not only to the bibici but to Radio Paris, German controlled. For there came a day when even the German radio admitted that Le Mans and Alençon had fallen and that the invaders were now little more than eighty miles from Paris. Eighty? What was 'eighty' when the invading armies had mastery of the air and could attack with bombs and rockets, guns and flame, every new trench line or river line that opposed them. Then it was Chartres that had fallen, and Dreux. Forty miles. And the Germans demanding, 'Where is the Luftwaffe? Why are these bastards allowed to come joy-riding over us at will? Lieber Gott, if the Americans are at Chartres and Dreux, they're over the last of the hills and there's nothing in front of them but the whole flat country of the Ile de France.'

A rain of fire was sweeping across the north-west of France and must surely pass over Paris. Soon the guns were loud to the south-east of Sainte-Marie, and the earth of Sophie's garden shook and shook beneath the near impacting bombs. The Germans admitted to fighting within twenty miles of Paris. Within ten. In the Forêt de Marly; in the Forêt de Meudon. Five miles from the Seine. Then across the Seine on both sides of Paris. The B.B.C. reported that the British Commander-in-Chief had addressed a Special Message to his troops: 'The end of the war is in sight. Let us finish the business quickly.'

Sophie one night lay awake in her bed listening to a roar and beat of engines and clamour of voices, presumably on the Beauvais–Paris road. When she lifted her head from the pillow to listen better, she distinguished the harsh clangour of caterpillar treads, endlessly continuing. It was as if an army was stealthily moving through the night. Then, when again she had lifted her head, came Marie-Louise's footsteps down the stairs. And a tentative tapping on her door that jumped her heart from its seat. 'Yes? What is it?'

'Madame, have you heard? Are you listening?'

'Yes. Come in. What is it that is happening? It sounds like soldiers.'

Marie-Louise entered. In nightdress with naked feet. 'Is it the Americans, do you think, Madame?'

'I don't know. What time is it?'

'Three minutes to four. Listen. Oh, listen. Something is going by.'

Ruling passions strong in death: Sophie's heart might be slain within her but she must still hurry out to see any new excitement. 'It'll be light soon. Could we go and see? If it's the Americans we mustn't miss it. It might be the English. It might be us. God, it'd be so wonderful. The end of all terrors for us. The end of pain. Shall we go?'

'Oh, yes, Madame. Do let us.'

'But if it's the Americans, surely there'd be cheering.'

'It's only four o'clock, Madame. There's hardly anyone awake.'

'Still, if it were the Americans, surely we . . . oh, what can it be?'

She had flung her feet out of bed, and they were feeling for her slippers. No need to say a word more to Marie-Louise. Marie-Louise went racing up the stairs to her clothes.

But it was fifteen minutes and more before they were out of the house. Sophie, however excited, must dress herself reasonably well for the public gaze. As Klem used to say, she would keep the whole agenda waiting on the Day of Judgment while she spruced herself up for such a public occasion. And perhaps this business now, whatever it might be, was part (so Monsieur Dupré had suggested) of an earthly Dies Irae. Marie-Louise, adequately dressed in two minutes, and listening to those noises in the night, beat a toe impatiently outside Madame's room, even goading her at times with an 'Are you ready, Madame?'

'Just one moment, Marie-Louise. Just coming.'

At last they were out together and hurrying through the grey of dawn to the junction of the Rue de la Forêt with the Rue de Paris. Before they reached it they saw the dark procession passing by and quickened their pace that they might miss as little as possible. At the cross-roads by the fountain, there were only a few watchers in this early hour. A few early labourers stood halted on their journey to work and stared.

An army retreating through the last of the night. Tanks with steel-helmeted men crowded on to them; armoured cars overfull; motor-cycles with side-cars holding three men and four—it was the same procession as they had watched in a daylight, heartlessly brilliant, four years before: a German army streaming towards Paris. But then they were fine disciplined men, proudly dressed in victory; now, though disciplined still, they were torn and tired and vested in gloom. And they hurried by, not only in their grumbling iron vehicles and big staff cars, but in small stolen French cars, Citroëns, Peugeots, Renaults; in horse-drawn farm carts, wagons, trucks, 'platforms', dung carts. Some even rode on heavy farm horses. Officers were speeding and weaving along on bicycles, snatched from where or whom? Some of them pedalled women's bicycles much too small for them. And not only disciplined soldiers, orderly to the point of pathos, were passing by. Who were these lonely soldiers without their rifles, without their heavier equipment which they must have cast aside as many of the routed French had done? None of the speeding officers troubled to ask them who they were or to shoot them. No time. And not German soldiers only; civilians too. German civilians who had served the Occupation and now had orders to get out of France as quickly as possible. Civilians with bundled possessions in their cars, on their bicycles, on their backs; they were the refugees now.

The wheel turns, my dear sir. So Klem had said to his German captor on that dreadful day.

'If only Monsieur were here to see this, Marie-Louise.'

'And Mademoiselle.'

'Do you think they know, Marie-Louise?'

'It is perhaps possible, Madame. The Abbé would have said so. Oh, shall we soon see him again? And Frédé?'

The road at this stage ran east for a long crooked stretch so that this wan cavalcade seemed to be snaking endlessly towards the far-away, rose-pencilled dawn. Endlessly indeed, for when the daylight was full and golden, it was still clattering by. And all the village had long been awake to it; faces at all the windows, the windows opening for fists to shake, hands to wave in sardonic farewell, voices to jeer 'Sauve qui peut. Sauve qui peut', mouths to spit. The crowds on the pavements were less ready to jeer, for the Germans in the tanks and cars looked sullen and still nursed their sub-machine guns along their right arms.

It was not the Germans who fired. A roaring overhead lifted all eyes to the sky, and here were the British Typhoons screaming down to plant bombs around the village roads and so to arrest with craters and the rubble of fallen houses this massive retreat; then they would have enclosed it in a barricaded killing-ground from which no vehicles could turn away and find safety in the fields. 'The RAF!' cried the crowd. 'Vive la RAF!' Behind the Typhoons came a string of Spitfires, flying at great speed and little higher than the house-tops. They turned their machine guns on every vehicle in view and then were gone, sweeping upward into the sky.

The watching crowd scattered to shelter as the first bullets hit the ground; all the windows swallowed their people into the dusk inside. Sophie, seeing men topple dead or shrieking off tanks, carts, and crashing bicycles, covered her face with her hands and called, 'Come away! Oh, Marie-Louise, come away!' flying from the sight of sudden death even more than from the fear of it.

§

All that day Sophie, shaken by this slaughter in the Rue de Paris, stayed within her house walls, much as a quivering hare will stay crouched in its form when frightened by the behaviour of humans without. And as an animal will peep from its earth she looked often from her windows that faced the forest because there were things to be seen there. The Beauvais–Paris road was not the only channel of retreat for German columns. What better channel than the roads through the forest, screened by great trees? And these roads, converging, debouched on the tilt of the Rue de la Forêt; their very mouth was up there before her windows. Orderly columns marched frequently down the slope, and she dreaded— and partly wanted, but for the excitement only—to see the Typhoons and Spitfires come diving on to them out of the sky. Sometimes Marie-Louise watched at her side.

It was not only these marching columns, pathetic and even splendid with their order and discipline shining in a dark hour, that came out of the forest; ever and again a straggler, with or without arms, came furtively, guiltily, from the cover of the trees, avoiding the open road. Deserters?

When next day in the late afternoon it was necessary for Marie-Louise to go into the village and get bread, she was gone for a long time, and Sophie, in fear, now watched for *her* from the windows. Once she even went out and watched from the corner of the avenue.

Marie-Louise returned at last, explaining that she'd gone to look at the terrible things of which everyone was speaking.

'What things?' asked Sophie, eager to hear. She followed Marie-Louise into the kitchen. 'Surely there can't be anything more. Surely we've had enough. Don't tell me there's anything worse than we've seen already.'

'May I sit down, Madame? I'm so tired. It's all so terrible.'

'Of course sit down and rest. You look pale as death. What things?'

Marie-Louise sat at her table. Sophie remained standing.

Marie-Louise's eyes stared into hers. 'The Germans only picked up their wounded; they left their dead lying on the road, and some of their dying too. All that our men have done so far has been to kick or roll the bodies into the gutters, and there they have lain all yesterday and all today. And you know what the sun's been like these last two days.'

'I do indeed,' said Sophie, for the sun in these mid-August days had been hot enough to lift the tar macadam from the surface of the roads and scorch and soften it.

Marie-Louise turned and looked through her window, as if she could not face Madame while telling the rest. The disabled tanks, she said, were now iron ovens and stank of the dead within. The gutters were ribbons of congealed and dusty blood. Those horses which had sagged to the road and died plunging before their eyes were swollen and bloated. Beyond the houses and in the fields the cows lay with their legs stiff in the air and their bodies blown up like balloons. Tales told in the streets were too awful, and some, it seemed, were true enough. The forest smelt of death, they said. The dead were hanging from the trees.

'*Why?*' gasped Sophie, sinking to a chair.

Marie-Louise explained why. The Allies had dropped leaflets calling upon the retreating Germans to surrender and promising them lenience and safety. Many had obeyed, deserting as individuals or in groups, and some of these had been caught by the still disciplined troops and hung on the roadside trees as examples to others who came by. Besides these corpses on their rudimentary gibbets other Germans were lying dead in the brush because the Maquis and other résistants had been sniping at any and every German they could see, anxious to kill as many as possible before this brief but grand opportunity for vengeance was lost to them. 'And one remarkable thing, Madame, is that here and there on the roads an officer lay dead with several wounds in his back.'

'You mean? You mean by that?'

'That he was killed by his own men who wanted to surrender.'

'Oh God, Marie-Louise, when will these things end? Do you think the last of the Germans have gone by? Shall we have some peace from them now?'

'Monsieur Fleury thinks we've seen the last of them in Sainte-Marie.'

'God grant that he's right. Some peace at last.'

'I think he's right, Madame,' Marie-Louise comforted her. 'They seem to have all gone from Sainte-Marie. Perhaps it's all over for us. Not over for our poor France yet, but over for us.'

Sophie went up to the breakfast-room, the only chamber she ever occupied now, the hermit-cell in which she lived an anchorite's life day after day, day after day, and all of every day. She looked from its window. Certainly all was quiet around the house. The dogs lay in the garden, half asleep in the warm evening sun.

XVIII

A Strong-Point in Sainte-Marie

'ENTER thou into thy chambers and shut thy doors about thee,' sang Isaiah. 'Hide thyself until this indignation be overpast.' Sophie and Marie-Louise might believe that the indignation was overpast, but what these two women, shut within doors, did not consider was this: if the forest was a good way for columns on the retreat, it was also a good way for columns advancing. And since the policy of the advancers was to surround Paris and enforce its surrender rather than to do battle in its streets, and since Sainte-Marie was an obvious point in the encirclement to be subdued and held, the Americans were likely to appear at any moment, streaming down from the forest.

They began to understand this the next morning when the dogs suddenly leapt up from the breakfast-room carpet and barked and barked as seldom before, and the little bell on the garden gate rang, and Sophie, hasting to the window, saw a body of men in field-grey uniforms, steel-helmeted and high-booted, filing into her garden and forming up before the house. 'Seen the last of the Germans,' did Monsieur Fleury say? Then look at these. No glum and hunted Germans, these, but smart and purposeful men, apparently firm in discipline, with two stern young officers in parade dress, their belts and boots glistening in the sunlight. One of these two, well-groomed as ever, his empty right sleeve in his tunic pocket, was Major Clauss.

It was he who, having acted as guide perhaps, mounted the steps and knocked on the door.

Sophie who had watched with a hand pressing on her heart cried out to Marie-Louise from the stair-top, 'Oh, what now? Have they come for us? But there are so many. They can't need all these to take two women.'

'Let *me* go,' said Marie-Louise.

Marie-Louise drew open the door; Sophie came half-way down the stairs; Major Clauss bowed and spoke.

'Pardon,' he said. 'We——' but then he saw Sophie on her stair and clicked heels. 'Pardon, Madame, I regret having to inflict this further distress upon you, but we must occupy your house. It is likely that the enemy will attack Sainte-Marie, and it is unfortunate perhaps that your windows command the forest. I well remember the view from the room you gave me, and I took it upon myself to bring these men here. They have come from Paris, to oppose any advance upon Sainte-Marie. If the enemy comes this way we shall defend the house to the last man.' The fanatical gleam lit up in his eyes like a carbon filament. 'We have orders from our Führer to stand and die, if need be, and we shall certainly obey.' Sophie perceived at once that he wanted her to hear this because he was remembering how Klem had scoffed at the Führer. 'Now may we come in, Madame?'

'I cannot stop you,' she said, with the dignity that was the gift of despair. She wished she had the courage to show, like Klem, a contempt for these heroics of their Führer, but she had no such thing. She could only manage this show of dignity even though her heart held nothing but an ultimate despair. 'What do you wish to do? Where do you want to go?'

'Everywhere. To begin with, the rooms that face the forest road. Come in,' he said to the officer at his side. 'Bring the men in. You, Madame, had better leave the house. Doubtless you have friends near by who will take you in. We do not know what is going to happen here. May I ask you to go quickly?'

'I am not going from the house. Indeed I am not. This is my

home. I don't know what you are proposing to do with it, but I happen to think that my place is here and I have no intention of scurrying for shelter to someone else. I would have you know, Monsieur, that my first husband was a soldier, and that my son is now one too.' So she stated, inaccurately in both cases. She had surprised herself with the bold answer. It was not just an hysterical answer; it seemed to be something that belonged to this sudden enforced dignity; something too that belonged to the love she had once felt for this house and for all that was in it; something that belonged to her love for Klem, so much more perfect now that he was lost to her. And certainly the proud attitude was strengthened by the thought that the Americans who were expected were no enemies of hers but friends. Strengthened too by a long-rooted desire to do better before this man than she had done when he came to take Klem away. 'I do not leave my house for anyone, Herr Major.'

'Very good, Madame. I could of course compel you to go— this happens to be war—but I have every desire to respect your wishes. You have a cellar, perhaps?'

'There is a cellar, yes.'

'Well, I must insist that you take shelter there. You too, Mademoiselle.'

'Thank you,' said Marie-Louise, 'but I will stay in my kitchen.'

'I am afraid you may not. The kitchen has a ground-floor window, I imagine, and there are such things as bombs.'

'Bombs?' Sophie could not stop herself echoing this word.

'Hand-grenades, Madame. Thrown through the windows. So you see we cannot permit Mademoiselle to stay in her kitchen.'

'I am not "Mademoiselle". My name is Madame Benoît,' said Marie-Louise, angrily providing this untimely information.

'I apologize. Is there any way of escape from the cellar if they throw incendiaries into the house?'

'Incendiaries?' Sophie's hand had sought her brow, but she had quickly drawn it back, not to be seen suffering dismays.

'There's a window high up, a little below the level of the ground,' said Marie-Louise. 'I suppose we could crawl through that.'

'Good. Then will you both kindly go there. Thank you. Take over, Leutenant.' This was shot at the young officer who was apparently in command of the section or platoon. 'This is the house of the traitor I told you about. We dealt with him at Fresnes.'

Some of the men were in the hall, some on the steps. The young lieutenant, standing on the doormat, waved them in front of him. 'Upstairs, you and you. Top floors. Second floor you. And for God's sake keep those dogs quiet. Can't they be taken away? Mademoiselle, take them away or I'll have them shot. One can't hear oneself speak. Ten. . . . Twenty. That'll do for the middle floors.' His hand arrested the flow. 'You in this room here.' The hand pointed to the salon. 'You to the kitchens. All glass out of the windows. Every bit of it everywhere.'

'*No!*' Sophie had almost screamed this, suddenly shocked out of her dignity.

'Please,' complained the young man. 'There are such things as splinters. Into the cellar with you, *please.*'

Sophie could only shrug and descend the cellar steps. The scale was fully down and no new weight could sink it further. The dogs followed her, tripping down behind her in obedience to her sad call.

Standing in the cellar, she listened to the glass crashing and splintering into the garden as rifle-butts dashed it from window frames; crashing down from her room and Klem's; from the breakfast-room, so long her lonely habitat; from Rennie's room above. 'Oh, God . . . God. . . .'

Marie-Louise had followed her with two kitchen chairs, and there was nothing to do but sit down in this cellar, poorly lit by its one shallow window partly below garden level. And here they sat, listening to the heavy boots and blended voices overhead. They heard clips going into rifles, bolts drawn back, butts hitting floors as arms were ordered. The young lieutenant's voice shouted, 'You with the axe: hack all branches off the fir trees. Never mind

the trunks if they're too thick; leave them. If you *can* hack them
down, leave about a metre and a half standing.'

'Oh, my fir trees,' Sophie bewailed. 'Why must they cut them
down?'

The young man's voice seemed to answer her. 'Make haste.
We want a full field of fire. No dead ground anywhere if we can
help it.' The branches came splintering down.

'Oh . . .' It was a long sigh, but what was there to do but sigh?

From all that they could gather, sitting dismissed from the battle
down here below ground, it seemed that Major Clauss, knowing
this house so well, had chosen it for a command post and that
orders were being sent from it to a chain of other villas which,
facing the forest, had been turned into strong-points. It seemed
also, since they were hearing much of the Major's voice, that he,
though but one-armed and only a disabled and administrative
officer, was playing an ardent part in this last desperate command.

Marie-Louise sat with her hands joined on her apron; and because
her kitchen chair stood on a red-brick floor, and there was bottled
sunlight above her, caught in the trench behind the shallow window, it occurred to Sophie, in one of those irrelevant thoughts
which intrude upon any preoccupation, however wretched, that
she looked like a figure in a Dutch painting. While she was thinking this, Marie-Louise was trying to comfort them both. 'I'm
waiting for the Americans, Madame. These Fritzes won't keep
them out. Not for long. The Americans are carrying all before them
everywhere. Vive les Américains.'

'You mean they'll surrender?'

'Or be killed. "Stand and die" was what the Major said. You
heard him? And I suggest it meant he agrees with me that there's
not much else they can do. For which the good God be praised and
blessed.'

'You mean they'll all be killed here in my house?'

'Probably. I have no great objection to that.'

'But, Marie-Louise!' Sophie was remembering things that
Klem used to say. 'Most of them are only silly misguided boys

just doing what they've been forced to do. That was what Monsieur used to say.'

'Madame, posted up on their police station there is a new list of hostages whom they've executed—boys I knew, boys who'd done nothing but were just tied to posts and shot, twenty of them, as a reprisal for one filthy German killed. They've blown up a village where Germans have been killed—shooting all the men in the square and shutting all the women and children in the church and burning them alive. The children, Madame.'

'Well, I don't know . . .' Sophie demurred. 'I know what Monsieur would have said.'

Apparently Marie-Louise didn't wish to hear what Monsieur would have said. She wished to hear nothing that would abate the flow of her vengeance. 'Old Nicot, who's taken over command of the F.F.I. in our area, tells me,' she said, 'that they've executed seventy thousand Parisians in the last four years—and old Nicot's no liar. And what about those they've deported to their concentration camps and there tortured them or starved them to death? Madame, I think we have not tasted their tortures. Perhaps . . .'

'Yes, perhaps . . . perhaps . . . but I don't know. There's always Monsieur. . . .'

Marie-Louise, declining to listen, went on, 'We don't want these men from Paris blowing up Sainte-Marie and burning us in the church. Let them die. Up there. One and all.' She pointed to the ceiling. 'They're shooting our boys daily in a room at Issy-les-Moulineaux. Very well; let the Americans come and shoot them in every room they can find them. In my room for one, I hope. It'll never have been used for a better purpose.' Then she changed the subject. 'The Americans will be good to us, I think.'

'But my home? It will be a slaughter-house. Is that what you're saying?'

'Yes. We can clear up after them. I will.'

'But everything will be ruined. The place will be uninhabitable. Where shall we live? Where do we go to live? There's nowhere to go.'

'We don't go anywhere. We stay here. There are plenty of carpenters and joiners and glaziers in the F.F.I. and I know they'll come and make it so that we can live in it, even if only in one or two rooms. They'll do it for me, I know. I am one of them. It'll be all right, Madame. So now, dépêchez-vous, s'il vous plaît, Messieurs les Américains.'

Sophie, sitting there, again and again turned her eyes to this small woman who sat with folded hands on her apron, waiting untroubled for butchery upstairs. Strange the shapes of life that kept company with her in these days. All that she said in one silent interlude was, 'When I first came to look at this house and saw this nice large cellar, I thought how useful it would be. For many things. I never really had this in mind.'

'No,' said Marie-Louise. 'But here we are.'

It was not the Americans who came. Suddenly, down in that cellar, the two women heard an angry burst of rifle and automatic fire from the rooms above, but addressed, not towards the forest— no, the opposite way: towards the avenue and the Rue de la Forêt.

At the abrupt sound of it the dogs, leaping up towards the high window, almost surpassed the gunfire with their barking. They were barking towards the village. A burst of fire from outside met this fire from the house. The women heard its bullets impinging on the house walls. Marie-Louise rushed her chair to the wall beneath the window and mounted it. She peered through the glazing that was above ground.

'It's the F.F.I.! *Madame! The F.F.I.!* And the Maquis! Can you believe it? The Maquis are with them.'

'Keep down! Keep away!'

But either Marie-Louise did not hear or she was too exultant to obey. 'And there's Nicot. Dear old Nicot. Oh, he will do everything. He is wonderful.'

Not only had the F.F.I., the Forces Françaises de l'Intérieur, embodied since May all forces of the Resistance into one command, but since the day of invasion the Maquis, the men who had taken to the bush and the forests, had been fully mobilized for guerilla tactics ahead of the invaders' onrush, and behind the Germans resisting it. And now F.F.I. and Maquisards had come from the village, a hundred strong, on a joyous expedition, having learned that the Fritzes were turning some of the villas beneath the forest into strong-points. Already this expedition had reduced one villa and left a sergeant and men in occupation; now for this house; was it not their Marie-Louise's house?

'Oh Madame, look. Come and look.'

Through the privet hedge on that side of the garden, which the Germans had not troubled to cut down, Marie-Louise could see the Tricolor armbands of grey figures crouching and moving. From the windows of the one house across the avenue Sten guns, rifles, and a Bren were issuing, all ready to open a covering fire for those who would rush towards this house. Further down the avenue she saw a captured German lorry with 'F.F.I.' daubed in white on its camouflage; and at the corner of the avenue the roofs of cars with Tricolors flying from their aerials. From the lorry's side a Lewis gun stared over the hedge at the house and a trench mortar pointed at the sky. Even as she looked at the lorry a huge black Senegalese in a khaki shirt with 'F.F.I.' on his armband, rose above the Lewis gun and addressed towards the house a brilliant white smile; then quickly dropped back into cover.

'I know them! I know heaps of them!' cried Marie-Louise. 'That's my darling Boule-de-Neige, the sweetest thing. Oh, bless him.' And she forced open the window and began to crawl through it.

'Come back! Come back, Marie-Louise. Don't be quite mad.'

'It's all right, Madame. I can get to them. They are my friends. They all know me. I'll be with them before anyone sees me. I can tell them we're here. I can see that they don't throw any bombs near us or set the house on fire.'

'On *fire*?'

But Marie-Louise had wormed her small body through the window. This was to have been their way of exit in case of fire; but it was not the house that the attackers had set on fire; it was

213

the heart of Marie-Louise. She was through. Sophie, climbing on to the chair, but leaning back for fear of bullets, saw her run crouching through the piers of the garden gate and disappear. Safely, because the bullets from the house were flying either towards the lorry and the cars at the corner or over her head towards the opposite house. She did not know that Marie-Louise was taunting invisible enemies as she ran, 'Trop haut, mes amis, trop haut.' As Sophie peeped, the first grenade burst against a wall, and she came quickly from her chair. She stood alone in her cellar now, her heart pulsing with the gunfire, and a thumb-nail at her teeth.

Marie-Louise was safe among her friends; and her friends were young men with baggy trousers thrust into their socks, hand grenades in their belts, pistols in their hands, or Sten guns slung on their backs. Some wore steel helmets and high boots taken from Germans they'd slain. They were boys and men who had left shop-counters, office desks, factory benches, class-rooms for their part in the uprising. Paris had now risen by order of the National Council of the Resistance; and Sainte-Marie, its outlying satellite, had risen with it. The Underground was above ground now, out in the open, attacking buildings still held by Germans, manning barricades, ambushing tanks and arming more and more of themselves with the weapons of Germans killed. The Secret Army was everywhere on its feet, guns at the ready.

And it was more than possible that some of the weapons and some of the skill now to be used against this house had been brought to Paris by a British agent, André.

Among these men of Sainte-Marie there were some women and girls with red-cross brassards on their arms or little red-cross flags in their hands to hold up before the enemy. They had cars and stretchers round the corner in the Rue de la Forêt. With them were two sullen women whose hair had been shorn down to their scalps; women who had lain with the enemy and were now forced to purge their treachery by doing menial work for the Resistance.

Back among the women Marie-Louise saw the attack upon the

house. The F.F.I., directed by 'Nicot', an old grey barrel-bodied 'lieutenant', seventy-five at least, whose rank in the previous war had been a full colonel's, comprised men enough to reduce it quickly. With his second-in-command, young enough to be his grandson, this old grey commander directed men to points all round the house from which they could maintain a rapid covering fire upon every window-space while the men with the Stens and the grenades went in to the assault. These young men crouched along the avenue in single file, each close behind the other, and each holding a gun poised or a grenade ready for the swing.

But first he cried to them all, '*Wait*. Wait till I tell you to go.' And he called Marie-Louise to him. 'How many Krauts went into the house?'

'About thirty, Nicot.'

'Thirty. Then they can't have any hope of holding out against us. They've seen what guns we've got. We can drop the house over their ears. Wait all. Perhaps they'll surrender.'

But no sign of surrender came from the house. Rather did it open fire again at the house across the avenue.

'Oh, well,' said the old commander. 'If that's how they want it . . .' And to all his gunmen covering the house he bellowed in a voice astonishing from so old and plethoric a figure, '*FIRE!*'

Instantly an endless covering fire forced all heads down below Sophie's window sills, and '*Go!*' he bawled.

Crouching low, the young men rushed into the garden, cracking over the shards of broken glass, while the covering fire flew above their heads. They swung grenades into salon and kitchen; they bowled them through the unglazed windows of breakfast-room above. A small part of the breakfast-room wall burst into the garden, leaving a jagged hole through which you could now discern Sophie's work-table, apparently unhurt, unashamed, indifferent. The only rooms that received no grenades were Rennie's and Marie-Louise's—they were too high—and Sophie's bedroom which was difficult of approach from a narrow strip of garden. The only grenade thrown towards Rennie's room exploded, well timed, against the gable above it, blasting its rough cast and sham half-timbering; the only one directed at Sophie's room burst on the bricks beneath it.

Their immediate task accomplished, the young grenadiers raced back into the avenue, leaving one of their number fallen and writhing on the grass.

The house had gone silent; almost as if no one was left alive in it. But there were still those upper rooms. Men must be unhurt there.

'Wait,' commanded Nicot again. And all watched the house. But no sign. Silence.

'All right then. Get ready to go. Are you ready?' Again that mighty bellow, '*Fire!*'

The covering fire blazed at the house; the young men waited the order to go; but then Marie-Louise, creeping closer and peeping, saw something which it had never entered her head to expect. Over the sill of Monsieur Rennie's room there issued, and continued to issue—though no face showed itself—a white bed sheet which she recognized at once; it had been snatched from her bed in the next room.

Cheers rose from all the men as this flag of surrender drooped and fluttered down the front of the house. The women screamed and skipped. 'Aha!' said Nicot. One or two of the wilder youths in their joy shot a victory salvo into the sky, and were instantly ordered by him to stop. Did they want spent bullets to kill half the neighbourhood?

Nicot led the way into the garden, and was just making ready to go with his subaltern and some men into the house when from the window-space of the breakfast-room appeared the figure of Major Clauss with his left arm—his only arm—stretched forward in what looked like a Nazi salute but was really a gesture counter-ordering the surrender. '*No!*' he called. 'No surrender'—and instantly shots sounded in the room behind him and he fell forward over the sill like a bolster joining the sheet for an airing in the breeze.

'Oh, *no!*' Marie-Louise cried aloud in protest. 'He was not wholly bad. Oh . . . *no!*'

'You knew him?' asked Nicot, hearing her.

'Oh, yes. He lived with us; he lived in that room there—Monsieur Rennie's. I made him food when he was ill. It was he who took Monsieur Burgermann away, but even then he was not wholly bad. He tried to help Madame and me.'

'Dead? Is he dead? I think so.'

But Major Clauss strugged up again so far as his breaking knees would allow, lifted the one arm in what, this time, was really the Nazi salute and, turning suffering eyes to the sky, called out, 'Heil Hitler'; then fell from view like a puppet when the Punch and Judy show is over.

'That looks like all,' said Nicot. 'If they're killing their officers from behind, that's the lot. Come, boys, it's going to be safe enough to go in.'

He turned to the women who had now come crowding around him. 'My dears,' he said, 'we'll wave for you when we're sure it's safe for you to come. There must be plenty of work for you in there. Most of them are only wounded, I expect. Bring all your stuff and do your best for them like good girls. Remember these are not the Gestapo who tortured your father and brothers. Most of them, I'm sure, are just lads who in their own foolish way loved their country just as your own boys here do. And, anyhow, they're suffering now. Bring the stretchers. Come, men.'

But then Marie-Louise rushed up to him. 'Can I come too, Nicot? You must let me because——'

'Certainly not, Marquise.' Marquise was a new trade name which Nicot had given her; a partial pun on her real name. 'Why the devil should you come? Go away at once, Marquise, and try to be good.'

'But Madame is in there.'

'Madame? Madame Who?'

'Madame Burgermann. It's her house.'

'Mon Dieu! Where is she? Where the devil——'

'In the cellar.'

'Mon Dieu! And where's the cellar?'

'Under the kitchen at the back. *My* kitchen.'

'Oh, well, she may be safe there. Perhaps you'd better come.'

'I could show you around the house.'

'Oh, we'll find our way around all right. But come along, and if anyone shoots you, I'll kill them all. I promise you that, Marquise.'

'Merci, mon commandant.'

'Do you speak German?'

'No, but Madame does perfectly. She was married to——' but here Marie-Louise stopped, thinking it no time to expound the history and opinions of Monsieur.

'Oh, well, perhaps she'll do for an interpreter. If she's not dead. Maybe she's lying dead. Horrible pensée. Come along, Marquise.'

Gripping his automatic, a Colt, in his right hand, and followed by his subaltern, Marie-Louise, and a mob of his men, Nicot went up the steps to the threshold, where the door was opened to them by a German corporal.

'Hands up, Kamerad,' ordered Nicot.

The corporal obeyed, lifting both hands to the level of his head.

'A little higher please, Herr Corporal. Thank you. Cover them all, you others.' And Nicot with a number of the men entered the house, which immediately embraced them with a smell of blood, reeking explosives and fallen plaster-dust. It was silent now except for the moans of wounded and heavy-booted steps moving to and fro. Marie-Louise rushed to the top of the cellar stairs. 'Madame, Madame, come up. It's all over. This is Nicot, Madame. There's no danger any more.'

Sophie appeared at the top of the stairs, followed by the two dogs whom the detonations of battle overhead had beaten into silence and a terrified suspense. Her face was blanched but otherwise expressionless, the face of one who has sat in the very cellarage of despair, where misery's other name is acceptance. At sight of her a jubilant young maquisard, guessing who she was, flung up his arms in triumph and said—or shouted—'C'est fini, Madame

C'est tout. Vive la France. Vive Sainte-Marie. Vive tout le monde.'
He danced a tap dance before her, hands still on high. 'Vive votre
maison. Vive tous vos jolies choses. Vive les petits chiens.'

She smiled sadly, and threw sad eyes around her riddled home.
The door of the salon stood open and she glanced into it. The
sun, unperturbed, uninterested, was shining through the empty
window-frame, and she saw two men lying dead or wounded
there, one on his face, the other on his side with knees drawn up,
like a man in a warm bed. Their blood lay dark on the carpet. A
Louise Seize chair and the chaise-longue stood unharmed amid the
fragments of plaster and on the stretches of bloodstained white
dust. A second fascinated glance showed her the hanging oval
mirror in its gilt rococo frame with asterisks splintered over its
face. Remembering the day when she bought it, she almost laughed
as she thought, 'It was never meant to reflect a scene like this.'

Men and women were now mounting her stairs, some with
folded stretchers on their shoulders. They caused her to hear, but
without feeling, the moanings of men in her rooms above.

Nicot said, 'Madame, I am desolated to have damaged somewhat
your beautiful home, but, believe me, we have boys of every trade
on earth in the F.F.I., builders and plasterers and painters, and we'll
do all we can to make it agreeable for you again. And for Marquise.
N'ayez aucune inquiétude, chère Madame. Marquise, where can
we put Madame for a few days. This is no place for her until we've
got it in some sort of order. There are friends near at hand who will
take her in, I am sure? Perhaps you and she——'

But Sophie interrupted him. 'Oh no—please—I must stay here.
Someone must be here to take care of everything——' she
said it sadly, meaning all her furniture and ornaments whether
broken or whole, and not wishing to leave even the ruins of them.
'If your men could really patch up a room or two where we could
live . . .'

'We will certainly do our best, Madame. But meantime, just
for a little while we clear the house, you must be away, I think.
This is no place for you, the middle of a battlefield.'

'Yes, Madame,' said Marie-Louise, laying a hand on her arm. 'There is Madame Donnay. She will welcome you in.'

'But why is it no place for me, Monsieur, even if it is a battle-field? I am ready to help with the wounded. My first husband was a soldier and died on a battlefield. Let me go now and give some help. This is, after all, my house.'

Nicot smiled understandingly but shook his head. 'We have plenty of young women to look after the wounded, Madame. Had we not, I would willingly accept your help. As it is, we would rather you were away for a while, I think; and perhaps before the day is over we'll have a room or two ready for you——'

But here a tall, harsh-faced man of the Maquis who had been watching and listening, said, 'Stop! You make a mistake, Nicot. This woman is a traitor.'

Marie-Louise swung round to him. 'What do you *mean*?'

'We know all about her. She was a secret collaborator.'

'She was *not*!'

'Oh, but yes, she was. We've heard all about her. She collaborated for a long time with the top Germans in her house, and when her English son came for help she turned him away. Her son was an English aviator who crashed, Nicot, and he came here for shelter and she refused it. The Germans have told us all about her. Why, it was Marquise herself who told all this to them when they came to take this woman's German husband off to Fresnes. That's why they spared her. That's why she's living in peace here now. And that's why she's on Balzac's list now.'

For Sophie this was a moment of death-in-life. Her heart seemed shot in her body, but she was standing in her own house, alive. Was she to be taken away like Klem? Hanged? Agony—death—in an hour? If so, could she go like Klem—with courage? Oh, God . . . courage . . . like Klem. Most strangely, for a second, a flash of time, she thought she might be able to do this. It was a proud, flashing moment, almost happy in its pride, almost a moment of peace.

But Marie-Louise had taken a step towards the man. He was

tall and heavy, and she seemed less than half his size as she stared up at him. 'And how long have *you* been in the Maquis?' she asked. 'Not much more than half a year, I think. You've learned all this very quickly. Where did you pick it up? It's not so long that *you've* been good enough to do anything to help us.' Face turned up to him, head thrust forward, she seemed to spit the questions up into his suddenly dazed eyes. 'I don't remember that *you* were around when Darc was killed and Monsieur, Madame's husband, was taken away. That's why all your information is ever so slightly wrong, you see. Picked up a year or so too late. May I suggest that you only decided it would be a good idea to join the Maquis when you knew the Boches were going to lose their war? Only just in time, in fact. Am I right, comrade?'

The man had lifted a fist in a threat to bring it down on her. 'How could I join the Maquis when it's only been organized a few months? Will you tell me that? I joined it directly I could. Before that I did what I could to help.'

'And precious little that was. And precious late in the day, I seem to remember. I've noticed that those who were a little late in getting into the Underground are always the loudest in denouncing others as traitors. It's safer for them.'

'Shut up, Marquise,' said Nicot.

'I will not shut up. This house has been working for the Underground for four long years. I was in it from the beginning. So was Darc—Mademoiselle Jeanne who killed herself in the end rather than give anyone away. She always told me she would. Two in this house have died for France while this gentleman, I suggest, was wondering what was best to do to save his skin——'

'Marquise, I will not have this!'

'Oh yes, you will. He's going to hear a little more. Two have died for France: Darc and her poor good father. And it should have been three. Why *I* haven't been killed more than once in the last four years I simply don't know. Probably because none of you thought I was sufficiently important to worry about. And to all this may I add that my husband who lives in this house with me was fighting for France when you, Monsieur, were God knows where, and he's been a prisoner all these four years. Madame knew all about me and all about Darc, and so did Monsieur. That was why they took him. She saw her husband taken away through that door to die.'

'*And* she turned her son away,' repeated the man sourly.

'So she did. Because she was afraid. Were *you* never afraid, my brave man? If not, I wish we could have had your help earlier. Yes, in a moment of fear to which we women, unlike you big brave men, are liable, she turned her son away.' As she said this, a sudden inspiration lit up in Marie-Louise's eyes; a wonderful inspiration it seemed; plainly she was wondering why she had not thought of it before. 'And do you know,' she said to the man, 'who her son is?'

'No, and I don't care.'

'Even so, it may interest you to know. His name is André.'

In amazement both the man and Nicot gaped at her. The man gasped, 'André? Do you mean——'

'Yes, our André. Oh, yes; and for all I know that pistol on your belt of which you're so proud, and with which, maybe, you want to kill Madame, was brought to you by him. His weapons were mostly given to you late arrivals.'

'Is this really so, Marquise?' asked Nicot.

'Of course it is. Wait.' Without further answer she rushed into her kitchen and dragged open a dresser drawer to fumble in it noisily. They waited in silence, while men bore on stretchers the dead or wounded past them. All the time the creaking footsteps and the loud voices and the few moans sounded overhead. Marie-Louise did not find in her first drawer what she wanted—where had she hidden it?—so she banged the drawer testily home, and dragged open another. Not here; and she cursed this delay while Madame's fate was in question. She found it at last, and rushed back with it. It was an unmounted photograph of Rennie in R.A.F. uniform, and across a bottom corner was inscribed, 'For my beloved Marie-Louise and for my dear Frédé of whom I am so jealous.'

'Is that André by any chance?' she asked, passing it to the man. As he looked at it she jeered. 'Perhaps you'll tell me that's not André. The Frédé he mentions happens to be my husband.'

The man passed it to Nicot who said to Sophie, 'This is your son?'

'Certainly he is my son,' said Sophie, acknowledging him at last, and Marie-Louise said, 'Now touch his mother if you dare.'

Both men were silent. So she added more quietly, 'She's known all about his being here. She even met him in the forest. André is still with us. Lay your hand on her and then go and tell him what you've done.'

Nicot only murmured, 'André! Mon Dieu!'

The angry man spread open palms at the side of his hips as much as to ask, 'Who was to know this?' and after some hesitation and a shrug, walked away.

Steps on the stairs coming down. Young men of the F.F.I., their automatics proudly held, were bringing the unwounded down as prisoners. These, mostly large young men, came without belts or arms, with their jackets open and their hands joined on the tops of their caps or the crowns of their steel helmets. They passed by and out into the garden.

'Madame,' said Nicot, 'we owe a great deal to your son. I thank you in the name of the Patron who commands us all.'

'My son is with you? Alive and well?'

'He was with us only yesterday. Today he is with Colonel Rol who commands in Paris.'

'They are fighting there? We heard they were.'

'Indeed they are. Fighting for the last five days, and largely with weapons brought by André. For which—' and he bowed with an old man's gallantry again—'je vous remercie.'

'Oh, but is the fighting severe?'

'Don't be afraid, Madame. If ever André was in the Underground he is now. He is with Rol and his staff who are controlling

the fight from all the tunnels and sewers of Paris. Their Headquarters is a hundred and eighteen steps down—and unfortunately
a hundred and eighteen steps up. As I know to my cost. I am not
as slight as I was. So don't worry: Monsieur André is probably
racing with Rol's orders along about five hundred kilometres of
sewers just now.'

'You are winning? Your F.F.I. is winning?'

'Bien sûr! The Boches are finished, and we shall remove them
from our beloved Paris just as we are removing them from this
house of yours Madame—either with their hands above their
heads or their feet first on stretchers. Then, no doubt, we shall be
able to send your son to you.'

'Oh, *will* you?'

'Yes, Madame. Do not be sad. This is a great day. And for sure
we will remake your home for you if only for André's sake. Now if
you will go with Marquise——'

'I must first make myself tidy,' said Sophie, so much happier
now, and relapsing into old habit. 'May I go up to my room?'

'But yes, Madame. But certainly. This is your house.'

'I will go with you,' said Marie-Louise, as if fearing what Sophie
might see there.

Nicot bowed to both of them in a graceful consent and farewell.

They walked up to Sophie's bedroom, picking their way through
fragments and chunks of plaster, crushing spent cartridge cases
under their feet, avoiding cavities and rifts in floor and stair-treads.
The sun poured into the bedroom as into the salon below, and
from the passage she saw two men lying side by side on the bed,
their faces upward and their bodies as still as two stone figures on a
tomb. Their glazed eyes showed that they were dead. Their blood
lay soaked into her counterpane. This room had received nothing
but machine-gun bullets from the house opposite, so it was only
superficially scathed and had been used as a place in which to lay the
dead. Presumably, she thought, young Major Clauss was now lying
on his old familiar bed upstairs—Rennie's. Schlafen Sie wohl, mein
Herr. Poor Jean's 'Good-night' to him, years ago.

'Pardon,' said an elderly F.F.I. man in the passage, apologizing for these unsuitable corpses in her bedroom, as he bowed Sophie politely through her door.

She gave another look at them but, inured now to all things, only turned aside and sat herself before her Louis Quinze marquetry poudreuse and such bottles and jars of cosmetics as were still intact and on parade below the splintered mirror. Occasionally, as she repaired her face, she looked at the reflection of those two, lying side by side on the bed where she and Klem had lain.

XIX

Tenez Bon Nous Arrivons

WHILE the F.F.I. were fighting in the streets of Paris on the day after the fight for the chateau, a light aeroplane flew above the running battles; and when it was over the Préfecture de Police which was now—the police having struck and risen against the enemy—a central fortress of the Rising, it let fall a message from General Leclerc, commanding the 2nd Armoured Division of the Fighting French, which was already drawing near the gates of the city. Yesterday, while the chateau was falling, the General had received his order from the G.O.C.-in-C. to 's'emparer de Paris'and to take his Frenchmen in, first of all the Allies. The message fell at the corner of the Préfecture on the Quai du Marché Neuf. It said:

'Tenez bon nous arrivons'

And they arrived. They arrived that same day as night darkened over Paris. A little before nine o'clock their leading tanks bearing great French names, 'Valmy', 'Papa Joffre', 'D'Artagnan', 'Père la Victoire', came roaring through the Porte d'Orléans and along the Avenue d'Orléans and the Rue Sainte-Jacques towards the bridges over the Seine, while the packed multitude cheered and roared and wept. 'Les Français! C'est la Division Leclerc!' Probably a majority could hardly say or shout it for weeping. The tanks rumbled over the bridges and were now in the heart of Paris, the Ile de la Cité. They crossed the further bridges and halted in the great Place before the Hôtel de Ville. The moment was twenty-two minutes past nine. Scenes famous and scenes terrible that great square had witnessed, but never one like this. Amid the uproar of cheers and the singing of the Marseillaise and the hysterical laughter that struggled with tears two oily, sweating, bedraggled and unshaven men from the heart of a tank, an officer and a private, Captain Dronne and Private Pirlian of the Tchad Regiment, who had been fighting their way for four years from French Equatorial Africa to Paris, were dragged and borne by men of the F.F.I. into the Hôtel de Ville, to be embraced by the President of the National Resistance Committee and the Prefect of the Seine. The President, holding the tired captain in his arms—and weeping a little—said, 'Mon capitaine, in the name of France's soldiers without uniform I salute in your person the first soldier in French uniform to reach Paris.' The Prefect, when his turn came, said with a like Parisian eloquence, 'Bienvenu, mon capitaine. Bienvenu, Monsieur Pirlian. And now will you who have been marching to Paris for four years, all the way from Tchad in Africa, meet our men of the Underground who have sprung out of its shadows and up from its pavements to fight with you and to greet you as their brothers.'

Among those in the Prefect's office who stood by his Colonel Rol, watching these embraces and gulping down a loud in his throat—was a British agent with the field name of André. He was thinking, 'Dear Uncle Klem, you are not here; nor you, dear Jean; but I feel I am watching this for you. May I represent you, and, yes, others in the Underground whom I learned to love quite a little, such lively lads and brave old boys they were; but they are not here tonight any more than you are. They are where you are. In your name and the name of these dear dead friends, bienvenu, mon capitaine. Bienvenu, Monsieur Pirlian.'

Next afternoon this André, in the form of Flight-Lieutenant Rennie Quentin, burst into the little chateau at Sainte-Marie. He had heard in Paris all about the joyous recapture of the house. It was not difficult to burst into it because the door was open and

227

men were in the salon, removing the temporary boarding from the window frame and substituting some sort of temporary transparent material. Sophie had consented after all to stay two nights with Madame Donnay in the village but was now back home. Marie-Louise had never left the house, but had enjoyed helping her F.F.I. friends in their work and seeing that it was sensible. 'Oh, lord, lord . . .' Rennie said as he saw the general wreck. 'God, they've made a fair old mess of it, haven't they?' But he was too excited to say or think more. He rushed into the kitchen, seized Marie-Louise round her waist and held her, as usual, high in the air, while he danced about and shouted, 'Paris is free. Surrendered half an hour ago. Come and see it all. Vive la France. Vive Marie-Louise.' Then he set her down on the floor and said, 'Come at once. Paris is liberated and Monsieur Rennie did some of it. But Marie-Louise did much more. Get your hat. One of your real festive hats. Your most celebrated hat. Where's the lady? She's got to come too.'

'She's upstairs in the breakfast-room. It's the only room your miserable F.F.I. have so far made fit to live in, after smashing everything up.'

'Good old F.F.I.,' he said inappropriately and dashed up the stairs. 'Come along, Madame. Come and see. The whole German garrison has surrendered and now a whole Frog division is going to pour into Paris.' He was in the breakfast-room and in her arms. 'You who have never missed anything are not going to miss this. Come on'; and he began to pull her towards the door.

'But, my darling, my darling, I must make myself presentable first.'

'Fiddle-faddle. Come at once before it's over. You who've always pretended to be crazy about Paris, you've got to come and weep with the whole population. I've been weeping all yesterday and today.'

'Yes, but . . . oh, Rennie, is the war over? Is it over?'

'No, it's not, but it's over round here, thanks very much. We've still got to take Berlin. But that can wait. Let the old Boche wait.

Sorry to keep him waiting. Come along. I've got red-cross arm-bands for you and Marie-Louise in case any pompous idiot tries to stop us anywhere. I've enrolled you both for the afternoon as "infirmières de la Croix Rouge". Don't worry about the house and the frightful mess it's in. My boys'll see to that. They'll do anything for me. Powder your nose and come. Or powder it in the car. I've got my little Citroën outside. She's the fastest little girl in Paris, and that's saying quite a lot. She'll get us there in twenty minutes.'

Now indeed two ruling passions of Sophie's life were locked in conflict, the one her need to decorate her person for the public view, the other, her need, her craving, to miss no spectacle that was at hand and that others were seeing. It was a speedy battle in which neither party scored a convincing victory but the craving could be adjudged the winner on points. For Sophie to give less than seven minutes to dressing for the street was certainly a victory of sorts and proof of a powerful contestant. Seven minutes while Rennie stamped impatiently in the hall or called sarcasms up the stairs or begged Marie-Louise, who was waiting at his side, to go up and drag the woman down, and while Sophie kept calling, 'I'm coming. Just coming. Oh, dear, oh dear,' so tormenting is it when one's soul is a battlefield; seven minutes and she was down with them and being drawn by Rennie's hand to the Citroën at the gate, while the F.F.I. workmen at the window offered encouraging cheers. It was remarkable what she had achieved in those few minutes. Rennie complimented her on it, as he dragged her into the car beside him; then the little springy car went bouncing and leaping over the few miles to Paris, while Sophie appealed, 'Oh, Rennie . . . Rennie . . . do . . . do be careful,' and Marie-Louise held tight to the straps at the back.

'Keep calm,' was all he enjoined. 'Keep calm and collected.'

'Collected?' Sophie questioned the word. 'I'm being not so much collected as distributed.'

'Well, never mind. Can't be helped for once. C'est la guerre, quoi?'

'But it's a pity, if the war is really over round here, to die like this.'

'Skip all that. No one's going to die. Here we are.'

He was entering Paris by the Porte de la Chapelle. The white-painted F.F.I. on his car won him an easy passage along the Boulevard de Strasbourg and the Boulevard de Sebastopol; and thence over the bridges to the Left Bank and the Rue Saint-Jacques. Here was his goal, for the whole French Armoured Division was rumbling and drumming along this ancient Roman highway which had once seen the Legions go by. In giant American Sherman tanks like giant prehistoric reptiles, drumming, drumming onward, with huge guns pointing ahead; in strings of armoured cars; in jeeps; in open staff cars; and on foot they were heading for the centre of the capital and the centre of France: the Place du Parvis Notre Dame and the Place de l'Hôtel de Ville. Tricolors and the Cross of Lorraine flew from many a tank, jeep or car. Rennie, Sophie and Marie-Louise were soon but three heads among the close-thronged cheering, bellowing people, to whom, only a little while ago, the policemen had been yelling, 'All civilians indoors. There are plenty of Germans about who haven't yet heard of the surrender and they may shoot'; a command which no one obeyed, the crowds merely answering, 'Vive la Police'. The crowds stayed packed on the pavements, hanging on to lamp-standards. Such civilians as were still indoors leaned from their window-sills to watch and cheer or stood for the same purpose on their roofs (if roofs can be said to be indoors). Girls pushed their way through the lines of police with apologies—'Vive la Police' —so as to climb on to the hulls of the tanks and embrace all the gentlemen thereon, and to do the like with the men in the jeeps and the officers in the staff cars. Many of these girls did not return but remained seated on the tanks or standing on the footboards of the cars or hanging permanently attached to men who marched on foot. Here and there one of them hung from the waist of a huge Senegalese, black as the oldest oak, and widely grinning.

Rennie, ever and again thumping Marie-Louise on the back in

his excitement, urged her to go and do likewise. 'Go on. I give you my full permission. Go on. It's your duty. How can you just stand there and not do your manifest duty by the poor boys? Kiss 'em all. I shan't tell Frédé.' And Marie-Louise, deeply infected at last, dashed through and struggled on to a tank, momentarily halted. She kissed one soldier, holding his cheeks between both her hands, and while she was so engaged the tank started abruptly, and carried her away with it. Marie-Louise was last seen that day seated in comfort on a Centurion tank.

Now overhead, many bombers came flying very low so that the roaring of their engines might join the roaring of the crowd and demonstrate a kindred joy. The Rue Saint-Jacques, already quaking beneath the iron rotation and drumming of the tank-tracks, now trembled even more because of this rolling thunder so near to the ground. Windows and shutters and doors vibrated in response and shared in the enthusiastic din. As one aeroplane after another roared up and away it saluted the company with a victory roll.

Rennie, left alone with Sophie, looked at the cordoned police struggling to hold back the crowds while unable to keep the girls from slipping under their linked hands or elbows and joining the army, and he was soon possessed by a pleasing idea. He submitted it to Sophie. As follows. When the police, seven days before, had struck work and turned their Préfecture into a fortress of the Rising, Messieurs les criminels of Paris had struck work too, saying, 'We also are Frenchmen. Vive la Police.' But now that all was victory and rejoicing there was really no need for them to desist from profitable labour any more. Besides, were not houses and shops and parked cars and coat pockets all unattended, and were not the admirable and patriotic police fully occupied? So Rennie suggested to Sophie, and was later proved to have been remarkably accurate in his reading of the situation, that Messieurs les criminels, rejoicing in the liberation of their city, were now occupied in liberating pocket-books, watches, bicycles, bags, and bottles of wine and packets of food for their own patriotic celebration in the evening.

There was hardly a happier woman in any of the massed crowds than Sophie on this day. She had her tall son at her side, her arm in his that they might not be torn apart, and often in his happiness he pressed her arm hard against his side. 'Is it really almost the end of the war, darling?' she asked, addressing the words into his ear so as to be heard in the noise.

'Almost. A month or two more perhaps while we take Berlin. Maybe six or seven months, but the end is sure, and nothing can stop it. The whole world knows that. Peace early next year perhaps, and then . . . ?'

And then? Had he really meant it, she asked, when he said she could go back to England and live near him? Not too near, of course. Not to be a nuisance to him in any way.

'Of course I meant it,' he roared. '*With* me, I hope.'

'Oh, but no, you'll get married. You're sure to.' And she thought how the citizens of Sainte-Marie had called him a 'beau jeune homme'.

'Well, we'll see about that, but you'll have to be near at hand so that we can often get together and talk about Paris and Sainte-Marie. Especially about these last days. And all this, all this. By the way, I wonder if we shall ever see Marie-Louise again. And will she be properly intact, if we do? I mean, there's no Frédé to protect her modesty. Nor me. I suppose some of it all will fade out of memory as the years go by, but—God, we should have enough to talk about till the end of our lives.'

She would go, she thought, saying no more. It wouldn't hurt her now to leave that little house in Sainte-Marie. It had seen too much. And every street in Sainte-Marie, and every glade in the forest, held its memories which were best left there, veiled a little, muted a little, by the mercy of distance.

The last of the Armoured Division passed by, and now the crowds were streaming, slowly because packed so densely, towards the great boulevards—des Italiens, Capucines, Montmartre—and the great squares—Concorde, Carrousel, Vendôme, Opera, Bastille.

Evening, and Sophie and Rennie, the drumming of the tanks still in their ears, wandered along these boulevards and from one famous square to another, pausing often to watch the dancing, for now there was dancing in the midst of them all. Every girl in Paris was dancing with a soldier, sailor, F.F.I. man, or her private boy-friend, accompanied here by a peripatetic concertina, there by a dancing fiddle, here by a radio set, there by a gramophone, each from a window open to the night. Paris had not danced in its streets for four empty years; but Paris was itself again tonight. Little traffic disturbed the dancers on the wide boulevards; only perhaps a jeep with cheering Americans inside it or over its bonnet, or a traditional fiacre from the Champs Elysées with Americans crowded into its seats and one of them astride its horse. Above the dancing, from many windows and motionless in the still evening air, hung the flags which for years had been hidden and waiting for today. And everywhere, ever renewed, from standing groups, or from gaily marching throngs, came the chorus, women's voices shrilling above the men's: 'Allons, enfants de la Patrie, Le jour de gloire est arrivé.'

Then, suddenly, the darkness being fully down, all eyes were drawn to a flood of light on the western sky. Two long searchlight beams had shot up from the Champ de Mars and written, almost from horizon to zenith, a giant V on the empty blue sheet of sky. It raised a roar of greeting, and Rennie flung his arm round Sophie's waist and crushed her against him, as they looked at it together. She felt the trembling of his arm. Victory for Paris. It seemed the answer to her old prayers that she should be watching it within the trembling arm of the son she had left so long unacknowledged and once turned out into the night.

XX

Three Return

THIS might well have closed our story of an ornate and rather pretentious little villa beneath the Sainte-Marie forest, and of its chatelaine, when waves of war beat up against, and all around, and into her home. But it seems there are three more things that should be touched upon before we leave Sainte-Marie for good.

It is eight months since that day when General Leclerc's Armoured Division marched into a liberated capital. And here comes another army marching along the Strasbourg-Nancy road with its eyes towards Paris. And yet not an army, nor strictly marching, for they do not come abreast but in straggling units of three or two or even one alone. And most are unshaven men, pale, hollow-thin, and wearing dilapidated civilian garments or the tattered remnants of French battle-dress reinforced, maybe, by newer and robuster parts of German uniforms. Refugees?

No, the opposite. Homecomers. The wide steel curtain of war, driving like a local storm-area out of France and into Germany, has broken open the gates of all the prison camps as it swept by. And since there were two million Frenchmen and more in the prisoner-of-war camps there are other columns like this one; they are flooding like tides on the Ludwigshafen–Metz road, and the Frankfurt–Luxembourg road, and all the other highways that converge from Germany upon Paris. In the happy phrasings of the Psalmist, these exiles have had their captivity turned as the rivers in the south; and now, their five Babylonish years behind them, they are coming again with joy, but like unto them that dream.

Our business is with one only on the Strasbourg–Nancy road. He is bigger than most Frenchmen and has kept some of the rotundity which he carried five years ago into captivity. His ragged uniform is remarkable—or it would be in any other company— because his trousers were once part of French battle-dress and his jacket, flying open, is the black tunic of a German S.S. man with all its insignia torn off. Yesterday, his own tunic being worn and ragged and cold, he dragged this one from the body of a dead German. Hat he has none, and his hair, close-cropped weeks ago, stands up *en brosse*. Under his arm is a bundle wrapped in a filthy blanket—though what he could have found to bring out of prison it is difficult to say. It is three days since the gate of his prison near Frieburg in Breisgau was flung open by the First French Army coming in power and wrath through the Black Forest.

Like all these others tramping with him he has not been able to wait for organized transport but has set out on impatient feet to make his way home. Already he has walked seventy miles without help from lorry or car, there being too many of these ghostly revenants on the highway for lorries and cars to do anything but gather up a few and help them onward. At last, however, the column thins out as the cars and lorries and American jeeps pick up more and more, or as men force themselves into stationary trains; and at Saint-Dizier this big man with the bundle has his turn of luck, for here the admirable Americans have provided several of their transport planes 'to bring these poor guys home'; and he with many companions is crowded into one of them. He slumps down into it with a sigh like a furnace and a grin and his bundle on his lap. Only a hundred and eighty kilometres to Paris. Why, an American aeroplane will do it in an hour.

It does it in less. There below is the square-pyramid steeple of Saint-Denis's great church. Oh, let him look. Almost, if his eyes sweep the green relief-map asway below, he can see his home in the north-west. There at any rate is the forest on its hills.

But no time to look properly. The plane is curving down to Le Bourget's airport. It touches down and stops, and all the men hurriedly rise to file out and feel their feet on an outskirt of Paris. Only think: from Le Bourget an autobus runs to the Gare du Nord and the Gare de l'Est and the Place de l'Opéra.

This man with the bundle, so eager his rising, dropped everything in it on to the floor, and some things rolled out of sight. He had to wait till all the men had crowded past before he could reassemble everything into the blanket again. It was not easy to find everything and he was alone in the plane for some minutes. This didn't seem to matter. Nobody came near him. So he took the opportunity to visit the toilette, to which he'd felt a strong call during most of the journey. Thus it was quite a time before he came alone, with his bundle under his arm, out of the aeroplane door and on to the waiting stairs.

He had hardly done so before he heard a loud voice call men to attention. Lifting his eyes, he looked ahead. There, between him and the reception building of the airport, he saw two ranks of French airmen facing inwards on each other and standing at rigid attention. They seemed to be all young boys as if specially selected for this duty. But why at attention, since they had no one near them but their young officer? Being modest and shy like many big men, he walked off at an angle to avoid them, but an airport worker in a blue smock, seeing this, called out, 'Non, non! Par là,' pointing to this odd little parade.

'But why?' demanded the big man.

'Par là.'

'But what is it?'

'Pass through them, Monsieur. Like the others. It is the same for all. They wait for you. They suspect that you have been relieving yourself and they wait.'

And now the young officer was motioning to him that he must come between the two rows—yes, even in his dilapidated clothes and with his dirty bundle. He spread his hands as if begging to be excused, but the officer cried severely '*Non, non!*' and then with a kindlier smile indicated the avenue between his young men. So this solitary man, as ragged as any hobo of Paris, obeyed; and as he neared the young men the officer called all to the salute. Their left hands slapped against their rifles held stiffly upright against their sides; the officer's hand shot to the peak of his cap; and all hands stayed at the salute till he, with his bundle, had passed. In his confusion, embarrassment and gratitude he saluted them all nervously, without a hat.

Of all the V.I.P.s who had arrived at this airport probably none, unless perhaps a royal person, had been given such a guard of honour.

Having passed through, he heard the officer stand his men at ease again, and later dismiss them.

From Le Bourget to the Gare du Nord; and there, to his delight, Frédé found a train that left in seven minutes for Sainte-Marie.

§

Sophie sat behind her sewing-machine in the breakfast-room. The wheel of the machine hummed round, and her thoughts were helped by its rhythm and music. In the eight months since the F.F.I. attacked the house much of it had been restored. All the windows had been glazed again and the fallen ceilings repaired. Only the walls, not yet properly replastered, and this familiar table at which she sat, showed their gashed and open wounds. She was thinking, hardly able to believe her thoughts, that it would be only days now before the war was over. And then . . .?

On the table at her side lay the new *Paris-Presse*, no longer German controlled. An hour ago she had been reading that the British army had driven more than eighty miles beyond the Rhine; that the Americans were west of Eisenach in Germany; and that the First French Army had reached Friedrichshafen after storming through the Black Forest. Total victory soon, and peace, and England. And Rennie.

The dogs barking; the little bell on the gate; steps on the gravel. At once she was at the window, but not quickly enough. Whoever it was must have gone round to the back and the kitchen door. Her own door was open in the warm spring afternoon and, as she dashed to it to listen, she heard the cry of joy from Marie-Louise in her kitchen and her sobbing—and two words, 'Frédé! Frédé. . . .'

Though the name set curiosity and excitement alight, Sophie did not rush downstairs. This was Marie-Louise's moment; she and Frédé must have it alone. After listening a moment longer she went back to her chair and her machine. Marie-Louise would come running up with her exultation soon—very soon.

'Madame! Madame!' Yes, here she was.

'Yes, Marie-Louise?' Almost as if one had no idea what she was coming to say. But one could go to the door again, justly, since one had been summoned like this. Sophie went to her door, and there was Marie-Louise dragging Frédé up the stairs behind her as a child brings a present or a prize to show to parents above.

She brought him to the door of the room, where he bowed to Madame and stood grinning awkwardly.

'Frédé! Come in. Where have you sprung from? Come in. Sit down and tell me all.'

'But I am in a very dirty state, Madame. Mucky. I have walked most of the way from Germany. My boots—look at them. It was only for the last hundred kilometres that I got a lift in a plane. I think I had better not sit down.'

Marie-Louise: 'No, he mustn't sit down.'

'Sit down at once, Frédé. You must be tired, walking all the way from Germany. And anyhow most of the furniture in this house is ruined. Sit down, both of you. This is a great moment. Let's hear all that Frédé has to tell us.'

But Marie-Louise, excitement driving her, did all the talking at first. Even in the act of sitting down, even while arranging herself on the chair, she poured out, 'He has come back loaded with presents, Madame. You should see them in the kitchen: bottles of wine, a huge saucisson, a packet of sweets, lovely flowers, a bottle of champagne. He met Madame Henriot in the Avenue de

238

la Gare and stayed talking with her a little, you see, and soon the whole street had heard about him and came rushing out to see him. And they all dashed back into their shops to find presents for him. Monsieur Hugues gave him a beautiful basket to carry them. He said it was his present. Frédé just walked into the kitchen with the dirtiest bundle you ever saw under one arm and a big basket of marvellous things on the other.'

Frédé, having gathered courage to speak a little, proffered one reason why the people should have behaved like this. 'They said Marie-Louise had been so good, Madame.'

'Well, that was no exaggeration, Frédé.'

'We must drink the champagne with Madame,' said Marie-Louise, evading this topic.

Then Frédé, further encouraged by Sophie, told them about his prison camps, while Marie-Louise sat there, hands joined on her apron, and gazed at him proudly. He explained that, compared with the deportees and political prisoners, a prisoner-of-war was a comparatively protected person. 'Conditions were bad enough, Madame, but the Geneva Convention prevented the Boches doing to us the things they were doing to the deportees in the concentration camps. Even if they'd have liked to defy the Geneva Convention, they couldn't very well because there was always, vous voyez, the danger of reprisals. We had rights. It was the poor civilian prisoners who had no rights. I saw some of them on the road in their horrible striped prison suits—long blue and white stripes up and down them, Madame, just like striped pyjamas— and they looked like walking corpses. Corpses in striped pyjamas, we said. We were not like that.'

Still, he gave them some examples of the brutalities, tortures and gross, unjust executions practised in the prison camps to which he'd been consigned; and he described them so quietly, and with so little heat, that Sophie asked with surprise, 'Frédé, hasn't it made you hate all Germans for ever and ever?'

He didn't answer at once. Then he said, 'I did feel like that at first, Madame, and for a long time afterwards. But five years in prison gives you a lot of time to sit and think, and at last I began pointing out to myself—I didn't want to, Madame, but somehow I had to, when I was thinking properly—that if some of our guards were mad, savage brutes, there were some who were not. There were some who tried to be good to us and help us. So I told myself there were probably other Germans like them outside the S.S. and the Gestapo. Plenty of them, perhaps. And of course, Madame, I thought of Monsieur.'

§

Only a few days later, the concentration camp at Schirmeck in Alsace having been burst open by the First French Army, a deportee arrived at the little station of Sainte-Marie. He was in a special train filled with other emaciated, convict-cropped, ill-clad deportees, but he was the only one who stepped out on to this platform— or, rather, was slowly helped out by willing, gentle hands. In face he looked little different from the others in the train, if only because all skulls are alike. The bone-structure of his face and head seemed hidden only by a layer of sallow-white skin and a bristling of white beard and hair. His eyes could have been a dead man's except that they moved to look up and down this platform and dimly lit with a smile as if glad to look upon a familiar scene. On the platform, because of his extreme thinness, and because the coat and trousers of his striped prison suit were too short, and greatly too loose, the trousers held up by string and the coat flapping in the draught of the departing train, he looked an unnaturally elongated figure, as if his body had been stretched outwards on a rack. And yet he was no taller than the two men who were now helping his tottering steps towards booking hall and street.

In the small oval Place de la Gare outside the station a crowd awaited him. Certainly nine tenths of the women in Sainte-Marie were there and as many men as could snatch an hour from work. In front of them, opposite the station doors, stood their mayor, Monsieur Philippe-Gabriel Galais. In his hand, folded, was the flag which five years earlier he had waved three times over the people from the balcony of the Mairie before folding it up by order of the Germans and handing it to the Curé, who, you may remember, made the sign of the cross over it, before letting it pass from sight.

When this deportee, coming so slowly between his two supporters, appeared at the station doors a great gasp, a long '*Oh!*' of amazement from many hundred throats rose in that Place de la Gare. They had meant to raise a great cheer but not one of them, on sight of that corpse-like figure being helped into the sunlight, could do anything but breathe out this '*Oh!*' Could that drooping figure be their Curé whose stomach had once been so large that he had to carry it with head and shoulders thrown back? 'It's impossible,' whispered Sophie, for she and Marie-Louise and Frédé were there in the crowd together. 'Who could believe it?'

'They nearly all look like that,' said Frédé, learnedly.

'Yes, but . . . the Abbé! He must have been seventeen or eighteen stone. Now he doesn't look to be seven or six.'

'Less,' said Frédé, who'd learned from Marie-Louise what a 'stone' was. 'But that's what happens.' Proud of having been a prisoner himself, he explained, 'Starvation does it, and dysentery. We were not starved as they were, but I've seen our dysentery lads go like that. Worse than that sometimes,' he added proudly.

'How can you be worse than that? It's a wonder that he's alive Oh, my *poor* . . . *dear* . . . Abbé.'

Meanwhile the people could only look silently at that skin-and-bone structure in the loose prison garb, and feel unhappy because they had not cheered and could not cheer; because they had done nothing as the mayor put the folded flag into the Abbé's hand, and he smiled at sight of it, put it to his lips and returned it; because they were all just standing silently in the street. But their discomfort was eased and some happiness given back to them by one of the women who, after emitting that '*Oh!*' with all the others, suddenly rushed forward and knelt before the Abbé, lifting up his hand and kissing it. Inspired, she had acted for them all; and they, as they saw him lay the hand on her head to bless her, began, one after another, to kneel too in the places where they had stood, till at last all were kneeling, even the men. It was an action unprepared, unimagined, and inevitable. One had knelt, and all must kneel.

Marie-Louise had shown no hesitation in kneeling with the others; nor Frédé, after a time; Sophie, English, and shy of kneeling in the public road, but yet more afraid of being the only one left standing, knelt too—and felt foolish. But glad to be doing this extremely difficult thing for the Abbé's sake.

This impulsive action by all his people seemed to pour new strength into the Abbé, for he now walked unsupported at the mayor's side and blessed the kneeling people left and right of him as he went, making the sign of the cross towards them. To those who could hear his weak voice he said, 'Dieu vous bénisse, mes enfants.'

When he had passed they rose and followed behind him all the way along the Avenue de la Gare, which runs between its acacias straight from Sainte-Marie's station to its church. The Abbé's triple-doored church, with the Rue de Paris running past it, gazes straight down the avenue. As he walked towards it in his clownish striped dress, too short, too loose, he laughed and said, 'Monsieur le Maire, that was my church. I am told that I am still the Curé of Sainte-Marie, but I feel like the prodigal.'

'How, mon cher Abbé? Comme l'enfant prodigue?'

'Mais oui. Parfaitement.' And still gazing at the church with its three arched doorways, he laughed and explained, 'J'étais mort et je suis ressuscité; j'étais perdu et je suis retrouvé.'

§

So Frédé and the Abbé returned to Sainte-Marie. The only one who never returned was Eric. To this day no one has ever known what happened to him. No one will ever know for certain now. But a man from Sainte-Marie who was imprisoned for long months in the concentration camp at Buchenwald for 'a crime against the Reich', having been apprehended in the act of defacing a German poster with a rude picture and a derisive word, has always believed that he saw him once in the camp and heard the name of O'Healy called one morning. 'Achtung! Achtung!' called the loudspeakers, 'the following prisoners must report themselves to the Turm (the entrance tower) forthwith: Lagrange, Caillou, Talbot, O'Healy. . . .' If that was so, it is more than likely that Eric escaped at last from Buchenwald through its only open way, the crematorium's low black chimney, disappearing with other wasted fellow-prisoners in the upward smoke, an unwilling victim of history.

§

Last year, sixteen years after the war's end, another man returned to Sainte-Marie; a man nearing fifty, of full heavy figure and face, with cheeks and chin that sagged a little and hair that was silvering. He walked from the station up the Avenue de la Gare just as Abbé and Mayor had done. No one in that wide road recognized him; some looked at him for a second from shop-doors or pavements and wondered who he was. It was not for them to know that he had come to look again at this village after many years; to find old war-time friends if any were still here; and, more than all, to stand alone and gaze at one house. Perhaps even to knock at its door and ask permission to walk about in it.

Wandering slowly along, he turned round by the Abbé's church towards the Place de la Forge, in the centre of which was the fountain where he had once met two men arguing in the first light of morning over a copy of the *Paris-Soir*. There were shops and cafés hereabout, but still no one recognized him; nor did he recognize any of the people who passed him by. Opposite the fountain was the Café de la Forge, and 'Surely,' he thought, 'Madame Paulet, if she's still the patronne, will screw up her eyes and stare at me, and suddenly let loose a scream. Of delight, one hopes. Let us put it to the test. We cannot go on like this, being greeted by no one, and no one according us more than a cursory interest.'

He turned into the café. It was greatly changed, he thought; changed for the better while he, alas. . . . It now had a mosaic floor, a curving counter all chromium-plated fittings, and tables and chairs of modish modern design. But, standing behind a shining coffee machine, was Madame Paulet, apparently quite unchanged. She had seemed plump and middle-aged and pleasant-faced twenty years ago; she seemed no more than middle-aged now; nor could he discern any difference in the plumpness of her bosom, the smoothness of her round face or the warm friendliness in her eyes.

'Bonjour, Madame Paulet,' he said.

She looked at him, screwed up her eyes, stared, and let loose a scream. 'It's Monsieur Quentin! Monsieur Rennie Quentin! Oh, my God. It is André. You came back as André and did wonderful things for us. But you have . . .' She outlined with both hands the portliness of his figure. 'Oh yes, Monsieur, you have.'

'Alas, yes,' he agreed.

'But sit down, sit down, Monsieur. Where have you come from after all these years? I make you an omelette. Oh, why isn't my poor foolish Gaspard here? We would all drink wine together. Quick! Tell me everything.'

'No omelette, Madame. Thank you a thousand times, but I have only a short hour in Sainte-Marie. The glass of wine, yes. I want to find friends on the other side of the forest, in Bouffemont and in Villiers-Adam, if I have time.'

'Ah, but yes. That was all your area, wasn't it? What great days they were. Et vous étiez un héros, n'est-ce pas? We heard how they gave you the Croix de Guerre.'

'Yes, your country gave me that, and do I value it? My own dear country gave me precisely nothing. But none of that seems to matter any more.'

'Oh, but we often speak of you, Gaspard and I, even though it's all getting so far away. And how is Madame, your mother?' (So they all thought that, did they? Well, let it be: what could it matter now?) 'She is still alive?'

'No. She died last year. A month or two after she'd thoroughly enjoyed her eightieth birthday.'

'And she kept well to the end?'

'Yes, yes. Vigorous right up to the end.'

'And fairly happy?'

'Oh yes. It was always her nature—rather like mine—to avoid discomfort and keep herself happy. She lived with me, you see, and she would always insist on my taking her out to anything the least bit exciting.'

'Why did you not bring her here? Were *we* not exciting?'

'She would never come back. Somehow, after we left, she felt she never wanted to come back. Certain memories, you see.'

'Oh, but one understands. How one understands. And you, Monsieur?'

'I always intended to be a schoolmaster but instead I stayed in the R.A.F. I am now, if you please, Squadron-Leader Quentin.' He said it not without pride.

'Ah! The great and glorious RAF!'

'Well . . . yes, in some ways.' He said it not without reservations.

'Vive la RAF. Its good health, Monsieur, and yours.'

He raised his glass to her. And Marie-Louise?—did she remember Marie-Louise?

Mais assurément—but they had not seen her this ten years and more. She lived now in Paris with Frédé, her husband.

'I know. She used to write often to Mother.' (Let them have it so.) 'Tomorrow I intend to surprise the life out of her. I am much looking forward to it.'

'Ah yes, she loved you. But not'—and here Madame Paulet let loose her rippling laugh—'not to the exclusion of Frédé.'

'Alas, no. And Madame Dubosquet and Brigitte—are they still in their cottage below the forest?'

'Manon Dubosquet is still there with one of the sons who were prisoners-of-war. Nice for her to have him after losing her husband so cruelly. Brigitte is married. She married an American corporal and now lives in San Francisco.'

'So far away! And I always said *I* was going to marry her. Oh dear, oh dear, I always felt she'd be unfaithful to me.'

'You are married, Monsieur?'

'Not yet. But there is time.'

'Certainly there is time. And you must certainly get married. You must not be wasted.' Again with both hands and a smile she outlined his thick and powerful-seeming figure. 'You must do your duty. You have had your mistresses, perhaps?'

'It could be so, Madame.'

'Yes, yes, yes. Naturally. And you have one now—is it not? Of course. One very sweet and agréable, I am sure. But you must marry and have lovely children.'

'I will consider it. The Abbé Belfort—what happened to him?'

'Ah, he lived among us for a year or two more after he returned. Only a year or two. He never really recovered from his treatment in prison. Ces Allemands-là! Nous n'aimons pas Messieurs les Boches.'

'Well, Madame, I must be going on.' He rose. 'Good-bye.'

'Au revoir, Monsieur. You will come again. Monsieur, I don't think I ever thanked you for all you did for us in those days.' She fell into almost the exact words that Madame Dubosquet had used nearly two decades before. 'Je ne sais pas comment vous remercier . . . mais . . . je vous remercie de tout mon coeur.'

And he, without knowing it, used words like those which Jean had spoken to herself before dying in the forest. 'Ça va bien, Madame. Je suis content d'avoir pu faire quelque chose pour la France.'

'Au revoir, Monsieur. Come again and show me your pretty young wife. No nonsense about that. Au revoir.'

On along the Rue de la Forêt, his heart speeding as he saw the mouth of the little avenue that led to the chateau. Turn that corner and he would see its cone-capped tower peeping above those fir trees on the garden side which the Germans had not troubled to hack down. Who would be living there now?

He turned the corner. Yes, there it was, behind trees that were older now and fuller by more than a quarter of a century since he had first come to them. He slowed his steps as he approached the gate because almost afraid of the emotions that would come as he looked at garden, porch and windows.

Now he was looking over the gate: at salon and breakfast-room and his own room above. Neat looped curtains in all these windows, but curtains too simple, too cheap, too undainty, for Sophie. To the unsuspecting no trace anywhere of a battle this little house had once known; to him, yes: pittings and chippings here and there on the façade, delved by bullet or splinter. For the rest, all in good order and clean.

A perambulator under a fir, and, no doubt, a fat baby under its hood. Then they were young people, the successors of Sophie, Klem and Jean.

Dare he knock and tell them? Yes, yes; cowardly to have come all this way and to turn round at the gate. He might never come again. So he went up the steps to the door and knocked—on Sophie's knocker, the brass ship in full sail, which she had forgotten to bring away. Here before his eyes was a trace of Sophie.

A comely if ample young woman in a gaily patterned apron opened to him, and he smiled and told his story. Would it derange her if he had a little look round?

'But no, Monsieur! Cela ne me dérangera pas. Je serai enchantée.' And indeed she looked enchanted. 'Come in. Come and go anywhere.' She wiped her hands on the apron and, as he entered and looked at the hall and up the stairs, she explained volubly how the children were at school, and her husband at the usine. Prosperous working-class people, these.

The salon. A family living-room now with good plain furniture, all very different from Sophie's baroque, rococo, and gilded pieces. No rosewood, tulipwood or marquetry; no ormolu to shine in this entering sun.

He went upstairs, she going with delight before him and talking all the way. By the time he had looked at breakfast-room and Sophie's room (where two dead men had once lain while Sophie arranged her face) and was on his way upstairs to his own room, he knew much of this new young chatelaine's life-story and not a little of her husband's. He knew the successes of her children at school.

In his own room he hardly heard what she was saying because he was looking from the window at the garden and the forest. He was remembering how a brave if foolish young German major had fallen dead over this sill. Murdered from the back. He looked again at the forest. The forest, unlike the house, seemed exactly the same as it had always been, unchanged by so much as a leaf. As eternal as the men who came to it and passed through it were transitory.

It was up here, looking at the forest, that he spoke about the battle for the house, and she, tidying an ornament on the mantelpiece, said Yes, she had heard 'something' about that.

'Something.' So a story begins to fade, like some old photograph from which the years are wiping all precision away, and which, in the end, will be too pale and evanescent to be worth keeping any more.

He said no more about it, but, after a few last and lingering looks at this and at that, as he descended the stairs, thanked her with a grateful smile and came away.